PRAISE FOR
THE ALASKAN NIGHTS

Come Fly with Me

"A sexy, emotional journey of the best kind."
—*New York Times* Bestselling Author Carly Phillips

Baby It's Cold Outside

"A fun, sassy, well-written, hysterical, heartfelt, and entertaining book." —Fiction Vixen

"Refreshing . . . this was a great book that had me laughing out loud." —Night Owl Reviews

"A cute, funny, fast-paced romantic novel filled with humor [and] heartwarming moments . . . a great read on a cold night in front of a warm fire."
—Manic Readers

"Addison Fox charmed the heck out of me with her first Alaskan Nights novel. I cannot wait to return to the wonderful town of Indigo, Alaska."
—Romance Junkies

"Steamy encounters . . . keep the blood pumping all the way to a sweet ending." —*Publishers Weekly*

continued . . .

"Heartfelt. . . . Readers will eagerly await the next novel in Fox's series after reading this poignant romance."
                                                      —*Booklist*

"[A] fun, sexy story."   —The Romance Dish

"Fox does a fantastic job. . . . The characters are dynamic and interesting. I can't wait to see what happens next in this sexy new series!"
                                    —*RT Book Reviews* (top pick)

"With plenty of humor mixed in with some sizzling sex, *Baby It's Cold Outside* proves that you better cuddle up with a hot man and a good book to keep you warm while it's cold outside. Grab this gem of a book before winter settles in too deep."
                                        —Romance Reviews Today

PRAISE FOR
THE SONS OF THE ZODIAC SERIES

Warrior Betrayed

"A terrific tale."   —Alternative Worlds

"Ms. Fox is definitely an author to watch."
                            —The Romance Readers Connection

Warrior Avenged

"Everything I love in a book: a sexy, enigmatic hero, a strong, capable heroine who is his match in every way, action, surprises, and plenty of steam! It's a fantastic series, and trust me, you won't want to miss a single moment!"   —The Romance Dish

"Another powerfully sexy and exciting entry in this dynamic series."   —Fresh Fiction

"An exciting series."   —Risqué Reviews

"[A] superb . . . urban romantic fantasy."
                            —Genre Go Round Reviews

Warrior Ascended

"[A] powerful romance."   *—Publishers Weekly*

"A delightful twist to the Greek Gods . . . will keep you turning the pages and begging for more. A great start to a promising paranormal series!"   —Fresh Fiction

"[A] blast to read, combining paranormal romance, enjoyable heroes and heroines . . . kept me turning the pages until I finished it."   —Errant Dreams Reviews

"Promise[s] plenty of action, treachery, and romance!"
                            —RT Book Reviews

ALSO BY ADDISON FOX

Just In Time

An Alaskan Nights Novel

Addison Fox

A SIGNET ECLIPSE BOOK

SIGNET ECLIPSE
Published by the Penguin Group
Penguin Group (USA) Inc., 375 Hudson Street,
New York, New York 10014, USA

USA | Canada | UK | Ireland | Australia | New Zealand | India | South Africa | China

Penguin Books Ltd., Registered Offices: 80 Strand, London WC2R 0RL, England
For more information about the Penguin Group visit penguin.com.

First published by Signet Eclipse, an imprint of New American Library,
a division of Penguin Group (USA) Inc.

First Printing, August 2013

ISBN 978-0-451-23973-0

Printed in the United States of America
10   9   8   7   6   5   4   3   2   1

ALWAYS LEARNING   **PEARSON**

For Holly Root

From our very first call, I knew I'd found a business partner who lives and works with the qualities I admire most: integrity, hard work and thoughtfulness.

You champion the work and you nourish the creative soul with an unfailingly kind hand.

You are equal parts sounding board, negotiator, ledge-talker-offer and cheerleader.

You are a friend.

Our partnership has enriched my career in a myriad of ways, but it is our friendship that has enriched my life beyond measure.

Chapter One

$\mathcal{W}$eddings were a big fat pain in the ass.

If she didn't enjoy them so much—or love the couple who'd be standing at the end of the aisle even more—Avery Marks knew she'd have taken the weekend off and run for the hills.

"Did the champagne arrive?" Sloan McKinley, the bride-to-be and one of Avery's closest friends, asked as upswept oversized blond ringlets bounced with every movement of her head.

"It arrived last week." Avery barely looked up from where she made a last-minute adjustment to a slight rip in the underskirt of her bridesmaid dress as she sat on the end of her bed.

"And the bouquets?"

"This morning, right on schedule. Mick picked them up himself on his morning run to Anchorage."

Avery hesitated to add she'd already confirmed this three times already. A bride was entitled to a bit of the crazies, especially with her walk down the aisle less than an hour away.

"My mother's driving me bat-shit." Sloan sat down with a hard thump in a small wing-back chair Avery kept in her room. The minuscule, stiff-backed torture device was too impractical to be good for much, but Sloan seemed unaware as half her frame got lost in a sea of crinoline.

Avery did look up at that as she cut off the dangling thread from her repair. "Doesn't she always? Even about the littlest things?"

"Well, yeah."

"So today isn't exactly the definition of a little thing."

"Right again."

A long sigh floated toward Avery and she couldn't help but smile at the melodrama. Boy, had she missed this. She'd loved her four glorious months in Ireland on a professional exchange program, but she couldn't deny how much she'd missed her friends.

"Besides, focus on the outcome. Marriage to Walker and two weeks in Fiji."

The lines of frustration smoothed out across Sloan's face, replaced with a bright glow and a warm, distant smile. "There is that."

"And lots of sex," Avery added with a philosophical nod before standing to hold her dress out before her. "The tropical kind."

"You have a one-track mind."

"Pretty close." Avery stood before her dresser mirror. "And as your designated friend who's not getting any, I have to say quit your bitching."

Sloan laughed as she stood up in her frothy bundle of underskirt. "Here. Let me help you get into that."

Avery dragged off her shorts and button-down shirt—a nod to the mass of hair that was currently arranged atop her head like a well-pouffed bird's nest—and stepped into the thin silk Sloan held out in a circle.

"Aren't I supposed to be helping you?" Avery took the dress from Sloan and shimmied it up her body. The dark red silk was particularly flattering and she settled the beaded fabric against her torso.

The bright smile faded quickly as tears welled in Sloan's perfectly made-up eyes.

"Oh, oh." Avery reached for a tissue on the dresser as she held the front of the dress against her chest. "No tears."

Sloan clutched the tissue. "I'm sorry. I can't seem to stop doing that."

"Come on, don't cry. Save that for the ceremony."

"They just won't stop. Every time I think I have a handle on it, I think about how different my life is from a year ago and how happy I am and I can't stop them."

Avery pulled Sloan in for a hug, mashing her dress and Sloan's underskirt between them. "I know."

"And it's wonderful."

"It is." She ran her hand in large circles over Sloan's back before stepping away. "Which is why you're going to quit blubbering like you just failed ninth-grade English and help me into this."

"You are such a slave driver."

"And you've got a hot man waiting at the end of a long white aisle." She swatted in the general direction of Sloan's ass—it was hard to tell through the layers of material—and turned back toward the mirror. "Let's get cracking."

The tears vanished as quickly as they'd come and

Sloan moved to stand behind her. Avery felt light fingers on the small row of buttons at her back as Sloan did up the dress.

"Speaking of bitching, the dry spell is all your own fault if the almost-daily calls from Ireland are any indication."

Avery saw her own eyes widen in shock as she stared at herself in the mirror. "Who's been telling?"

"Sandy Stringer's beside herself to share the news. Says he sounds like a dream, with this deep, seductive masculine voice that sounds like a cross between James Bond and Gerard Butler."

Avery shook her head at the report from their summer front desk clerk and made a mental note to suggest Declan call her cell phone from now on.

And no matter how much she wanted to fault Sandy, the woman had described Declan's voice to a T.

"I didn't go to Ireland to get laid."

Sloan stood up after fastening the last button. Avery appreciated the warm, comforting hands that gripped her shoulders. "I didn't come to Alaska to get laid but it didn't stop me. And, for the record," Sloan added before placing a quick kiss on Avery's forehead, "it's not getting laid if you really like the person."

Avery knew that. Knew it with every fiber of her being. She also suspected that for all her talk about being a lonely single girl not "getting any," it was the fact that she wanted it to be special that kept her waiting.

Not that Declan O'Mara wasn't awfully special. But it just hadn't been right, no matter how many times she'd tried to lose herself in his kisses before the big fireplace in his B and B in County Clare.

Perfect location.

Perfect timing.

Perfect man.

And still, she'd held back, a memory of vivid green eyes, dark hair and a mischievous smile she could remember since roughly the age of five haunting her thoughts and holding her back from taking the next step with Dec.

Shaking it off, Avery ran her hands down the fitted bodice. "Sandy's got a big mouth. There's nothing going on between Declan O'Mara and me."

"But there could be." Sloan's voice singsonged next to her as she reached for a small, silver hair clip on the edge of the dresser. "That's part of the fun."

"She's blowing it out of proportion."

"And I love the fact that there's something to blow."

Avery caught Sloan's wry expression as her words registered to both of them.

"You know what I mean." Sloan giggled.

"Oh I do. I'm also thinking with thoughts like those, maybe you shouldn't be wearing white." Avery winked at her, unable to hold back her own laughter.

The door slammed open as Grier Thompson—the third member of their self-proclaimed Musketeers—walked through. "I hate both of you. I'm stuck downstairs calming Winnie's nerves and the two of you are in here having a grand old time."

"How'd you escape? Did my mother finally pass out in a fit of the vapors?" Sloan glanced sideways from the dresser mirror as she positioned the silver clip in her hair.

"Or did you just come up here to retrieve my crucifix?" Avery added as she began the hunt for the strappy heels that completed her outfit.

"She's mental, Sloan." Grier dropped into the small chair Sloan had recently abandoned. "Scary mental."

"You were only with her for fifteen minutes." Avery spotted the sexy shoes on the far side of her bed. "How bad could she be?"

"You do not want to ask that question. In the fifteen minutes I was with her, she made the caterer cry, sent the florist off to redo her corsage, and she went toe-to-toe with Sophie. And we all know that's saying something."

Sloan whirled from the mirror, her vague air of concern shifting into a clear case of bridal jitters. "She's fighting with Walker's grandmother? Oh God, I need to get down there."

Avery sensed Sloan's intention and beelined for the door, closing it with a firm snap. "You don't need to get in the middle of things. It's your wedding day."

"Avery's right. I made my escape because Sophie wanted to have a little conversation with *Winifred*. She shooed me out and forbade me to allow you anywhere near your mother until the photographer arrives for pictures."

"There will be no pictures if the mother of the bride and the grandmother of the groom end up having a cage fight in the bridal suite."

Grier was already up and out of the chair as Avery reached Sloan's side. The two of them pulled Sloan toward the edge of the bed, and Grier put a soothing hand on Sloan's back. "Come on, Sloan. Calm down."

"But it's my wedding day."

"Which means both women will come to their senses and refrain from engaging in said cage fight." Avery hoped like hell she was right about that one.

"Avery's right." Grier patted Sloan's back. "They'll wait and save that for the baby shower."

A powerful laugh escaped Sloan and she leaned forward and clutched her stomach as several more giggles followed.

Avery caught Grier's eye over the top of Sloan's head. *Are we out of the woods?* flashed between them as clearly as if they'd spoken to each other.

"Some bridesmaids you two are." Sloan gave each of them a teary smile before wrapping an arm around each of their waists.

Avery hugged the two of them back, Sloan's earlier words echoing in her ear. Her life had changed over the past year. In ways she'd never imagined.

And two of the biggest reasons it had changed were the women sitting right here.

For the first time in her life, she had good girlfriends whom she trusted implicitly. Women who had her back. Women who believed in her. Women who wanted the best for her.

Sloan and Grier were her family, and she hadn't realized quite how much she missed having one until the two of them arrived in Indigo, Alaska, and raised its population to 714.

A light knock on the door broke the spell.

"It's Lou. Can I come in and take a few pictures?"

"I'm not dressed!" Sloan's gaze shifted quickly to the dress.

"Hang on!" Avery hollered toward the closed door

as she and Grier worked in unison to remove Sloan's gown from its hangers. "Okay, Sloan. It's time to put on your wedding dress."

Avery didn't miss Grier's misty smile as she held the other side of the silk confection open for Sloan to step into. Nor could she miss the way her own throat tightened as they buttoned up the back of the dress.

"Gorgeous," Grier sighed.

Sloan pulled both of them into a hug before her gaze drifted toward the door. "I'm ready."

"Come on in!" The three of them hollered in unison.

In an act that ensured Sloan would have a day of photographs full of the most spontaneous memories, Lou came through the door with his camera up and caught the three of them wrapped up in one another's arms, bright smiles reflecting their joy.

Roman Forsyth reached for another round of longnecks from the small cooler his mother had kindly thought to provide. He made quick work of the metal caps and handed the bottles to his two best friends, Mick O'Shaughnessy and the groom-to-be, Walker Montgomery.

Walker took the bottle midpace across the hotel room they were using as a groom's suite. "Did everything get here?"

"I left all of it in Anchorage." Mick took a long drag off his new bottle as Walker's mouth fell. "Oh for God's sake, I put everything in the damn plane myself this morning. And I was out of here at six a.m. The least you could do is believe me when I tell you I have everything. Again."

Walker scrubbed a hand over his freshly shaven face. "Damn it. I'm sorry. It's like I can't keep anything in my head."

"Name the Bill of Rights," Roman suggested. The finger gesture he got in return pretty much told him what Walker thought of that idea, but it did give him an opportunity to poke his friend a bit more. "You were able to name them, along with all the other amendments in the sixth grade. If you've forgotten that, Sloan McKinley has really gotten you good."

"Legs like that'll do it every time," Mick added as he raised his beer.

"Yeah, but the brains, the smile and the open welcome for everyone she meets were the clincher." A funny, lopsided grin spread across Walker's face. "And she wants to marry me."

"There's no accounting for taste," Roman offered as he took a seat, careful to select just the right one.

"Isn't that the truth." Mick nodded.

Walker glanced up at that, the dreamy haze evaporating from his gaze. "You've got room to talk. Grier let you put a ring on her finger."

"And I count myself the luckiest of men," Mick intoned, his voice solemn. "I count myself even luckier that she wants a wedding that's small and intimate, with a minimum of fuss."

"Which is an improvement over her wanting you to drag her to Vegas," Roman couldn't resist adding. "I still don't understand why you turned her down."

"I'm a romantic fellow, and Elvis officiating just didn't fit the bill for what I have in mind."

Roman shook his head, a subtle sense of bemusement humming in his veins. He was happy for his friends' leap into the married phases of their lives, but couldn't quite understand when things had gone so sideways.

They were the eternal bachelors.

And now he was the only one left.

"What time is it?" Walker's voice pulled him from the maudlin thoughts that had dogged him with uncomfortable regularity these last six months.

Roman stuck out his arm in an exaggerated gesture and dragged up his tuxedo sleeve to look at his wrist. "He's improved, Mick. It's been six minutes since the last time he asked."

A good-natured round of "You're an asshole" later—a standard response the trio had practiced since middle school—ended with the three of them sitting in quiet solidarity.

Walker broke the silence first. "You and Avery were awfully distant last night."

Roman chose his words with care, but couldn't stop the slight edge of resentment that coated them. "I barely saw her. She was so busy flitting around the room talking about Ireland."

"Don't tell me you've got sour grapes about the Irish, Boy-o." Mick affected the lilting notes of his heritage in his tone. "Our fine lass was simply regaling our townsfolk with tales of the Emerald Isle."

"It's more the Irish asshole who can't seem to leave her alone."

The words were out before he could stop them, and as Roman took a reflective drag on his beer, he had to admit he didn't want to.

"So that's what has you so torqued up." Walker took the seat next to Roman, who stood to pace. It was bad enough he'd already let the cat out of the bag about Avery; he'd be damned if he'd share every fucking thing going on in his life right now.

"He lives in Ireland. What the hell is he getting her hopes up for?"

Mick's words stopped him midpace. "So that's why you're pissed? You're afraid she'll get hurt?"

"Damn straight. The man lives like a billion miles away. What is he expecting, calling her every damn day flirting with her?"

Mick shook his head. "That's how it works, man. I realize you've been living in the rarefied air of a celebrity athlete, where women throw themselves at you with wild abandon, but the rest of us have to work at it."

"Some call it a courtship ritual," Walker added. "Maybe you've heard of it."

"What the hell is he courting her for?"

Shitty peripheral vision or not, Roman didn't miss the glances and raised eyebrows Walker and Mick exchanged across the room. It was Mick who spoke first. "He likes her, Roman. Is that so hard to believe?"

"No. Of course not. She's spectacular."

But it was Walker who put the proverbial nail in the coffin. "I hope you'd at least agree she deserves it."

Avery watched Sloan walk down the aisle of the small, A-frame nondenominational church that dominated the end of Main Street and thought she'd never seen a more radiant bride. But it was Walker's incandescent smile as their gazes met that would put any woman into sighs of ecstasy.

Grier reached over and squeezed her hand, a bright smile shining through her tears. Avery squeezed back, the sappy feelings that had swamped her earlier winging back through her chest in a heady rush.

So why the hell—in the middle of a moment of sweet, glorious perfection—did she clamp eyes on her ex-boyfriend across the aisle?

Roman stared back at her, that green gaze as compelling as it was when she was sixteen. Add in the fact that all six-foot-four feet of him was decked out in a tuxedo that had to be custom-made and her traitorous body gave a leap of appreciation that wasn't quite appropriate for church.

One dark eyebrow lifted in silent challenge and Avery fought the urge to stick out her tongue.

Damn the man. He'd make a stripper blush with those bedroom eyes and thick, luscious hair that begged to be mussed.

And wasn't that the problem?

Everything was way too easy for Roman and it always had been.

It had just taken her too long to understand that fact.

Dragging her gaze away, Avery focused on the bride. Grier took Sloan's flowers as she took her place beside Walker, and Avery did a quick refluffing of the train so it lay evenly on the aisle.

Jobs completed, she and Grier met Mick and Roman where they escorted them the few brief steps to their front pew seats. Roman took her arm, and it took everything inside her to keep her gaze straight and her smile firmly fixed as the entire town of Indigo looked on with interest.

"You look beautiful."

Avery swallowed hard at the warm breath in her ear, those inconvenient feelings rising once more in a hard clutch of her belly.

"Thank you."

She took her seat, the words playing over and over in her mind.

So many images stood out in her memories of the two of them, but the one that held the top of the list was the year they began to notice each other as more than friends. Roman had whispered in her ear in the middle of a soccer match on the town square. He'd told her where to line up a shot and she'd nearly melted into a puddle as his words skittered down her spine, light as a feather and as powerful as an avalanche.

The sensation—a mixture of inexperience and the sudden change in a relationship she'd had since grade school—had taken her so off guard that she'd pushed him away with a smart-ass retort. But she'd thought about his words long into the night, wrapped up in her tiny bed in the back room of her mother's house.

Clearly not much had changed in eighteen years.

"You ready?"

Avery felt Grier's quick poke to her thigh and realized she'd nearly missed her cue along with most of the ceremony. She and Grier returned to the altar to help Sloan with her dress, then moved to the side as Mick and Roman stepped forward to flank Walker.

Mick produced two shining platinum bands from his vest pocket and laid them on the reverend's open Bible.

Avery watched with rapt fascination as Walker slid the band effortlessly on Sloan's finger and moments later when her friend returned the gesture. And when the couple kissed for the first time as husband and wife, the entire church let up a cheer.

Walker and Sloan began their walk back down the aisle, and Mick and Grier followed. It was only when Roman took her arm once more to begin their procession through the church that a thin layer of panic seized her.

Broad smiles greeted them as they moved down the aisle, making slow progress as many guests stopped Walker and Sloan with hugs. Hooch MacGilvray even threw her a big wink, which his wife, Chooch, responded to with an oversized elbow to the stomach.

Roman seemed oblivious as they walked, his arm locked steadily with hers. She snuck a glance at his chiseled profile and—miracles of miracles—it looked as if he'd missed Chooch and Hooch's antics. As if sensing her attention, he turned with a smile.

"I haven't felt this on display since I did a calendar shoot for charity."

Avery sucked in an involuntary breath. She'd seen that calendar when someone had brought a copy for Roman's mother, Susan. She'd even given herself permission to go look at it late one night when she was manning the front desk by herself.

Long ropes of muscles defined his arms from shoulder to wrist, and thick ridges sculpted his abdomen.

He'd always been well built, but the man that stared back at her from the photograph, wearing nothing but a strategically placed towel, had taken her breath away.

He was magnificent.

A warrior.

And he had been as foreign to her as if a stranger stared back from the page.

Pulling herself back from the heated memory, Avery just shrugged as those inconvenient flutters once again filled her stomach. "Small towns."

A slight smile grooved his cheeks as he leaned in once more. "So why don't we really give them something to talk about?"

Chapter Two

Roman shifted his feet to bring Avery's face more clearly into view.

"What's that supposed to mean?" Her hiss was low enough not to be heard by anyone else, but no one in the remaining pews between them and the door would miss the fury in her eyes.

"If you're so worried about what everyone thinks, let's make it worth our while. Have a little fun."

"I'm not worried about what people think."

Fresh air greeted them as they finally made their way through the doors of the church and Avery pulled her hand from his arm.

"Could have fooled me."

Avery flung a hand in the direction of the church, even as she stomped across the small front lawn to give them some privacy. "Did you not miss how we were on display in there? The oversized winks and broad grins, everyone so delighted we were walking down that aisle together?"

Roman couldn't resist poking at her a bit more. "Cupids in their eyes and all that shit."

"Exactly!"

"Which was all I was really pointing out." He kept his tone reasonable, but no matter how hard he tried he couldn't hold back a grin.

"You were talking about sex and that's something else entirely."

"You've got a dirty mind."

"And you weren't talking about sex, Mr. Big Shot Hockey Player?"

"While I never turn down sex with a beautiful woman, no, that's not what I was talking about." He'd turned down plenty of sex, but Roman decided he didn't quite need to share that tidbit now. Instead, he moved closer to Avery, intrigued when she held her ground. "I was actually talking about a little slow dancing. A few whispers in dark corners. Maybe even a well-placed kiss or two. You know, all the things people expect from the single members of the wedding party."

"This dress is not a neon sign for sex, despite what conventional wisdom—and *Cosmopolitan* magazine—suggests."

"And there you go, right back into the gutter again."

As if suddenly realizing how close they stood, she moved back, but he didn't miss the light flush that suffused her chest and cheeks.

"We're going to behave like civilized adults. Just because we have a past the entire town knows about doesn't mean we have a present. We can be nice and cordial to each other."

"I agree."

"You do?"

"Sure." He shrugged, deliberately casual, even as a flash of something very much like a flaming sword to his guts ripped through him. "You've got a new boy-friend you're all excited about. I'm big enough to wish you well and want what's best for you."

Whatever smart-ass remark was about to come out of her mouth—and he knew Avery Marks well enough to know there was going to be one—floated away on a light stammer. "You do?"

"Of course."

The urge to rip something apart—preferably the Irishman he pictured in his mind—gripped him, but Roman refused to show it. He'd spent far too long in the spotlight, hiding what he really thought about things in favor of doing what was politically expedient. He'd be damned if he didn't put the skill to good use now.

"Well, good."

Her wide-eyed stare didn't waver, and Roman saw the effort she was making to shift gears, but he kept the stupid, fucking, *understanding* smile pasted on his face.

A loud shout from the direction of the receiving line broke the moment, and Avery turned back toward the church. "I'd better go see if Sloan needs anything."

"You do that."

"I'll see you at the reception."

"Count on it."

Roman watched her go, her long, lean frame filling out the dark-red silk dress to perfection.

And only then did he let his smile drop.

"Are you okay?" Concern lit up Grier's dark gray eyes as Avery took her place in the receiving line.

"I'm fine," Avery said through gritted teeth.

"And I'm Mother Teresa."

"That's a bit hard, seeing as how you're not only not dead, but you're no saint if the rumors about you and Mick out in the airplane hangar last weekend are true."

Grier's mouth dropped in a surprised O, but she recovered quickly, her voice prim and proper when she spoke. "We went out to the see the meteor shower."

Avery hip-bumped her, desperate to keep the conversation off her and Roman. "I've also heard he's got a nice set of etchings out in that hangar as well."

"Hey, don't point the finger at me. I'd have been a married woman by now if I could have convinced my fiancé to elope to Vegas."

"Every man's fantasy."

Grier shook her head, her bewilderment evident in the gesture. "He refused to bite."

"Are you surprised? That man oozes chivalry."

"It's one of his best traits."

"Amen." Avery smiled, both because she loved Mick O'Shaughnessy with the sort of lifelong affection that made family out of friends and because his sense of honor really was one of his most lovely qualities.

She was halfway through congratulating herself on shifting the subject when Walker's secretary, Myrtle Driver, and her husband, Mort, hit her stretch of the receiving line.

"Nice ceremony." Myrtle's voice was a mixture of gravel and vinegar.

"It was lovely." Avery nodded.

"They're stupid in love, but I think they've got what it takes to make it. They're crazy about each other in and out of bed. It's worked like a dream for me and Mort."

Avery tried not to choke as she nodded solemnly.

"Saw you eyeing Roman. You two had the whole good thing in and out, too. Shame you were both too young and stupid to understand it."

Whatever polite manners her mother had managed to scatter into her through the years fled. "He's the one who left, Myrtle, for a big contract in New York."

"Well, he's back now. Pick up where you left off."

"He's not back. The season's done."

"So go back with him. You've been content to roam the world the last few months. Go have yourself another adventure."

"It's hardly that easy." The crucifix she'd mentioned to Grier earlier flashed through her memory and Avery was suddenly sorry she'd left it in her room.

"Life's as hard as you make it. Remember that."

With those ominous words, Myrtle marched off, the silent Mort following in her wake.

"She's scary," Grier whispered low enough so the next person in line couldn't hear.

"Demonic is more like it."

The receiving line finished up quickly, Indigo's denizens eager to get to the reception. As soon as everyone was out of earshot, Grier returned to their conversation. "Myrtle did have a good point before."

Avery whirled on her friend. "Do not tell me you're in on it, too?"

"In on what?"

"The cupids that have magically started flying

around everyone's head where Roman and I are concerned."

"I'm not in on anything and I don't think you should just fall back in his arms like almost fourteen years haven't passed. I just think she's got a point, that's all."

"It's been nearly proven on several occasions that Myrtle Driver is the spawn of Satan. Do you really want to side with her?"

"I happen to have it on good authority Satan wouldn't wear that shade of lipstick."

Try as she might, Avery had no response.

Grier reached for her hand, the squeeze quick and light. "All I said was she had a point. Do me a favor and think about it."

Avery was still thinking about it an hour later as she floated around the transformed town hall. If "the grandmothers"—Sophie, Mary and Julia—made the hall a wonderland each and every December for their annual bachelor competition, a wedding had given them an excuse to bring a fairy tale to life.

She'd been here fifteen minutes and still hadn't seen every inch of the bedecked space. Everywhere she looked was absolutely enchanting, and Avery eagerly took in the acres of roses, tulle, twinkle lights, ice sculptures and even a handcrafted bower that looked like something Martha Stewart might aspire to.

"What do you think, dear?" Julia, Roman's grandmother and Avery's own fiercest champion, sidled up to her.

"It's incredible. How did you do all this?"

Avery would have to be deaf to miss the slight sniff

underlying Julia's tone. "Sloan's mother helped. She's been in here like a drill sergeant all week."

Although Julia and her two cohorts were pretty good at the drill-sergeant routine, Avery opted for a good old-fashioned dose of diplomacy. "I can see you, Mary and Sophie stamped all over it." She gave Julia a quick hug. "The very best parts."

"You are too sweet by half."

"Nah, I'm just half as sweet as I should be."

"A woman needs a bit of an edge. Keeps people on their toes. Speaking of which"—Julia's green eyes narrowed—"I saw Myrtle spent a while with you and Grier in the receiving line. Mary commented on it, too, and you know Mick's grandmother isn't known for missing tricks."

"She's relatively harmless—you know that. And somewhere down deep inside, I actually think she means well."

The stubborn frown didn't quite fade from Julia's normally serene face. "Doesn't mean her delivery doesn't need work."

"I'll give you that." At the expectant look, Avery added, "She was seeing stars in her eyes as Roman and I walked down the aisle. Thought she needed to give me a quick bit of advice."

"She won't be the only one. Are you all right with that?"

"Of course."

"Oh, don't pull that with me." Julia lifted two glasses of champagne from a circulating waiter and handed one over, her smile bright, as if the two of them were discussing nothing more than the joys of the day. "I may love my grandson to distraction, but I'm not as besotted as the rest of this town. You can't erase years of bad behavior and just expect things to go back the way they were."

"No, you can't."

"You also can't live your life for other people's expectations and that's the bigger reason I wish people knew when to keep their mouths shut."

"Julia. It's okay. Really. He's only here for three weeks. I'm not going to break."

One delicate, aged hand settled on Avery's arm. "No, darling, you're not going to break. And I never thought for a minute you would. But you've had to do a lot of bending, and I, for one, am glad it's your time to stand tall."

Julia raised her glass for a quick toast. "To the future."

"Now, that's worth drinking to."

Roman pasted a smile on his face as he heard his name ring out. The lovely Myrtle, her long-suffering husband in tow, had her sights set straight on him. The reception had dragged slower than the day before a play-off game, and all he wanted to do was escape.

Yet every time he turned around, one of Indigo's denizens wanted to have a word with him. When you added on Sloan's bewildered family from Scarsdale—an entire school of fish out of water—he'd spent most of his time running interference to keep them comfortable and entertained as they peppered him with questions about the upcoming season.

A fucking season he had no idea whether or not he'd be a part of.

"Roman!"

Myrtle finally caught up to him, Mort shuffling in her wake. Both had full glasses of what appeared to be strawberry margaritas, and Roman abstractly noted Myrtle's tongue appeared to be about the same shade as her lipstick when she licked a bit of sugar off the rim of her glass.

And then he tamped down on the shudder that he'd actually noticed Myrtle Driver's tongue.

"Damn, but you are a difficult man to catch up with."

"It's a lovely party, don't you think?" Roman slugged down the glass of club soda he'd switched to at the start of the reception. While the blessed oblivion of scotch continued to beckon, he'd resolved to stay on his toes.

"Good food and good booze. It's my kind of party. Now, Mort's got something he needs to talk to you about."

Roman had known Mort and Myrtle Driver for all of his thirty-four years and he could probably count on one hand how many times he'd heard Mort speak. The man lived his life content to let his wife do the talking, so his deep baritone and cultured voice was something of a shock.

"Our grandsons are hockey players and they're in desperate need of a coach. The town's been looking for a replacement but we don't have one as of yet. Would you be willing to do a clinic with the kids? Help them out and keep their skills sharp over the summer? Maybe even show the team some drills so they can keep it going after you leave?"

Interest welled up like an oil strike, even as the sudden urge to drag at his bow tie tickled his fingertips. He loved talking about hockey—gloried in the moment his skates took the ice—but he was hardly qualified to coach.

Hang out with the kids and goof off, maybe shoot a few pucks, yeah. He always enjoyed that.

But to actually teach them something . . .

"You want me to coach the kids?"

"Work with them and help them. It won't take up too much of your time, but they're a good bunch and they love the game. We just can't seem to keep a coach in place."

"No one in Indigo's qualified enough and everyone we brought in leaves as fast as their skates'll carry them," Myrtle commiserated. "What's so bad about living here? It's good enough for all of us."

Mort patted her arm, his affection for his prickly pear more than evident. "Don't get upset about it, baby. We just haven't found the right one yet."

One rather indelicate sniff later, Myrtle turned her attention back to Roman. "So what do you say?"

"I'd love to help out. I've got a few commitments scheduled over the next month so I'll be in and out but I'm sure we can work around it. Is there anything booked at the rink besides the kids?"

"No." Mort shook his head. "The rink's in a bit of disrepair. We wanted to get it fixed but other things around town have needed more urgent attention, so we make do. It's just frozen water, after all."

As if inspired by the frozen water reference, Myrtle looked into her large—and empty—margarita glass. "Let's go before he changes his mind."

A spear of annoyance lanced through him; it was as if Myrtle thought he were some mouse she was trying to catch in a trap. "I'm not going to change my mind, Myrtle. When I say I'll do something, I will."

Through what could only amount to years of quick saves, Mort placed one hand on his wife's arm while offering up a wide smile. "Why don't we meet for breakfast? I'll take you over to the rink after and we can work out a schedule."

"Sounds good."

Roman's ire faded along with Myrtle's slightly tipsy totter on her three-inch red heels. He needed to get a grip on this pervasive streak of annoyance that lay just under his skin now that he was back home. While he enjoyed the relative anonymity of living in New York, he'd been missing Indigo for some time. Coming home with the temperament of a wild boar wasn't going to get him very far.

So why couldn't he shake the sense that these people he'd known since he was a child really didn't know him at all?

"You look like you want to punch something." Mick sidled up to him, his distracted gaze roving the room until it alighted on Grier. Just like that, his shoulders relaxed and he shifted his focus 100 percent to their conversation.

"Myrtle."

"Since Walker utters that single word a minimum of eight times a day, you're going to need to give me some context."

Roman glanced down into his glass and shook the ice. "Nothing. It's nothing."

"You sure?"

"I'm not an asshole, am I?"

"You're fairly likable most of the time." Mick took a casual sip of his beer before adding, "What prompted what I can only assume was a rhetorical question?"

"Nothing, it's stupid." Roman scrubbed a hand over his cheeks, sorry he'd even brought it up.

"No, it's not. What happened?"

"It was just something Myrtle said. She's half lit on margaritas. It's nothing."

"But it *was* something."

"Mort asked me to help out with the kids' hockey team. Running drills and teaching a few days a week since the kids' coach left town. And I said I'd do it and then Myrtle made a stupid crack about getting away while I was still saying yes."

"People don't have much sense when they drink. Case in point: Sloan's uncle laid a hand on Grier's ass, which I'm still trying to calm down about."

"Is that who you were giving shit to over at the bar?"

"It was a quietly worded suggestion as I got him a Coke to sober up."

"Suggestion?"

"I told him if he didn't keep his hands to himself I knew a cold, remote place on Denali I could drop him so no one would be any wiser."

"I can't imagine Grier was too happy about that?"

"Since he's still babying his instep from where her heel accidentally slipped on it, I'd say he got the message."

"I love a woman who's not afraid to use her stiletto."

"And seeing as how I love that *particular* woman

and her best friend, I figured a quietly worded statement would be much preferred over a physical battle." Mick shook his head as the uncle with dubious morals zeroed in on one of the town's divorcees of a more appropriate age. "So summing up my original point, people make bad choices when they drink."

"The problem is, I think Myrtle would have said the same thing stone-cold sober."

"And you're taking her word as gospel?"

It was dumb to bring it up—even dumber to give it more than a passing thought—so Roman held off on saying anything further. He knew Mick was only trying to lighten the mood, but it wasn't helping. And try as he might to ignore it, the truth was more than evident.

No one in Indigo had any sense of who he was anymore.

But they would.

Chapter Three

*A*very fought the urge to order another glass of wine and made the game-time decision to switch to a ginger ale instead. As she turned to look at the room, midway through another eighties dance hit, she had to give credit to Sloan and Walker. Despite some initial concerns that the two families wouldn't have anything in common, four hours later the bride and groom could consider the day a wild success.

Sloan and Walker had originally planned to spring the wedding on Sloan's mother to avoid her involvement with the planning, but Winnie had steamrolled straight through their surprise attack. To avoid the embarrassment of canceling the lavish wedding her mother was intent on setting up at the Plaza, Sloan had come clean and told her what they were planning and how they really wanted to celebrate their day.

The fact that the change had then necessitated transporting roughly sixty guests up to Indigo from New York had kept them all hopping over the past six months. Avery had even gotten into the act from Ireland, helping to coordinate transportation.

"The 'Y.M.C.A.' does it every damn time." Grier

moved up next to her at one of the makeshift bars and reached for her soda before Avery could even take a sip.

"What?"

"The 'Y.M.C.A.' It's like a wedding drug. Start playing that and everyone's on their feet and dancing. Whether they're from Scarsdale or Indigo, it's like they've known each other for a lifetime."

"I'm sure the open bar and the wine served with dinner didn't hurt."

Grier shook her head and guzzled another sip of the ginger ale. "Nope. It's the sweet, magical voices of the Village People. The DJ played that first and now look at everyone a mere three hours later. Dancing like it's their job."

"How much wine have you had?"

"Enough that I did the Macarena with Chooch."

"I saw that."

"And, I'll have you know, I was sharp enough to keep Mick from kicking Sloan's uncle's ass."

"Nice."

"Which is why I deserve another glass of that delicious Cabernet." Grier gestured at the line of bottles at the back of the bar with the now-empty ginger ale.

"But you will like yourself far better tomorrow morning if you have another soda and get me one in the process."

Grier nodded, a small moue pursing her lips. "You're a spoilsport, but you're absolutely right."

"Why do you think I ordered myself a soda?"

"So you won't lose your head and put that bridesmaid dress to good use with Roman?"

"I'm not putting anything to good use with Roman."

"Shame." Grier sniffed as she caught the bartender's attention and ordered two more sodas.

Avery refused to let Grier's words ruffle her. The knowing glances she and Roman had both received all day had grown tedious, but she refused to give in. It would only give everyone's not so subtle winks and exaggerated eye raises credence.

"No, it's not a shame. In fact, like these sodas we're selecting, it's damn smart."

Grier lifted one of the glasses the bartender set down and handed the other to Avery. "I still say it's a shame."

"Do not tell me you're as gaga as the rest of them."

"Nah, I just want my dear, bestest friend to have some good lovin'." Grier's expression had a distinct, philosophical—overlaid with alcohol—bent to it as she scanned the room. "And if you're going to ignore the very insightful suggestion of cuddling up with Roman, perhaps you'll finally put Ronnie out of his misery and jump the poor man. His eyes follow you around like a pound puppy."

"I am so not going down that path with you again. I used to *babysit* him." When Grier just continued to stare at her—a careless shrug added for good measure— Avery enunciated further. "I changed him into his pj's. It's just creepy."

"You can't deny he's completely hot and adorable."

Avery refused to look across the room, well-aware of the googly-eyed stare from their town bartender she'd get in return. "Of course not. And he needs someone who is completely hot, adorable and age appropriate for him."

"Your loss."

"No, someone else's gain."

"You're no fun."

"I'm plenty of fun. I'm just not cheap and easy. There is a difference."

Unwilling to discuss it any longer, Avery waved a hand to the room at large. "You really don't want this sort of thing for your wedding?"

"Nope. This isn't me." Grier took a sip of her new soda before moving them toward a small table at the edge of the room. "I really would have been happy with Vegas, but I know Mick wants to get married in front of his family."

They both took seats, and Avery didn't miss the dreamy look that suffused Grier's face. "And funny enough, once I heard him talk about standing up in front of his grandmother in church, I realized I like what he sees in his head. I like the idea of something small and personal, but still public. And I like the idea of doing it in my new hometown."

Avery knew Grier had had a rough go of it at first. Indigo's residents were less than enthusiastic about her arrival the previous November. How glad she was that everyone had come around and seen exactly what she'd seen.

A bright, warm woman with love to give and an easy way about her that invited people in.

Even if she'd suddenly turned into the love police, bound and determined to make everyone around her as happy as she was.

Mick, spotted them and crossed the room. "Mind if I join you?"

"Of course not." Avery gestured to one of the open chairs. "We were just talking about you, as a matter of fact."

"Should I be scared? Or blushing?" he added as an afterthought.

"Neither. Grier just mentioned what an inspired idea you had to get married in a quiet, intimate ceremony here in town."

Mick laid his hand over Grier's. The gesture was small, but the intimacy struck Avery as incredibly sweet.

His blue eyes darkened as he looked at Grier. "The guys think I'm nuts to skip Vegas."

Avery took a sip of her soda. "Well, I think it's romantic."

"I believe that's their underlying point. I seem to be ruining an opportunity to live every man's dream wedding and instead, feeding the female wedding beast."

A quick glance across the room to where Walker and Sloan danced in each other's arms had her smiling. "I hardly think Walker's complaining."

Mick's gaze followed hers. "I don't think so."

Strains of Etta James streamed from the speakers as Avery pointed toward the floor. "You two should go dance. This is a good one."

Grier took another sip of her soda. "We're talking."

"Well you should be dancing." Avery waved toward the dance floor. "Go on." Within moments, the two were in each other's arms, moving to the thick, sensual strains of the music.

The fleeting thought that she should be jealous hummed somewhere in the back of her mind, but no matter how many ways she looked at it, she couldn't muster up the emotion.

Would she like to have a relationship, too? Yes, no doubt. Would she begrudge her friends for having it?

No way.

"Care to dance?"

The deep voice pulled her up short, along with the realization she'd stopped paying attention to her immediate surroundings.

"Um, I can't."

Roman looked down at her, his half-quirked smile rapidly fading as he pulled his hand back. "Since when don't you like Etta James?"

"I love Etta. We just don't need to put ourselves on display by dancing like this. And especially not to a song with a title as full of innuendo as 'At Last.'"

"Right. Because all these people need a specific, innuendo-fueled reason to stare at us?" Roman took Mick's recently vacated chair. "Ignore them."

"You've had a lot of practice ignoring people staring at you. I can't say the same."

"It's easy, Ave. Just look somewhere around the top of their heads, your smile firmly intact."

Her heart rumbled in her chest at the endearment he'd used since they were young. Ignoring it—just as she'd tried to ignore him all day—she offered up a small smile instead. "You don't have any perspective anymore. The great unwashed masses of us don't know what it's like to be stared at all the time. And we don't like it much, either."

"It's a necessary evil of what I do." He paused and pondered his glass. "And I never said I liked it."

"Oh please. You've posed nude for pictures, with nothing but a towel. That does not scream, 'I'm shy and retiring, please don't look at me.'"

Whatever somber thought had been behind his last comment fled as his smile spread. He leaned in, his grin almost wolfish in the soft, muted glow of the room's twinkle lights. "You liked that one, did you?"

The gleam in those gorgeous green depths had her heart pounding again. Damn it, how did she get herself into these things? She had no business discussing nude photos with her ex. Especially when those photos were of him.

Forcing a bored note into her voice, she gave him the same generous smile she reserved for his grandmother. "You've got an amazing body, Roman. Everyone who looked at it liked that picture."

The ploy obviously worked, because he leaned back in his chair, his smile falling. As the moment grew tense once more—the normal state between the two of them—Avery fought the momentary urge to apologize.

It was all about self-preservation. And when faced with the impact of Roman Forsyth in the flesh, a woman needed a full suit of emotional body armor.

Satisfied hers was back in place, she shifted the conversation. "It's been a beautiful wedding. Sloan and Walker will look back on this and know they pulled off a winner."

"Everyone has gotten along."

"Grier thinks it's solely a result of the 'Y.M.C.A.'"

"That song is the great equalizer. No one can be all uppity and pompous while throwing their hands in the air and spelling letters over and over again."

"So it's got nothing to do with everyone making an effort?"

One dark eyebrow lifted at her assessment. "Did you somehow miss how chilly last night's rehearsal dinner was?"

Avery had to give him points for honesty. "It wasn't the most rocking evening I've ever attended."

"I've sat through postgame screaming matches from the coach that were more enjoyable than last night."

"Maybe that's why Sloan was nervous all morning. She almost flipped out when Grier let her know Sophie was taking her mother to task."

Roman's laugh was slow and easy. "Now, there's a conversation I'd have paid to witness. Walker's grandmother only looks sweet."

"I won't argue with you there. I don't think Winifred McKinley knew what hit her."

"She did look a bit shell-shocked during the ceremony."

They sat companionably, the moment a funny mix of easy camaraderie and frustrating self-awareness. She'd missed this, Avery acknowledged to herself. The casual conversation and comfortable understanding between the two of them.

They'd had it since they were young—and if she took her romantic emotions out of the equation, she knew the loss of this companionship had been nearly as hard as losing her first boyfriend.

The last strains of the song faded, and Avery didn't miss the quick tempo that took its place. Before she could register his movement, Roman was on his feet and pulling her to hers. "You can't skip this one. It's just not allowed."

His large hand engulfed hers and Avery felt herself dragged toward the dance floor as the crowd parted to make room for them, the strains of "Oh, What a Night" blaring through the speakers.

Avery lifted her arms, the tension flying away as the voices of the Four Seasons floated over her. Their ode to lost virginity was as enjoyable—and dance-worthy— at thirty-three as it was at eighteen.

Grier and Sloan made their way toward her, the three of them laughing and dancing to the freedom of the music.

"My mother hates this song!" Sloan finally got out after a particularly impressive half spin, half pirouette. "Thinks it's undignified."

"Can we get 'em to play it again?" Grier suggested as she added some nimble footwork to complement the movements of her arms.

Sloan shot a glance at her mother, who'd managed to join the floor and who was doing a rather impressive dance of her own with Sloan's father. "Actually, I'm not sure if we'll appreciate the outcome. My mother appears to be enjoying herself."

"Quick. Where's the garlic?"

Avery swatted at Grier's arm, laughing in spite of herself as Mick moved in to wrangle his wayward fiancée. Avery threw back her head and lifted her arms as Frankie Valli's voice layered over the happily singing wedding attendees. It was only when Roman moved right in next to her, his large frame dwarfing her own, that she dropped her arms, stumbling and losing the beat.

And just like that, whatever joy had her firmly engaged in the moment evaporated, replaced in her mind's eye with a vision of their prom night.

He'd stood above her so many years before, looking surprisingly similar. The tuxedo wasn't custom-made and his hair was a bit longer, curling at the nape of his neck, but the rest was the same.

And the same hungry expression that rode his gaze then was the one he wore right now.

Roman stared down at Avery, his heart throbbing somewhere around the middle of his throat. A need so sharp it was nearly painful struck him with blunt force, like a body slam against the boards while skating at full speed.

Damn, but she got to him.

Nerves buzzed around his stomach with manic need, and he realized with a start he hadn't felt the same around a woman since he was sixteen years old. When he'd schemed every conceivable way to ask her out.

His relief had been palpable when she'd said yes, her agreement to go to the diner for ice cream so simple—so natural—he'd wondered why he had worried at all.

Somehow he didn't think it would be quite so easy this time.

Or that a hot fudge sundae could fix what had gone wrong between the two of them.

Pulling himself firmly off memory lane, he smiled

and executed a neat two-step that he'd perfected in the eighth grade. "Your footwork needs some help, Marks."

The heat that flared in her dark eyes shifted at the whiff of competition. "I can dance circles around you. I always could."

"Prove it."

The pulsing beat kept up around them as Avery took his challenge to heart. She lifted her arms again and his gaze traveled the familiar paths of her long, lithe frame. The pert fullness of her breasts peeked over the edge of her gown, and Roman imagined peeling it off her with infinite slowness.

As the music reached its final chorus, she tilted her head back, her eyes closed to the music, and Roman felt himself pulled into her orbit.

Why had he ever left it?

Happy shouts filled the room as the entire crowd finished off the dance. Roman could only thank the magical power of an oldie-but-goodie that no one was focused on him and what had to be a besotted haze covering his face.

"You all right, Roman?"

The moment shattered as Walker slapped him on the back. Roman didn't miss the dark glare Sloan shot Walker, who was oblivious to his new wife's distress.

Suddenly inspired, he reached for Sloan as he turned to Walker. "I'm fine, buddy. And I'm getting my dance with the bride."

Sloan went willingly into his arms as the band moved into a slower number. Not nearly as torchy as the Etta James song, but one designed to slow down the room.

Sloan laid a hand on his shoulder as he clasped her hand. "I swear he's completely oblivious sometimes."

The thought flitted through his mind to play dumb but he respected Sloan way too much for that. "I'd say his timing was impeccable."

Other than the subtle tightening of her hand in his as Roman moved her into a turn, her expression stayed neutral. "I don't know about that. You were dancing with a beautiful woman. I'm not sure you needed your best friend's interference."

Roman ratcheted up his smile. The megawatt version he used for the press. "Yet here I am, dancing with another beautiful woman."

"You know what I mean."

"Yeah, well, my last dance partner had to be dragged onto the floor, so I'm not sure that's a ringing endorsement."

He watched several emotions flit across her face before she settled on whatever it was she found acceptable. "I realize there's a lot of history there. But you both have a chance to make the best of the here and now. Isn't that worth something?"

It was worth more than something, but Roman was damned if he'd say so.

He'd blown his chances a long time ago, and no matter how badly he wanted Avery—or how badly he missed having her in his life—he'd made his choice years ago.

And there was no getting around it.

"Come on, Mrs. Montgomery. I'm a rolling stone and you know it. Hell, you interviewed me, and I believe said as much in your article."

The delight she found in his use of her new name faded quickly, along with her smile. "That was a few years ago. And it certainly was before I knew you."

"Don't look so upset. And for the record, you were correct in your assessment."

"No, Roman, I wasn't." She held his gaze, an apology flickering clearly in the depths of hers. "I was horribly presumptuous and out of line, waxing poetic when I should have reported what was told to me."

He wasn't sure why the article had stuck with him, when it had been long forgotten by others. And he found it even more curious that it was his best friend's future wife who had written it.

One of the odd circles of life, he supposed.

But despite the reason, the article had stuck with him, Sloan's words haunting him for their strange measure of truth.

But when you dig down deep and pull away the layers, it's hard to understand what truly motivates Roman Forsyth. He's at the top of his game, the pinnacle of a hall-of-fame career, yet this reporter couldn't help wondering why the depths of his vivid green eyes hold a tinge of sadness.

Pulling himself from the memory, he leaned in and gave her a quick kiss on her most special of days. "You weren't horribly presumptuous, you were one hundred percent truthful. There's a big difference."

"Well then, I'll try for presumptuous once more and then I'll drop it." She made a quick cross over her chest. "Promise."

He could hear the song winding down, the last, lingering strains floating over the room. "Okay. Shoot."

"Don't miss out on something because you think

you can't have it. I almost made that mistake and if I had, I wouldn't be here today." She was on her tiptoes and pressing her lips to his cheek. "So just think about it."

Walker swooped in before the last notes faded, pulling his new wife away, but Roman didn't miss the somber light in her vivid blue eyes.

Nor did he miss the small smile she sent his way before turning into Walker's arms.

Julia propped her stockinged feet on a folding chair and lifted her glass of champagne toward Sophie and Mary. "To a very successful day."

Their town hall showed the evidence of a good time had by all, and they'd said good-bye to the last of the revelers a short while before.

And then made the unanimous decision to break into a bottle of Dom Perignon Julia had saved for a special occasion. Her dearest friends clinked their flutes in turn and each sat back with a satisfied smile on her face.

Sophie's gaze turned speculative. "I had a few moments where I thought things might not go off as planned, but everything did fall into place beautifully."

"Sloan's mother is"—Mary coughed—"unique."

"She's a grizzly bear." Sophie let out an indelicate harrumph. "But I saw a few moments of real genuineness so I suppose she's not all bad."

"I saw her tears when Sloan and Walker exchanged their vows." Julia let her thoughts drift to the ceremony. "I suspect she means well; she simply doesn't know how to show it."

"I thought I was supposed to be the diplomatic one." Sophie took another sip of her champagne. "You know, as mayor and all."

Mary let out another cough but Julia didn't miss the grin she hid behind her hand.

Or the quick wink she shot Julia when she came up for air.

Sophie missed all of it as she reached for the champagne bottle they'd set between them on another folding chair. "What is it about a wedding?"

"The promise—" Mary sighed.

"The passion," Julia added at the same time.

"Are you sure you're talking about the bride and groom?"

Julia heard the not so subtle notes of innuendo lacing Sophie's words. "Of course. They looked so happy."

"I meant Avery and Roman. Did you see the way the two of them looked at each other?"

"It's electric. Just as it always was," Mary added.

Julia understood their need to talk about it. Heck, she'd been more than happy to talk to her friends about their grandsons' romances, but something felt off and she couldn't quite define why. "That was a long time ago. I'm just glad the two of them can be in the same room together."

"But the way they look at each other." Sophie's tone was persistent. "Don't tell me you don't see it?"

It was hard to miss, but she'd be damned if she'd discuss it.

Her grandson had made some poor choices with Avery. Oh, she'd never begrudge him his opportunity to pursue his dream, but she also knew the pursuit had come with a price.

And Avery had borne the payment.

"Come on, girls. They have a lot of history there. It doesn't mean anything more. He's headed back home in a few weeks and our girl's still glowing from her trip to Ireland."

A merry twinkle lit Sophie's eyes. "Sounds like she had a wonderful time there. And the phone lines have been burning up ever since. Maybe it'll kick Roman's butt into gear and he'll do something about her. It's clear he still has feelings for her."

Julia wasn't sure why the words were so irritating, but she resisted the urge to say anything. Roman and Avery didn't need their interference. In fact, they'd both be far better off if they were simply left alone.

She hadn't missed the speculative gazes and whispered comments that had floated around the room all day. And the denizens of Indigo had turned practically purple holding their breaths and craning their necks watching them dance near the end of the wedding.

It was no one's business, but all anyone saw was hearts and cupids floating around their heads.

And it worried her.

From the earliest age, Roman and Avery had been compatible, their friendship easy and genuine. It hadn't shocked her when that friendship turned to something more in high school.

Nor had it shocked her when her grandson left a few short years later in pursuit of his dream.

He'd spent his life under a veil of missed opportunity; his grandfather dying before he was born and his own father dying when he was a child. She'd known—even if he'd never overtly said it—that he wasn't going to let his life go unfulfilled.

Roman had a dream and it hadn't been rooted in a small town in Alaska.

Even if the woman he loved with all his heart was.

Chapter Four

*A*very slipped out of her heels as she walked across the parking lot of the Indigo Blue. The July night had grown cool, but the purple twilight above her ensured no one could forget it was actually summer.

The midnight air swirled around her and she hovered in that delightful stage between drunk and sober.

Comfortably numb, she'd heard it referred to, and it fit.

Shouts still echoed around town, several of the wedding revelers headed to Maguire's for a nightcap or the diner for more fun, but they were all far enough away that she was blessedly free from making small talk. Susan had declared the hotel bar closed for the night, and Avery was determined to enjoy what was left of a quiet evening.

The front doors slid open at her approach and she walked into the hotel, the familiar lobby welcoming her home. She'd lived here for almost two years now—had worked here for nearly fifteen—and the sense of belonging she felt every time she entered the large structure that dominated the end of town never failed to strike her with a jolt of surprise. It had been a strange sort of comfort, knowing she was always welcome at the Indigo Blue, despite the failure of her relationship with the proprietor's son.

Even more comforting was knowing Roman's mother and grandmother continued to love her anyway.

Several of the wedding's out-of-town guests sat around the lobby in small conversation groups. Although she'd declared the bar closed, Susan had left complimentary waters and soft drinks in a cooler in front of the bar and a bottle of wine in each guest's room. Avery saw several people had taken advantage of the hospitality as they wound down from the revelry of the day.

The urge to stop and check on them was strong, but she willed her feet to keep on moving toward her apartment. She'd been up since five, doing last-minute prep work for the hotel before firmly morphing into her role as bridesmaid.

Her apartment was on a small corridor off the lobby and she headed that way, fumbling in her clutch for keys.

"Avery."

Awareness skimmed over her skin, and her fingers shook as she closed over the cool metal. On a small intake of breath, she turned away from the door.

"Roman."

"Did you enjoy the wedding?"

"It was a beautiful day."

His bow tie hung haphazardly around his neck and the top button of his shirt was undone. The awareness humming in her veins amped up another few decibels as she took in the column of his throat and the light growth of beard on his jaw.

How did he manage to look like he'd just walked off a photo shoot at midnight, after a full day of revelry?

"That wasn't my question."

"Hmmm?" She tried to focus on his words and not his large, tantalizing form as he moved closer toward her.

"I asked you if you enjoyed yourself."

"Of course I did." She brushed the question off.

"Liar."

"I am not. Besides, what wasn't there to enjoy? Two of my closest friends had a beautiful day and they threw a mighty fine party to seal the deal." A small hiccup punctuated her words. "And the wine was delicious. It wasn't quite your quarterly delivery of the mother lode, but it was damn good."

Roman had sent a quarterly shipment of some of the world's finest wines, the crates arriving with alarming regularity, starting the first year he received a seven-figure contract. Although she'd resented the large boxes that Mick delivered from Anchorage, she'd never been able to resist what was inside. Rothschild. Screaming Eagle. And on one rare occasion a case of Petrus she still hadn't had the courage to drink beyond one bottle.

"I know you like wine."

"I like lots of things. Doesn't mean I need you to buy them for me."

"It's a gift, Avery. That's all. Besides, I have it on good authority from my grandmother you're not the only one who enjoys the wine."

Avery couldn't resist offering up a small smile.

"Your grandmother is sitting in the lobby waiting every time Mick brings in a shipment."

A lazy smile spread across his face as he moved in another step closer. "I'll just bet she is."

Electricity hummed between them, sparking each time their gazes met, despite the silence that closed around them in their deserted stretch of hallway.

She really should be over *this*.

Over him.

It had been years, and enough was enough.

"Why are you here?"

"I wanted to see you."

"You saw me all day."

"I wanted to see the girl I remember."

A sigh floated up from deep in her stomach, full of lost opportunities. "That's all she is, Roman. A memory."

"I don't know." He moved forward and Avery wanted to move back. Wanted to raise some measure of resistance. But comfortable and numb and a raging case of curiosity had her standing still.

"I think she's still in there somewhere. That sassy girl who told me I'd never make the big leagues if I didn't get better on the boards. And who made me practice my debate skills so I wouldn't look like an asshole on TV."

A long forgotten image flashed through her mind. The two of them sitting in Susan's living room, practicing for their debate class.

"Do you really want to look like a Neanderthal doofus tomorrow? Come on, all we're debating is if Pearl Jam is worthy of the title of best grunge band ever."

A light flush of red crept up his neck. "No one wants to hear what I have to say. And for the record, they suck ass."

He'd been playing with her hand, distracting her as she tried to convince him to practice for debate class. Although his large fingers felt divine as they kept swirling over her palm, she tugged her hand away. The low clench in her stomach every time she got near him—or thought about him or looked at him—was hard enough to fight when he wasn't touching her.

And those damn swirls on her palm were way too distracting.

"Then convince me of it."

"Of what?"

"Why Pearl Jam sucks."

"I don't know why they suck. They just do."

"Nope. Not good enough." She stood, trying to put some distance between them. Her feelings for him had been overwhelming and she needed some distance from time to time.

"I'm going to say something and all you have to do is respond." His crossed eyes and folded arms only had her more desperate to make her point. "You think people won't make fun of you when you're in the big leagues if you can't put two words together? Because they will."

"The big leagues are a long way away."

She hoped so. God, how she hoped so, but even she knew he was special on skates.

She knew it.

And she'd have known it even if there weren't scouts up here every month or so watching him play.

So she forced bravado into her tone and dangled the bait he could never resist. "That's probably a good thing since you need a lot of practice. And you still can't do shit in the crease because you act like a girl when you get slammed against the boards."

The light of battle sparked in his green eyes and he sat up straighter. "I kicked ass in Fairbanks last week."

"You got lucky with that goal. Your only goal."

His deep voice grew heavy with anger. "They had it out for me the entire game. The asshat defenders wouldn't let me move."

"Excuses, excuses. Just like your crappy debate skills."

"Pearl Jam sucks. How will talking about it make me a better speaker?"

While their teacher was trying to make the class fun, she knew Roman had a point and he was just stubborn enough to ignore the lesson as it had been assigned. "Fine. What do you want to debate about then?"

"The Metros' defense."

Avery waved a hand. "Have at it."

"Have at what?"

"Debate the Metros' defense for me. Tell me why it's the best."

"It just is."

She hit him on the side of his head, the chance to touch him too wonderful to resist. "Listen to my question and then answer it. Teach me something."

Her words hovered in the air between them for a moment as his dark pupils expanded. He reached for her hand—the one she'd used to swat at him—and his thumb rubbed over her wrist.

"Fine. I'll teach you something."

The nerves in her wrist tingled under his hand, and she wondered why she never noticed before—not once in her whole life—how sensitive her arm could feel.

With a quick exhale, she forced her attention back on their conversation.

And her goal of ensuring Roman wouldn't flunk their debate class and miss the spring formal.

"Roman." Her voice sounded funny in her ears when she finally spoke. "Many say the New York Metros have no shot at the Stanley Cup this year and even more say their defense isn't playing to their full potential."

"I disagree, Ms. Marks." His thumb flicked again and she forgot to breathe.

"Ave?"

"What?" The remembered flush that suffused her body was replaced with the reality of an adult Roman standing before her.

"You look a million miles away."

"I was just remembering your high school debate lesson."

"Why Pearl Jam sucks?"

Her mouth dropped. "You remember?"

"Sure I do. I think about it every time someone shoves a microphone in my face."

"It was just a dumb debate subject by a teacher desperately trying to make class interesting."

"As I recall, you were the interesting part. But the lesson buried underneath ended up being important, too."

"What lesson?"

"Listen before you respond." A broad grin split his face and she sensed he held something back.

"And?"

"Nothing."

"No, not nothing. What?"

"I was so horny that night. I thought you'd never shut up about that stupid class and let me kiss you."

The urge to cuff his head like that long-ago study night filled her but she kept her hands at her sides. "Men. One-track minds."

"Only for the good memories."

"I find it hard to believe an unfulfilled hard-on was a good memory."

That same look—the one that had darkened his gaze so many years before—rose up and edged out the laughter in his eyes. "You have no idea."

Those notes of unfulfilled longing that had dogged him as a teenager grabbed him as if they'd never been sated.

One look at her and all the grown-up self-control he'd gained since actually growing up vanished.

And he wasn't kidding about the Pearl Jam debate lesson. It did come to mind every time a reporter shoved a microphone at him. You'd think he'd be used to it after all this time, but that memory—and the desperate need he'd had for a crazy, sassy slip of a girl—hadn't ever faded.

"Since you keep avoiding my question, I'll answer it instead. I thought today's ceremony was beautiful. I've never seen Walker so happy, and I think Sloan is the perfect match for him. And if one more person asks me how long I'm staying I may leave a swath of bodies along Main Street."

"Everyone is very concerned with how long you'll be here."

"I think they're hoping for the love equivalent of a hat trick."

Avery's eyes widened as his words registered. "Well, we need to ensure everyone knows that there's one love match that won't be happening."

Roman wasn't sure why but the quick refusal stuck in his craw. With deliberately lazy movements, he leaned against the doorjamb of her apartment. "Why say anything?"

"This town is crazy about love. You know that. And now that the grandmothers have two of you married off, you know they're not going to stop. This town loves seeing its bachelors settle down."

"We're grown-ups, Avery. I think you and I are more than capable of making up our own minds."

"They can be persuasive."

He couldn't resist. The lightly hissed words—as if she were afraid of drawing the devil out of his lair—hovered in the air. With a streak of devilish amusement of his own, he snaked out a hand and grabbed one of hers in a tight grip, pulling her forward. "So can I."

Without giving her a moment to think about it, he wrapped his other hand around her back and pulled her in for a kiss. A light "oomph" of surprise was the last thing he heard before their lips met.

She stiffened for the briefest moment—whether it was to fight him or run from him, he didn't know—before she made the clear decision to stay. The lithe, supple lines of her body went soft under his fingers and Avery took the last few steps into him.

And then he feasted.

The memories of her that had haunted him for years fled with the reality of having her in his arms again. The soft cavern of her mouth and the erotic play of tongues both took him back and moved him firmly into the here and now.

And as her tongue wrapped around his, drawing him deeply into her mouth, he realized that the memories he'd carried were of a girl. The woman in his arms was real, and so much better.

As if he needed any further evidence of that fact, her curves spilled into his hands as he shifted his grip from her back to her waist. With his other hand, he skimmed his fingertips up the side of her body, brushing ever so lightly against the side of her breast.

A light moan whispered through her lips and he did it again, satisfied when her breathing hitched at his touch.

She'd always loved when he touched her breasts and had grown more demanding about it as they'd learned each others' bodies. Each other's rhythm. On some level he couldn't define, it was gratifying to still know where to give her pleasure.

And how to make her moan.

So many things had changed in the time he'd been gone; he reveled in the sensation of knowing that they still fit.

Which was why he wasn't surprised when her hands came up hard against his chest.

"Roman—"

"What?" He marshaled his resources and skimmed his fingers once more over her torso, using his thumb to put additional pressure over the fullness of her breast.

"Roman." She stepped back, her lips wet from their kiss and her dark eyes glowing with an arousal he knew mirrored his own. "We can't do this."

"We can do this." He levered his hands at her hips to pull her closer.

"No. We can't."

Like a shutter slamming closed over the light streaming through a window, her passion-filled gaze shut down, replaced with an icy cool that stopped him from reaching for her again.

"We can dance around this, Avery. Or we can do something about it."

"Don't let nostalgia cloud your judgment, Roman. We stopped doing anything a long time ago. Dancing or otherwise."

Before he could muster up a response, she unlocked her door and slipped through it, not even turning to say good night.

The aftereffects of kissing Avery still hummed in his veins the following morning as Roman did his daily run through town. He had waved to a few early risers, but most of Indigo was still indoors, sleeping off a night of revelry.

Fresh air flowed in and out of his lungs with each step he took, and he appreciated the change in routine. July in Manhattan was usually stifling, and the tang of cool, crisp air was a welcome respite.

He followed a curving path out of town and along the river that ran outside Indigo. He'd done this run more times than he could count and the familiarity was a comforting presence as he processed the events of the last few days.

The overheated moment in front of Avery's doorway had haunted his dreams last night and he'd stood there for several moments, imagining what it would have been like if she'd allowed him to follow her inside. Long, soulful kisses like the one they'd shared in the hall. The languid removal of the silk material that showcased her figure to perfection. The press of their slick flesh as they came together after so many years apart.

He could see all of it—every taste and touch—and it filled him with a quiet desperation he'd never had a name for.

All he wanted was Avery. *His* Avery.

And for the next month he'd be in close proximity to the one woman on the planet who drove him absolutely crazy.

A rush of anger surged and he used it as an added incentive to push his body. Increasing his speed, despite the three miles he'd already covered, Roman fought the need that pumped through his bloodstream with good old-fashioned sweat and effort.

His feet thumped over the ground, the occasional twig or branch making a satisfying crack as his weight split it in half. Cool air swept in and out of his lungs with increasing force and he reveled in the effort, satisfied when it required more of his attention.

God, how she twisted him up and made him forget—

Without warning, one second he was upright and moving at a steady clip and the next he flew ass over head down a slippery embankment.

"Fuck!"

The words tore from his lips as he used his hands to stop his momentum. He closed his eyes against the ground that rose up to meet him and tucked his shoulder at the last minute, as if approaching contact with the boards at the rink.

"Effective, Forsyth," he muttered to himself when he ended up facedown in a pile of wet leaves and grass.

Roman rolled over, opened his eyes and looked around. A slight twinge echoed through his shoulder— more the result of an old injury than any real damage— and a quick assessment of his body ensured the fall had been more of an embarrassment than truly damaging.

A massive fucking embarrassment when he looked back up at the embankment and saw what he'd missed.

The path had a divot about the width of a foot and he'd stepped right into it. And he hadn't seen it at all because the hole had been in his peripheral vision.

Something he hadn't had in his right eye for almost three months.

Fuck, shit and damn.

He stood and brushed the grass off, swiping at his shorts. A large cut gaped at his knee and he could see blood on the cap.

"Great way to start the day, asshole," he muttered to himself. "Horny and banged up. Welcome the fuck home."

Chapter Five

Avery walked into the café around seven. Although there was plenty of breakfast at the hotel, she wasn't interested in making small talk with the guests, and Susan had taken pity on her.

Or had recognized she'd scare off any repeat visitors with an attitude that could rival a grizzly bear's.

"You're up early." Mick smiled at her from a booth near the door and waved her over.

"I could say the same for you. What are you doing here by yourself? Where's Grier?"

"My little party animal is sleeping off last night's fun."

"She was sobering up when I left the reception."

"Jell-O shots," Mick explained as he took a sip of coffee. "Someone had them in a cooler on the way out and she thought they'd be a good idea."

"I bet she feels a bit different this morning."

"Which is why I made about as much noise as one of my planes this morning as I got ready to head out."

Avery couldn't help but smile at that. "You're an evil man. It's one of your most charming qualities."

"I'm not sure Grier thought it was so charming."

"Actually, when she comes out of her self-induced stupor, I think she'll probably applaud you for it. She's twisted that way. Which"—Avery picked up the mug of coffee their waitress set down in front of her—"is the reason she's so damn crazy about you. You give her a run for her money."

"Sort of like you and Roman?"

Her good humor fled, replaced immediately with the grizzly attitude. "It's nothing like me and Roman."

"You sure?"

"Positive."

"The whole town thinks differently."

"Then they're going to be very disappointed to realize how wrong they are."

"Ah, but the real question, my friend, is, are they wrong?"

Avery mulled his words over as she looked at her menu. She knew exactly what she wanted—had known before walking in the door—but the menu gave her a handy excuse to stall.

She'd carried her feelings for Roman so close to the surface for so long that it hurt in a way she could never have imagined to have him dangled in front of her once more. She truly understood that everyone's hopeful eyebrow raises and happy gossip weren't meant to be hurtful, but they simply had no idea what it did to her.

With a casualness she didn't feel, Avery glanced up from her menu. "He left, Mick. A long time ago. I've gotten over it, and there's no reason to think we need to start things back up."

"Believe me when I say I know what a royal pain in

the ass all the attention is. But take it away, the innuendo and the gossip, and what are you left with?"

"Nothing, Mick." She folded her menu and picked up her cup of coffee. "Absolutely nothing."

Roman's royally shitty morning went from bad to worse when he walked through the door of the café. All he wanted was a damn omelet and a cup of coffee, not a resounding reminder of what he didn't have last night.

Yet there sat Avery and Mick, having breakfast and talking.

Their position in one of the front booths also ensured he couldn't just order at the counter and walk out without looking like a world-class jerk.

"What happened?" Avery's gaze ran the length of him before she was up and out of the booth. "Are you bleeding?"

"I'm fine."

"You're a mess."

He brushed off the concern and slid into the booth she'd just gotten out of. His knee did throb like a blinking neon sign, but he'd deal with it later. "I'm fine."

"What happened?" Mick's voice was calmer, but Roman didn't miss the sharpness to the question.

"I tripped on my run this morning. No big."

"You're covered in grass stains and you really need to put something on that knee."

Before he could brush it off as nothing, Avery's hand was on his thigh and she had a handful of napkins out of the small metal holder on the table, pressed against his throbbing knee.

And just like that, something else a few inches from her hand began to throb worse.

Way worse.

"I'm fine, Ave." It wasn't until the words were out that he realized his teeth were clamped so tightly his jaw ached.

Sudden awareness flashed in her gorgeous gaze. For a moment, he delighted in the simple sincerity of her actions and the fact that the walls usually standing high and impenetrable between them weren't in evidence.

Until that gaze flashed once again—this time to his groin—and her eyes widened in surprise.

Gruff instructions rang out as she lifted her hand from his thigh. "Here. Hold the napkins against your knee for a few more minutes."

"Thanks." *Even if I'd rather you hold something more interesting than a stack of napkins.*

Mick's averted gaze and focus on his coffee was the only thing that kept Roman's comment from being voiced. Add in the not so subtle fact that Avery had pulled her hand away from his body as if scalded—along with the reason for his tumble—and his humiliation was complete.

"What are you both having?" Roman asked.

"Pancakes," they said in unison.

Although he'd been set on the omelet, the thought of all those carbs had him reconsidering. Maybe the morning could be salvaged after all. "Hangover fare if I've ever heard it."

"Which is why I'm going to be a good fiancé and bring a stack home to Grier when I leave."

"Grier have a tough night?"

"Tougher morning," Mick said with a speculative gaze at his mug. "There's coffee at home for when she wakes up but I left her sleeping."

"What about you?" He turned toward Avery. "You look well rested and hangover free." Yet another battering to his ego at the evidence that she must have slept like a baby.

"I had my moments. I'm just lucky I stopped before I could do any real damage."

Because they sat side by side Roman couldn't see a full view of her face, but he didn't miss her meaning. "Well, the things we miss out on are often the most fun experiences. Even if we pay for them in the morning."

Avery did turn toward him at that, her dark eyebrows a hard slash over expressive eyes.

Served her right. She could say whatever she wanted, but he wasn't alone in that damn hallway last night. She responded to his kiss like she remembered all the ways they were good together.

Damn good together.

They were prevented from extending the argument by the arrival of their waitress bearing coffee. Roman ordered the omelet he'd planned on—the years of strength training had drilled too much discipline into him to act on the pancake impulse.

"Myrtle's got the whole town excited that you're coaching the kids." Mick eyed him over the rim of his coffee cup.

"It should be fun. I want to keep up my workouts in the off season, and their enthusiasm will be the extra kick in my old ass."

"The coach ran out near the end of the season. Jack and I didn't even have to fly him, he just packed his few bags and hopped on the train."

"Asshole," Roman muttered as he doctored his coffee. Three spoonfuls of sugar and about as much milk.

Avery had always teased him about how he put more stuff in his coffee than what was already in the mug. Annoyed that he'd think of their shared past over a damn cup of coffee, he attempted to get his mind back in their booth.

"He was that. No one in town liked him, so other than disappointing the kids, no one was sorry he left." Avery reached for the sugar after he set it down and doctored her own coffee. Although she didn't layer up with a heavy dosing of cream, he saw that age hadn't diminished her love of sugar.

And just like that, Memory Lane decided it wasn't quite done kicking his ass.

He remembered kissing her, that sweet coffee fresh on her tongue as they skated out on the river that ran along the edge of town. He'd used a debris-free quarter-mile stretch of river for his skating practice and she always found a way to cheer him on, pushing him to work harder.

To skate harder.

To sweat and toil and ache for what he wanted, even though it meant all that work would take him away from her.

It had taken him a long time to understand how selfless she'd truly been, pushing him all along.

The image of hot kisses on the cold river faded and

Roman tried to focus back in on their discussion. "How long was he here?"

"Less than a season. Claimed the winter was longer than he expected it to be."

"Where did you guys find him?"

"California." Avery snorted. "He thought he had the balls to handle Alaska."

"Clearly he missed the mark," Roman said.

"Or we did."

"Oh come on," Avery needled Mick. "You had your doubts from the day you flew him up here from Anchorage."

"I didn't say anything, though. He was already hired. What good would it do to bad-mouth the guy?"

"It might have saved Trina a big dose of heartache."

"She still playing the field?" Roman keyed in on that, a long-forgotten memory of Trina and the going-away "present" she attempted to bestow upon him the night before he left an image he'd prefer to forget.

"Sadly, yes." Avery's tone held a distinct note of sympathy, and Roman had to admit it was probably better he'd kept Trina's offer of a going-away present a secret.

"Add to it he wasn't from around here and you had her perfect target. Unlike you"—she swatted him on the elbow as their waitress placed three heaping plates on their table—"who denied her from giving you a proper send-off."

"You knew about that?"

"How do you think I knew to show up at the exact proper moment? She'd spread it around to anyone who would listen, including my friends, that she was going after you before you left."

"And you never told me?"

"What was the point? If I'd thought you were going to do anything about it, I'd have cut your balls off with the blunt end of your hockey stick."

Mick winced along with Roman's own audible "Ouch."

"I can't believe you knew and didn't say anything."

"I knew." Avery grinned, the first genuine smile he'd see since getting home. "And I figured I'd give you enough credit not to make a big deal about it."

Her words caught him up short and he marveled at the insight she'd managed to have at eighteen. He'd dated plenty of women over the years—some more successfully than others—and every single one had shared something in common.

All of them got territorial when another woman came into view.

Although he'd never been ready to commit to a life with any of them, he was a one-woman man. If he was dating, he was committed, and he'd never insult a woman by cheating on her.

How was it that Avery had understood that at such a young age, and women far more world-weary hadn't?

"I knew, too, if it makes you feel any better," Mick said.

"You knew because I told you."

"No." Mick shook his head. "I knew before that. Not much was a secret in our pea-sized high school."

"Yet you allowed me to face my fate alone."

"I was probably up in the air when it all came down."

"Likely story."

Roman couldn't stop the smile, the good-natured ribbing and memories of a far-simpler time too nice to resist. He'd been lucky through the years, making some good, lasting friendships in the NHL, but none of them was as long-standing—or as solid—as what he had with Mick and Walker.

Avery, too, he realized.

She'd been there from the first.

Which was why leaving her behind years ago was the only answer.

Avery smiled when the bright morning sun and cool breeze greeted her as she, Mick and Roman walked through the door of the café. Whatever bad mood she'd come in with, the pancakes and good conversation had gone a long way toward assuaging it. She realized that this was the first time since Roman had arrived back in town that their time together had been comfortable and easy instead of mired in thoughts of the past.

And even more enjoyable than she'd remembered.

While it had become habit to think about all the years they'd missed together, she couldn't help but be glad for the new moments they were able to share. Which had to be the reason for her tragic mistake.

"Do you guys want to go with me to the rink?" Roman asked. "I want to check it out before seeing the kids. Mort was supposed to meet me, but Myrtle shared the unfortunate news that something on the wedding menu didn't agree with him."

Mick lifted a take-out carton, a grimace on his face. "I've got to get these pancakes home and then out to the airstrip. I've got a late-morning run to Fairbanks."

"I'll go." Avery shrugged, unable to resist that warm, green gaze. "Susan doesn't need me back until lunch."

"Good."

Avery saw Roman's satisfied nod—along with Mick's momentary hesitation—before Mick spoke. "You still in for poker tonight?"

"You still prepared to lose?"

"Jackass."

"Count on it."

The two shook hands and offered up a few more insults before Mick headed for his SUV.

Avery at least gave Roman the courtesy of waiting until Mick was out of earshot. "You suck at poker."

"Not anymore."

"You understand the game and you bet well, but you have no poker face. At all."

"Like I said, I'm better now."

"That's not a skill you change, Roman. It's like eye color or black hair. You are who you are and either you have a poker face or you don't."

He gestured her forward down Main Street and in the direction of the town rink. "I beg to differ. You get your ass kicked enough times and you figure out how to stop getting it kicked. It's survival instinct, pure and simple."

His words held an odd measure of truth and she couldn't resist looking at his profile as they walked. The bright sun kept part of him in silhouette, but the side of his face that she could see was more guarded than when they'd been kids.

Tougher.

And sexier than ever.

Had he developed a poker face? Or had he simply learned how to be more cautious as age, wisdom and a lifetime spent in the spotlight took their toll?

"So the rink's in pretty bad shape? I got the sense from Mort at the wedding it hasn't been taken care of very well."

His question brought her out of her musings to focus on the large dwelling that sat just past the WELCOME TO INDIGO, ALASKA sign. Where the Love Monument—his grandmother's ode to her late husband—stood at the far end of town, the hockey rink stood proudly at its entrance.

Avery had always thought the two were an odd juxtaposition. The hockey rink announced they were a good, old-fashioned Alaskan town that loved the winter sport with a passion, and the Love Monument was hidden away, a treasure the locals kept close to the vest.

Outward expressions and inward feelings.

Like Indigo had its own poker face and it just dared anyone to discover who it really was, deep in the heart of the Alaskan wilderness.

"Yeah, it's not good. I don't think there's been a single update made since you skated there."

"That was years ago. And it was pretty bad then."

"Exactly."

The front doors were unlocked when they got there, the large, cavernous space echoing as the heavy door slammed behind them.

"John Wilcox still manage the place?"

"His son does now. John retired to Texas and fishes all day."

Roman smiled as his gaze roved around the lobby. "Good for him."

"He started an e-mail loop and sends notes all winter long, taunting us with how warm it is. He also has quite a following on Twitter."

"No shit?"

"Yep. Retirement agrees with him."

"Who knew? I thought he was the meanest man in town. Clearly he just needed an infusion of Vitamin D."

"Sunlight and heat do seem to agree with him."

Roman pointed toward the large double doors that closed off the rink from the lobby, anticipation hovering around him like a cloak. "Come on. Let's go look." He grabbed her hand—whether intentional or unconscious, she didn't know—but the small outreach felt so right she shrugged off her questions and went with it.

And if a small wave of heat ran from the tips of her fingers to her shoulder, well, she'd worry about that later.

"There's not much to look at—"

The words weren't even out when Roman stopped up short and she nearly tripped over herself to avoid barreling into him. Cool, moist air coated her skin and a heavy, dank smell assaulted the senses through the open door. Although the distinct notes of cold sweat were always in evidence at an ice rink, Avery knew there was something else layered underneath.

Years and years of disrepair and neglect.

"The kids actually play here?"

"They make do."

"How? It's disgusting." Roman dropped her hand as his attention caught on something near the penalty box. He moved down the first row of bleachers, his heavy footfalls echoing off the metal. Kneeling gingerly on the knee that wasn't injured, he ran his hands over the battered, splintered wood that made up the back side of the boards.

"This is rotten almost all the way through. Someone's going to get hurt in here."

"The kids don't hit that hard."

"This would splinter under the weight of a kindergartener."

"It's not that bad, Roman." Why she felt the need to defend the mess, she wasn't sure, but there was something in his face that had her defenses rising.

He looked so sad.

And very disappointed.

"It's a disgrace."

"People do the best they can. Other things have taken priority over the years."

"So much so that no one can even spend a Saturday hammering up some new wood?" Where she'd seen anticipation when they walked in the door, anger now set his shoulders in a hard, stiff line.

"It's not that easy."

"It's not that hard, either."

A response waited on the tip of her tongue, but she held it back, refusing to give words to the anger that swelled in her breast.

He regained his feet and turned to face her, his big hands on his slim hips. His six-foot-four-inch frame—honed to perfection as a professional athlete—was rather imposing as he stood there. "What? I can see you want to say something. Out with it."

"No, it's nothing."

"Ave?"

She hissed out a breath. For all her belief in her own poker face, he managed to call her bluff each and every time. "I just think you could be a little less judgmental."

"I'm not being judgmental, I'm being practical. This place is a disaster and it needs to be fixed."

"Then do something about it."

"Why me?" His hands dropped and he turned to walk farther down the bleachers, inspecting the boards as he went. She couldn't drag her gaze off his athletic body or the way his shoulders tapered down to a firm ass that looked outrageously magnificent in shorts.

Damn, but the man's body was a vision. A living, breathing monument to fitness, athleticism and sheer animal magnetism.

And just like that, the cold arena was suddenly way too hot.

She could only assume it was frustration that had her words coming out far more clipped and harsh than she meant as she followed him down the hard metal pathway of the bleachers. "Why not you?"

"Well why not everyone else, too?"

"What's that supposed to mean?"

"It means I shouldn't be the only one to care about this. Or notice it needs to be fixed. Hockey's important to this town, or at least it used to be. If we got everyone in on it we could have this place fixed up in no time."

"You want to do that?"

"I don't think there's a choice." He flung a hand at

the room at large. "I'm not teaching the kids in this disaster zone."

Avery knew he spoke the truth. After Roman left town, she had a hard time coming here, but she'd found a way to keep supporting the town pastime. The last few years, though, she'd simply found it too depressing to continue.

"Damn, how could everyone let it get like this?"

"Because no one cares about it like you do."

He turned to face her again. "Maybe they should care."

He kneeled once more and she was curious when she saw how he twisted himself on the way down.

"How bad does that knee hurt?"

"It's not my knee," he muttered before she moved closer.

"Are you all right?"

His entire body stilled before he turned to face her once more. "Fine. I'm fine."

Roman wanted to scream in frustration, the reality of his injury a roiling embarrassment in his gut. He hadn't missed the way Avery had zeroed in on his inability to fully see the board without shifting his position. To compensate, he made a big show of examining his knee and brushing at the tender spot.

As Roman stared at the cut on his knee—evidence of his monstrous professional problem—one question pounded in the same heavy beat as his pulse.

How was he going to keep this from her?

Pushing bravado into his tone, he focused on the immediate problem at hand in hopes of distracting her.

"I'll talk to Sophie about it. As mayor, she needs to understand what a liability this is for the town. More so because the town owns the rink."

"I hadn't thought about that. But no one here would sue."

"Avery, it's not about someone with a grudge. A kid could really hurt himself. The boards are dangerous enough as it is, but to physically go through one? It would be a disaster."

She nodded and he saw her acceptance. "You're right."

They continued around the perimeter of the rink and he pulled out his phone to take pictures and document some of what he was seeing.

"It's not as fun anymore, you know."

"What's not as fun?"

"Coming here. The games. They're not as much fun to watch anymore, since you've been gone."

"I've been gone over thirteen years. This town turns out good players. I have to believe there's been a good game or two played since I left."

"None of them are as good as you."

"Maybe if they played in a half-decent rink they might be. The kids must be scared half the time to take a hit or to play hard."

"I doubt that. Don't you remember being fourteen and invincible?"

"I'm thirty-four and I still feel that way."

"Modest as always."

He only grinned, finally relaxing now that the immediate threat of discovery was well past. "Did you expect anything less?"

"No."

"Good."

The cool air felt good on his skin and that sense of invincibility roared up and grabbed him as he stared at her. The friendly camaraderie fled on swift feet as something deeper and more intense took its place.

He wanted her.

It was so simple, really. And once acknowledged, he was forced to accept the fact that the feelings for her—his need for her—had never really gone away.

He'd simply buried it in hopes it might vanish with enough time and distance.

His gaze roamed over her face, the lines so achingly familiar. The vivid, interesting brown eyes. The soft flush of pink that perpetually rode her cheekbones. The long, solid strength of her athletic body that was both strong and feminine at the same time.

He reached for her hand, the simple gesture a tentative question as he tested the waters.

"Roman!"

The moment of awareness vanished as if it had never been. Avery pulled her hand away and turned toward the greeting, all the while putting a few feet of distance between them.

Roman held back a curse and turned to face the interruption.

Chapter Six

*I*f given the opportunity, Avery would have gladly strangled John Wilcox Jr. to within an inch of his life. His poor timing, coupled with that odd, worshipful expression the entire damn town seemed to take with Roman, chafed at her like sliding across the rink naked.

He wasn't a bad guy, per se, but he'd always lumped around town with about as much personality as his father. And now that he had a bona fide sports star in his rink—an event he could bandy about town for the next few days—he was sure as hell not going to let the moment go without a long, drawn-out conversation.

"You had a good season, Roman. Damn good. I was sorry to see the Metros kicked out of the play-offs."

"Not as sorry as I was," Roman quipped with a good-natured smile to round it out.

The tall form and stature she'd noted before grew impressively aloof as he shifted into what she often thought of as his "on-camera" mode. His vivid green eyes lost their luster, and the pitch of his deep voice altered. What came out the other side was a guarded, near-automaton set of responses she'd have bet her last dollar had been used before.

"What do you think next year looks like?"

"Management's working on some acquisitions over the off season. We'll see when training kicks off again."

"You like your odds?"

Roman's smile amped up until he practically glowed like a hundred-watt bulb, and patted John's shoulder. "I always like my odds, buddy."

Lost in the glow, John just nodded and smiled back, and Avery marveled at the change in the guy. Where he usually barely tolerated everyone, John was practically ready to do figure eights down the ice.

"Look, John. I wanted to ask a favor of you, if I could."

"Of course. Anything."

"I'm going to be giving the kids a few lessons over the next couple of weeks and I noticed the boards are looking a bit rough. I'd like to talk to Sophie about getting the town rallied around this place to help fix things up."

"Sure thing."

"Great. You'll be hearing from me." Roman gave him a quick handshake and turned for the door. "We're going to get going. I'll be in touch."

"I look forward to it."

Roman ushered her out the door, and Avery didn't even bother with a backward glance. She might have been invisible for all John cared.

"He looks like you just asked him to the prom," she muttered as they cleared the front door.

"That doesn't require a comment, but I'll give you one anyway. Eeew."

"No, I mean it. He totally fan-girled all over you."

Roman moved off the front walkway and into the grass. "I was buttering up the locals."

"Locals? You've known him since you were four, Roman."

"Yeah, well, he looked at me like he'd never seen me before, so I call it a fair trade." The pitch of his voice was back to normal and she sped up to keep up with his long-legged strides as he circled the building.

"What's that supposed to mean? And where are we going?"

He glanced back over his shoulder and slowed his step. "It means no one in this town talks to me like I'm a human being. And we're marching around the building because if the inside looks that shitty, I'm sure the outside needs work, too."

"The roof does have leaks." The angry expression that narrowed his jaw and tightened his lips had her taking a step back. "They put out big tubs to catch the runoff."

"It's a fucking disgrace."

He turned from the building, his hands on his hips, and Avery knew what was coming next when his gaze caught on the outdoor bleachers about fifty yards from where they stood.

The town used the indoor rink most of the time, but the site had been selected so they had a second practice area as well as a larger set of bleachers for outdoor games on one of Indigo's larger ponds.

"Those bleachers are falling apart, too."

"They did get fixed a few years back but they require so much upkeep no one's been taking care of them."

When he didn't say anything—just stared—she questioned his earlier comment.

"And people do think you're a human being."

"No, they don't. I've had a long time to deal with that, but don't delude yourself, Ave. I'm the homeboy who made good and that's all I will ever be to these people. They don't see me as a real person."

She watched as he crossed back to the building with those same long-legged strides but stood where she was. Roman had his phone out again and was snapping photos every few feet.

He did have a point, she mused. Hell, she'd spent her entire adult life hearing about the great Roman Forsyth, hockey god and living legend. Even when they were kids, his talent was already manifesting itself and he was as feted as a teenager as he was now as an adult.

Indigo's hopes rested on Roman Andrew Forysth's shoulders. For the first time in her life, she began to wonder what a terrible weight that must be.

Crier rolled over at the sound of heavy footfalls from the front room. Her voice came out scratchy and she grabbed at her head as a single syllable echoed through her skull. "Mick?"

"Yeah, babe?" He came through the bedroom door, looking all hot and rangy and delicious, a big smile on his face. "How are you feeling?"

"Like an idiot."

"Well, I have something that may make you feel a little more human." He pulled the take-out container from behind his back and the distinctly blissful smell of pancakes wafted toward her as he opened the lid.

She scrambled to sit up, her headache be damned. "I love you."

"I love you, too."

"No, I mean I'd cover myself with honey and let fire ants crawl all over me. I have that sort of love for you for bringing me this amazing breakfast."

He produced a fork and a small plastic container of syrup as he sat down next to her on the bed.

"Why don't you leave off the side of fire ants and save the honey for later." His firm lips came down on hers before he moved back to settle himself against the headboard.

"You're on," she murmured, secretly thanking the heavens she'd brushed her teeth a short while ago while hunting in the bathroom for aspirin.

Grier made quick work of the syrup and dug in. "Oh my God," she moaned around a mouthful. "You're like a breakfast ninja. These are awesome. You are so getting the honey later."

They sat quietly and Grier thought about how lovely it was to just sit there. Together.

Even with her raging headache and sizable embarrassment for the massive drunk-fest, he was with her. And he loved her enough to not only not be upset about that fact, but to also bring her pancakes.

"To add further credence to my breakfast ninja skills, I also come bearing a significant piece of gossip."

"Do tell." She reached for the coffee he'd placed next to the bed earlier. It was cold, but still packed a punch.

"I had breakfast with Avery."

Grier eyed him sideways. "Was she hungover?"

"Nope, fresh as a daisy after she got over her precoffee morning puss."

"Bitch."

"Would you let me finish?" He snatched a piece of bacon from the open container.

"Go on."

"Roman joined us, looking like he'd gone a few rounds with a pissed-off moose."

"What happened?"

"He was all scraped up on his leg. Claimed he took a fall on his run."

Mick's words set off a string of alarm bells and she set the container on her lap. "Claimed? Why would he lie?"

"I can't explain it, but something's up with him."

"How so?"

Mick shrugged and reached for a cube of roasted potato, dipping it in a pool of syrup. "I'm not sure. He just seems off and that's the best I can explain it."

"The entire town is giving him and Avery the full-court press. That's got to be difficult. For both of them."

"There is that, but I think there's something else he's holding back."

"He cares for her, too. And despite her protests, she cares for him. It's got to be tough for them to be around each other."

"He about came off his chair when she started tending his wound." Mick must have seen the question in her gaze because a big, cocky grin spread across his face. "Sweetheart. It doesn't matter how badly wounded a man is, if a woman goes sticking her hands all over his thighs he starts suffering a bit differently."

"I see." And she did, Grier realized, as the image of Avery tending to Roman's wounds rose up in her mind's eye.

She'd seen it—hell, they'd all seen it—the way the two of them fell into this natural pattern they probably weren't even aware of. There was a history of genuine love and affection between Roman and Avery, and when neither was busy fighting the here and now, that history reached up and grabbed both of them by the throats.

Or by the thighs, as it were.

She took another bite of pancake and chewed for a moment. "You think there's something there? Something that can be salvaged?"

"I know there's something there. But as for salvaging it? I'm honestly not sure."

"Everyone deserves a little hope, babe. I think we're a product of that."

He kissed her once more, this time lingering over her lips. "I know. I also know we got very, very lucky."

"Let's hope a little of it rubs off on our friends."

Roman was pleased the outside of the rink wasn't nearly as bad as the inside, but it still needed a new roof and there were sections of brick that definitely needed some repair work. He shoved his phone back into his pocket and resolved to talk to Sophie about it that afternoon.

"Where am I going to take the kids?"

"You can take them on drills until things get fixed." Avery had done her part, snapping photos with her own camera and taking some notes she'd promised to e-mail him. "Hockey's not only about the ice."

"They're going to be expecting time on the ice, though. Not jogging drills through town like they were at boot camp." He turned over a few ideas in his mind. "We could use my mom's van. The one she does airport runs with."

"Most of the wedding guests are leaving tomorrow. She needs it."

"Tasty still have his Suburban?"

"Is the Pope Catholic?"

"What about Hooch? He and Chooch have to transport all their sled dogs somehow."

"He's got a big SUV and a trailer."

"I'll see what I can work up. Call a guy I know in Talkeetna to see if I can borrow his rink for a few hours."

"Do you really want the responsibility of taking fourteen kids on a field trip?"

Roman shrugged. She had a point, but he'd made a commitment and he wasn't shirking it. "In for a penny."

"Or a pound of crazy."

"I'm the great and all-powerful Roman Forsyth, hockey god and revered town son. What could happen?"

Even as he spoke the words—solely in jest—an immediate vision of paying for his hubris hung in the air like a storm cloud. What *could* happen?

"Please tell me you haven't forgotten our class trip to the Denali National Park."

Memories lit up his mind like a pinball machine, and he had to give Avery points for picking one of the worst moments in his entire school career.

"The guinea pig was an accident."

"Is that what you've consoled yourself with after all this time?"

Roman could still recall the trip vividly, the images so clear they could have happened the day before. "It was Walker who stole the fourth grade's class mascot, not me. He just had no idea it would spend the trip peeing and pooping in his coat pocket."

"Which was why he let it go the moment he set foot off the bus."

"He was only going to set it down for a minute. Told Mick and me to watch it. Who knew they could run so fast?"

"Poor, sweet Randall. He'd spent his life in a cage and that single moment of freedom was all he needed to make his escape."

A happy grin lit his features. "That little thing could run. He was off down a trail and out of sight before we even knew what happened."

"I looked over and all I could see was you and Mick, high-stepping your way through the far side of the rest area we'd stopped at before heading into the park."

They walked back toward the front of the building. "How did you manage to escape detention for that one? Nearly every memory I have of getting in trouble involves Mick and Walker as well as you."

Avery's voice rose an octave with fake politeness, and Roman didn't even need to look to know that her spine stiffened along with the change in her tone. "For whatever reason my mother decided to chaperone that trip, and right about the time Randall took off on his adventure I discovered the doctored coffee in her thermos."

Roman remembered Alicia Marks coming along to chaperone the day, but didn't know about the liquored coffee. "You never told me that."

"I didn't tell anyone."

"Why did you keep it from me?"

"It was a long time ago, Roman."

"Doesn't matter. It had to have been upsetting. And we were dating at that point."

"I hadn't told you yet. About her drinking problem."

Roman came to a halt and reached for her forearm, effectively stopping her in place. "My mom told me about last year. About the end."

She nodded and he wished there was something he could do about the pain. The horrible, emotional roller coaster she'd spent a lifetime dealing with stamped her face with a mix of emotions.

Grief.

Sadness.

Shame.

It was the last that he questioned—she had nothing to be ashamed about—but he knew her too well not to understand that emotion accompanied the others. With infinite gentleness, he ran a finger down her cheek. "What's that look for?"

"It was pretty bad."

"I know."

A loud breath whistled through her teeth on a heavy exhale. The cautious, hopeful light he'd seen in her eyes when he touched her vanished, replaced by something dull and lifeless.

And empty.

"Do you really, Roman? How? Because someone

told you? Your mom or grandmother? Mick or Walker? Because I never talked to you until that lone call after it was all over. I never even saw you while any of it was going on."

Her anger was justified and Roman knew it. More than justified, if he were being honest with himself, but he tried to bring the moment back around.

"Come on, don't do this. We were having a nice time."

A dull frisson of panic brushed the back of his neck. He knew his words were empty, just as he knew he'd unleashed something with them.

And when the dam burst, he had no one to blame but himself.

"It doesn't go away, no matter how much you want it to. Us. All the years in between. It doesn't just vanish."

Each word was like an arrow, piercing through the armor he'd put up long ago when it came to Avery Marks. His own shame welled up, and with it a white-hot anger that incinerated everything in its path.

"What the hell do you want me to say, Avery? I'm sorry! I'm so fucking sorry for not being here. I don't know what else to tell you. It doesn't change how I feel for you. How I ache that you suffered while your mother was alive and when she died. It doesn't change the fact that I have empathy for what you went through."

"I didn't need your fucking empathy. I needed you."

She turned on her heel and took off, the speed she'd had in high school still in evidence as she ran toward town. Those long, coltish legs carried her farther and farther away and he stood stock-still, watching her take each and every step.

Julia and Susan looked up from the front desk of the Indigo Blue as Avery raced in through the lobby. She kept her head down as she headed toward her apartment at the back of the hotel and it didn't take much guesswork to figure out why she was upset.

"I'd hoped giving her the morning off would have put her in a better mood." Susan sighed as she punched some paperwork into the computer.

Julia chose her words carefully. Her daughter-in-law had a deep love for Avery, but it was that same love that had often made her blind to the girl's pain. "She's under a lot of pressure, Susan. Roman's staying for a few days and it's going to be hard on her, the way everyone scrutinizes them."

"It doesn't have to be hard."

"Oh no?"

"Of course not. He's not going to play hockey forever. Maybe it's time he'll finally start thinking about settling down. The wedding and his visit couldn't have been timed more perfectly. It's the off season and he has some time on his hands to stay put in Indigo for a few weeks."

Julia laid the stack of plastic key cards she was erasing onto the counter and turned to face Susan. "You're not still harboring that fantasy, are you? The one where they fall into each other's arms, decide they're madly in love and find a way to make it all work out?"

"Why shouldn't I? Anyone who sees them together knows what they have. What's between them. It's always been there."

"That doesn't mean it's what either of them needs."

"Of course it is. They both had to do some growing up but now's the time. They'll figure it out."

Susan walked back to her office with a serene smile on her face and Julia abstractedly wondered how she'd misread her daughter-in-law's behavior all these years. Yes, she knew Susan had always harbored the belief things would work out in the end, but it had always seemed somewhat sweet and nostalgic.

This near-blind belief was something else entirely.

"Everything okay?"

Julia slammed a handful of cards onto the counter, straightening their edges, and nearly fumbled the stack as those calm words pulled her from her reverie.

"Ken." She laid the stack on the counter. "I'm sorry. I didn't see you standing there."

"No, it's my fault. I don't mean to interrupt but you looked upset."

His dark, quiet eyes were so serious, she thought as she looked at him. So trustworthy.

She'd known Ken Cloud for more than four decades, and in all that time, Julia didn't think she'd ever heard him even raise his voice.

"I'm sorry. It's been a busy few days here and I thought I'd give Susan a hand. I'm afraid we may have been a bit loud."

"It was your body language that gave you away." He smiled, understanding painting the gentle curve of his lips. "I read my paper here every morning and the energy is usually quiet and fairly benign."

"Not this morning."

"Exactly."

"Care to discuss it?"

The impulse to do just that struck her at the same time a little curl of lust settled low in her belly. Both were foreign and more than a little surprising, but she'd never been a woman to waste an opportunity.

And her thoughts about Roman and Avery simply couldn't be discussed with Sophie and Mary, no matter how much she loved her friends.

They were basking in the glow of their grandsons' marriages—either completed or impending—and all they saw were aisles, veils and great-grandbabies in their futures. There was no way they'd understand her reservations about her own grandson and the girl she loved as a granddaughter.

"I'd like that. There's some hot coffee down in the dining room. Would you like a cup?"

"I thought you'd never ask."

Chapter Seven

Avery couldn't keep her gaze from returning to Sloan's left hand and the white-gold band that winked there, the metal bright and shiny. "I just can't believe you're married."

"Me, either." Sloan's smile was broad and effervescent as she danced around the luggage and clothing scattered throughout her hotel room. "It all happened so quickly. A year ago I didn't even know Walker, you, Mick, the grandmothers or Indigo even existed."

Avery jumped up and hugged her, the impulse so strong she knew she couldn't have sat still if she'd tried. "I'm so happy for you both."

Sloan hugged her back; then Avery felt her reach for her hand as she dragged them to the one empty spot at the end of the bed. "I'm disappointed I'm going to miss the next few weeks, though. I heard Roman's staying in Indigo. He's never done that, has he? Since he left?"

"You're going to Fiji. On your honeymoon, with the promise of nonstop sex. How can you want to stay here?"

"I'm being serious."

"So am I."

"Come on. What about Roman?"

Avery knew it was a losing battle to argue with her, so she tried to give the required information and get in and get out. "No. His visits are usually much shorter."

"How do you feel about that?"

Avery thought about her morning with Roman and the jumbled thoughts that had haunted her ever since, and tried to fake her way through an answer. "Fine. It's fine."

The bright blue stare Sloan leveled on her—one that was so direct it bordered on scary—indicated her friend didn't believe her.

Not for one single minute.

"Look. I'm not trying to be nosy or push at you around something that I know is terribly painful. But it's like I told you back in December. You're different people now. It would be a shame not to get to know each other as adults."

"I tried."

"When?"

"This morning." Before she could stop it, the story was tumbling out. She filled her in on everything. The trip to the rink. The fight. The uncontrolled anger that sprang up every time she thought about the fact Roman wasn't there for her when her mother died.

"You have a right to be upset."

"I know I do. But I can't stop thinking about this thing I read, years and years ago. It's about anger and forgiveness. And holding on to anger is like holding on to a hot coal. You're the one who gets burned."

"I guess." Sloan's blue gaze was gentle when she next spoke. "Maybe the real anger is at his limitations."

"In what way?"

"I mean, he looks so big and strong, but his actions aren't those of a man who doesn't care. In fact, I'd say they're the opposite. He cares so much it's like he fumbles over himself."

"So I should forgive him."

"I think you have a right to tell him how you feel and how much his actions hurt you."

Avery knew Sloan had an incredibly valid point. She also knew it was something she needed to take the time to digest later. "Look at me, being all selfish when it's your wedding festivus. We need to get you packed up and downstairs for the send-off picnic."

The concern in Sloan's eyes lingered a few moments before she let out a small sigh. "Did I really need a send-off picnic?"

"The picnic's an excuse to eat and drink some more."

"I'll give you that."

"And as for the festivus, it's what I've dubbed the entire week of events your mother has been bound and determined to give you, whether you wanted any of it or not. Although, to be fair, Sophie wasn't entirely out of the game, either."

Sloan sighed once more before heading for one of her open suitcases. "It's like some strange mania descended on all of them. They're like wedding zombies."

Avery couldn't help but laugh at that, the crazy compulsion that had driven all of them for the last few weeks fading in the light of a well-enjoyed event. "It feels more like childbirth. Everyone's forgotten the pain."

Sloan lifted a summer blouse and folded it before

laying it in the case. "I honestly don't care if I ever have another discussion about cut flowers, the shade of mauve for table runners or what is an acceptable train length for a woman over thirty."

"Amen, sister."

Sloan chewed on her lip for a moment. "Do you think that's why Grier wants something small? Because mine's been such a circus?"

"I doubt it. Grier's already given Mick a hard time because he just won't elope."

"Yes, but do you think it's because of this . . . this craziness?"

Avery saw the concern and couldn't resist teasing about their absent friend. "You've known her longer than me, but can you really see Grier having any part of something like the last week?"

"She'd rather be strung up by her fingernails."

"Exactly. You, on the other hand, my dear." Avery walked up and took Sloan's face in her hands. "You were destined for a wedding festivus the day you came out of Winifred McKinley's womb. Stop fighting it and let's go down and greet your adoring public."

She dropped a kiss on Sloan's forehead before pointing toward the bed. "After, of course, we get you packed for your honeymoon."

Roman popped the top on a can of Coke and tried to brush off his crappy mood. He'd been pissed off since that morning and nothing had pulled him out of it. Not his visit with a distracted Sophie, telling her what he wanted to do with the rink, nor his attempts at a nap before heading over for the wedding send-off.

At that, a question popped into his mind, and Roman turned to Walker, who was getting a lingering hug from one of Sloan's old aunts. He at least waited until the woman was out of earshot before asking what was on his mind.

"What the fuck is a wedding send-off?"

"Something my grandmother cooked up."

"Because the last few days haven't been enough?"

"Neither Sloan nor I had the heart to discourage her, but it's pretty dumb." Walker took a drag on his beer. "But since by this time tomorrow I'll be in Fiji, I'm trying hard not to argue with anyone."

"Thanks for the reminder."

"Anytime, buddy. Anytime."

They stood there in companionable silence for a few minutes, watching the various partygoers in small conversation circles. Some of Sloan's uncles had started a horseshoes game in the corner of the town square and Roman saw Tasty and Skate watching with avid interest.

"I heard you visited my grandmother."

Roman gave a smile, his earlier visit going so smoothly he wanted to suggest there be a wedding in Indigo every weekend. "She wanted to talk to me about as much as she wanted a hole in her head, so it was a quick visit."

"What's up?"

"I want to fix up the rink."

"Thank God." Walker took another sip of his beer. "I've told her that place is a disaster waiting to happen. Thanks for taking it over."

"Sure. Sure thing."

Roman took another sip of his Coke and allowed the

sweet soda to assuage the raw ire in his throat. The fact that the rink had been allowed to get that way burned in his gut, and he knew he couldn't say anything that would contribute positively to the conversation so he kept it to himself.

Instead, he put on his brightest smile—the one he reserved for reporters—and turned toward his best friend. "Well, she thought it was a great idea. I'm going to get a group together and we'll get it fixed up next weekend."

"Sorry to miss it."

Roman slapped his friend on the back, unable to maintain his shitty mood in the face of such happiness. "I know, I know, Counselor. You'll be in Fiji."

"You bet I will. With my blushing bride in a string bikini."

"Rough life."

"I consider it my reward for putting up with this circus"—Walker gestured to the field before them—"for the last six months. And I believe my bride feels the same way."

"It's been a rough go?"

"I just wanted to marry her, you know? All this. It's nice but it's not the marriage. It's just a wedding."

"Interesting point."

"They think men don't pay attention. My grandmother and mother-in-law, in particular. But I do. I've watched Sloan go from happy, engaged bride-to-be to frantic sobs when her mother did something that upset her. She's earned two weeks in Fiji as much as I have."

"Well, I wish you a ton of honeymoon sex and the time to relax from the madness."

Walker hesitated, and Roman felt what was coming next before his oldest friend even spoke. "So what about Avery?"

"What about Avery?"

As the words left his mouth, Roman saw her walk into the square next to Sloan. She had on a vividly colored dress that had bold slashes of red, blue and violet streaked through it. The sleeveless swatch of color fell to the knee and only served to highlight her long, lightly tanned legs and toned arms.

"We all see it. And that's not just the crazy love for my wife talking."

Roman deliberately pulled his gaze from Avery and turned to his friend. "Keep your crazy love talk to yourself."

"You two looked like you were having a nice time at the wedding."

"That's because we know how to be civil to each other. How to have a nice time with each other. We were friends for a long time, Walker."

"Until you weren't."

"What's that supposed to mean?"

"What I said. You were friends until you weren't."

"We've always been friends."

"You know what? It's a happy day, and I'm really not trying to fuck it up being an asshole, so I'm going to leave it alone and go say hello to my bride."

"You do that."

Roman didn't want to think about it—or Walker's underlying point—so he headed for the horseshoe match in progress. Maybe a change of scenery with people he didn't know would provide a nice diversion.

If nothing else, throwing something might calm his raging nerves.

Avery wasn't sure how Sloan had talked her into the dress, but now that she had it on and was in public, she practically felt naked. She never wore stuff like this.

And why in God's name had she accepted one of the outfits Sloan had bought for her honeymoon?

Sloan's argument—that she'd bought far too much and Avery would look great in it—had sounded inspired at the time.

Now she just felt like she was trying too hard.

And the small wink Sloan shot her before she headed toward her smiling new husband confirmed it.

Before she could dwell on it too long, Walker's law partner, Jessica McFarland, was at her side, two fresh beers in hand. "Care for one?"

"God, yes. How'd you know?"

"You had that look."

"What look?"

"The one that screams 'I'm naked in public and I just want to wake up from the nightmare.' "

Avery turned toward her friend, horror slowly spreading through her body and coalescing into a greasy knot of nausea in her stomach. "Oh God. I knew it. This dress looks awful."

"The dress looks fabulous. No one can stop looking at you, including our dearly beloved bartender." Jess inclined her head in Ronnie's direction, where he stood with a small cluster of the guys he hung around with.

"You really do need to do something about that,"

Jess said with a bright smile. "He's too prime to leave him wallowing in misery every time you're near."

"How many different ways do I have to make it clear I'm not doing anything with Ronnie?"

"It doesn't mean it's not a shame. He's adorable."

Avery didn't even turn around, knowing what she'd get if she did. Ronnie hadn't been too overt in his interest, but she knew it was there all the same, and she didn't want to embarrass or encourage him. She'd thought her four months away in Ireland would have helped the situation, but days like today made it clear her absence had only made him grow fonder of her.

And he was adorable. If she were looking for minimal strings and a good time, Ronnie would be at the top of her list, their age difference—and her junior high baby-sitting sessions for him—be damned.

But she wasn't looking for casual.

And despite her best intentions, she had a fascination of her own for someone else who was entirely inappropriate for her.

"Someone's looking sexy today."

Avery shot Jess a desperate look before she turned toward the older woman who owned the cackling voice. "Chooch. Are you enjoying yourself?"

"Sophie and those McKinleys sure as hell know how to throw a party." Chooch nodded her head, the ringlets she'd managed to curl over her entire head winking in the breeze. "You need to show those legs off more often. You're smoking."

Avery met Chooch's gaze head-on. "Thank you. I think."

"Damn straight. I meant it as a compliment. Legs

like that'll get all the boys to notice. And then maybe that'll kick some sense into Roman Forsyth's thick skull."

"I wore this dress for me."

" 'Course you did. Men come second when it comes to feeling good about ourselves." The woman moved in closer, her voice dropping to a whisper as she gestured Avery and Jess near. "Never make your decisions for a man, no matter how stupid over him you are."

"That's good advice, Chooch." Jess nodded her head solemnly, and Avery thought the older woman's advice was sweet.

Until she branded it in a way that was uniquely her own.

"And even if he's giving you several orgasms a day, you don't let him boss you around. You can give 'em to yourself just as easy and you don't need to let him know he makes you crazy or has such power over you."

Jess actually dribbled some of her sip of beer she was trying so hard to hold back the laughter, and Avery could only thank her lucky stars she hadn't taken a sip yet. "Equally good advice, Chooch."

"Don't forget it."

"Oh, we won't." Both women waved at Chooch's departing figure before falling against each other in a heap of giggles.

"How does she do that?"

"I'm not sure." Avery leaned down, clutching her stomach as another wave of laughter overtook her. "But I'm quite positive I've never thought of Hooch McGilvray as a master of the female orgasm."

"Maybe they'll erect a statue in his honor next to the Love Monument."

Avery and Jess collapsed in a fresh heap of giggles at the innuendo as well as the image. It was only when a deep voice interrupted them that Avery came back to her surroundings.

"You both look like you're having a good time. Can I get you fresh beers?"

"Ronnie. Hi."

"Hi." His smile was as broad as his wide, T-shirt-clad chest, and Avery wondered once more why she couldn't see the man past her image of him in Garfield pajamas. "I can only assume Chooch was dispensing advice?"

"Was she ever." Jess mock shuddered before she made the inevitable ploy to remove herself from the conversation. "I need to get going. I'm going to give the bride and groom a big kiss and then I have to get home and get the food put together for poker night."

"How'd you get roped into that?" Avery shot her a dark look even as she kept her tone bright, fun and oh so slightly manic.

"Because I love my man and want him to have the bestest poker night ever."

"That doesn't sound like you're following Chooch's advice."

Jess smiled—broad and wide—and shook her head as she walked backward across the grass. "Ask me if I care."

Avery shook her head as she watched Jess float off. "She's really happy."

"She is." Ronnie nodded. "I meant it about that beer. Can I get you one?"

A quick glance down at her nearly full bottle and Avery shook her head. "I'm good for now. Are you enjoying the party?"

"I am. I was in and out of the wedding because we had to get the bar ready last night for anyone who was coming in afterward, so it's nice to be out here enjoying the day."

"It was a great wedding."

"You looked beautiful." He took a sip of his beer. "In your bridesmaid dress."

"Thanks."

"Did you have a good time?"

"Oh yeah. It was quite a party."

They stood together in awkward silence before Ronnie nodded toward a group of kids playing a round of touch football. "My brother, Mike, is beside himself about the hockey lessons this week. He can't stop talking about it. He's really good and this should help him get a whole lot better."

"I've heard several kids talking about it."

"It's awfully nice of Roman to do it."

Avery heard the stiff formality in his tone and smiled. She knew Roman wasn't Ronnie's favorite person, so the fact he could see something good in the lessons was yet another sign Ronnie was a stand-up guy.

"It is."

"So, um, I was wondering if you wanted to grab a beer some night or something. I don't have to work every night, and it's been really pretty this summer. We could grab a picnic or burgers from the diner or something."

"Oh. Well. Um, I'd need to check my calendar. Susan's taking a lot of nights off in the coming weeks because of Roman being home and, well, um."

She saw his tentative smile hover in place, even as he put a few feet of distance between them, and wanted to shoot herself between the eyes.

Damn it, why couldn't she do this? And why did it have to hurt someone else in the process?

"Sure. Well, it's no big deal. Just drop in to the bar some night if you change your mind."

"Maybe I will."

She watched Ronnie amble away and felt like the lowest scum. How had a polite rejection—albeit a poorly worded one—managed to hurt him so badly?

And why couldn't she just take what was being offered?

She was young and healthy and vibrant and interesting and—*damn it*—why was she unable to just do something crazy and fling-worthy?

"Your admirer had his puppy-dog eyes on."

Avery turned to see Roman standing next to her and every unpleasant thought running through her head coalesced into a fiery ball of anger. "Shut up."

"It's a joke, Avery."

"It's mean and unnecessary. You're the big, bad hockey god so you have no fucking idea what it's like for the rest of us."

Alarm painted his features as he turned toward her. "Look, I wasn't trying to be nasty. And what the hell does the fact that I play hockey have to do with anything?"

"It's the bigger point. Not everyone's blessed with a larger-than-life existence. He's a nice guy."

"So go out with him."

"I don't want to go out with him."

"So what are you all up in my grill for about it?"

"I wish I wanted to go out with him."

The anger in his eyes changed as his brows slashed further over those green orbs, and Avery knew she was looking at the distinct notes of jealousy reflecting back at her. "What's that supposed to mean?"

The conversation was so absurd—almost as absurd as the fact that she was actually having it with Roman—that she threw up her hands and took off for the edge of the field.

She'd hurt Ronnie's feelings and had put her own on display in the process.

And damn it, she'd gone and ruined a perfectly good afternoon in a hot new dress.

Chapter Eight

An unpleasant surge of frustration, anger and misery carried Avery across the town square and back to the hotel. She could only thank the heavens everyone was so wrapped up in getting in line for the fresh burgers coming off the grill that they didn't pay her much attention as she stalked off the town square.

She hit the parking lot of the hotel and realized she wanted to head back inside as much as she wanted a root canal. A quick glance at the Jitters had her reconsidering.

An oversized mocha would go a long way toward assuaging some of her anger and guilt. It wouldn't fix it, but the chocolate therapy would at least make for delicious company as she tortured herself replaying the afternoon over and over in her mind.

The Jitters was practically empty, as she'd expected it to be, and she couldn't hold back the smile at the teenager's resigned face behind the counter. On one hand, she looked happy to have something to do, and on the other, she seemed moderately irritated to have her issue of *Seventeen* magazine interrupted.

The girl—Stacy, Avery thought her name was—

handed over the extra-large mocha and beelined for her magazine. Avery turned to grab a few napkins when her gaze alighted on Trina Detweiler.

For the briefest instant, Avery couldn't hold back the thought that something looked really wrong, but then Trina caught sight of her and her expression changed.

"Trina. Hey."

"Hey."

"You okay?"

"Of course."

"What are you doing in here?"

Trina's slim shoulders went up and down. "I felt like a coffee."

"Oh. Me, too." Since she was doing the same, Avery figured she couldn't quite argue the point, but it was still odd.

Trina was usually in the middle of everything, so it was a surprise to see her holed up in the empty coffee shop while the party raged on outside in the square.

Add on that Avery was picking up on an inexplicable sense of sadness that had softened Trina's features and made her normal, barracuda-like features almost human—and she couldn't help but wonder what she'd walked in on.

"You want some company?"

"If you want."

For the life of her, Avery had no idea why she'd asked the question or why she was sitting down, but it just seemed like the right thing to do.

"That's a pretty dress. Those colors look great on you."

"Thanks. Sloan's inspiration." Avery looked down

and smoothed the skirt. "Are you sure everything is okay?"

"This town is so boring, I miss having Kate around, and I'm just not feeling very celebratory. That about sums it up."

While she knew all of those things were true, she couldn't quite believe Trina wasn't holding something else back. But she opted for a slightly different tack. "Grier said Kate's doing well."

"She is. And I'm so happy for her." Trina looked up from her foamy coffee. "Really happy for her. But I miss her."

"I think Grier does, too."

"And it doesn't sound like she's coming back anytime soon. New York's her new home. Not that I blame her."

"You should go visit her."

"The last thing she needs is a visitor as she's trying to set up house with Jason."

"You're friends. She'd be happy to have you."

"May . . . Maybe I'll look into it."

Avery heard the slight hitch and wondered what else was at play. Was it the money?

While most everyone managed to get by, Indigo wasn't a bastion of wealth by any means. Everyone worked pretty hard for what they had, but most people weren't traveling the world, either. Could that be what had Trina down?

Before she could dwell on it, Trina shifted the conversation. "Speaking of new relationships, what's going on with you and Roman?"

"Nothing."

"Oh come on. The two of you generate so much heat it's surprising the whole town doesn't go up in flames."

"It's not like that."

"So what's it like?"

Avery took a sip of her coffee and tried to figure out what she wanted to say. She and Trina had never been close, and if you added on the woman's inability to keep a confidence, she was likely to have whatever Avery said repeated across town in a flash.

On the other hand, no one seemed to believe her when she said nothing was going on, so maybe she needed to be more specific.

"Just because Roman and I have a history doesn't mean we have a present. It also doesn't mean we're not friends."

"You two always just sort of fit."

"Yeah."

"So why haven't you kept in touch? Seems to me, if you had a friendship that was that good and that strong, a few thousand miles shouldn't get in the way."

"It's complicated."

Trina's gaze sharpened and Avery realized that there was a whole lot more going on behind those blue eyes than anyone ever gave the woman credit for. "Lots of stuff's complicated. Doesn't mean it's not worth it."

"Trina. Are you sure you're all right?"

"Yep. I'm sure."

"Okay. Well, I'm going to get back." Avery stood and was surprised to feel Trina's hand on her forearm.

"Avery?"

"Yeah?"

"Look. I know we've never been close and that

dumb stunt I pulled in high school before Roman left sort of ensured a friendship would be impossible. But if you really have feelings for him, don't let the past keep you from your future. I think you have a real shot with him."

"Oh . . . okay. Thanks."

Trina dropped her hand. "I'll see you around."

"Yeah, you, too."

Avery thought about the conversation as she walked back to the hotel and long after she'd curled up on her couch with her coffee. Trina wasn't the first to tell her to focus on her future—heck, her friends had been saying it since the previous winter.

But it felt different coming from someone who was essentially a stranger.

Maybe Trina had a point.

And what was with Trina's weird mood? Despite years of annoyance or, at best, indifference toward the woman, Avery couldn't help hoping whatever had put the distinct notes of sadness in her eyes would resolve itself soon.

Roman was still fuming over horseshoes at Avery's determined march off the square. He'd played a few rounds—poorly—and had resigned himself to a position of watching.

While he fumed.

Jess crossed the square, a bag of ice in hand, and Roman waved her over. He reached for the ice as she came to a halt.

"I'll hold that."

"I totally forgot it and had to come back. Thanks. It's heavier than it looks."

"What was that about before? Was Ronnie giving Avery a hard time?"

"What do you mean?"

"Oh come on. Ronnie was looking at Avery like he could eat her up."

"And well he should. She looks gorgeous." Jess gave him a good hit to the shoulder. "Like you don't feel the same way. And if it bothers you so bad, why weren't you there hitting on her?"

"I—" Roman broke off, then switched tactics. "I want to know what Ronnie said to her. She yelled at me for not understanding and then stomped off, upset."

Jess's face fell at that as she turned to look back across the wide, open lawn. "When I left them to head home, they were just talking."

"Well something happened."

"I don't know, Roman. I left to give them some privacy. They seemed fine."

At the implication that there was some reason to give Avery and Ronnie privacy, Roman felt his entire body go cold.

Damn it.

He'd thought the kid was over this stupid fascination with Avery, but clearly not.

Jess's eyes narrowed as she watched him. "What's this all about, Roman?"

"Nothing."

"Really? Because she's entitled to some attention. She's young and attractive, and since you've chosen to do nothing, the girl deserves someone who will put himself on the line. Ronnie likes her. He always has."

"Jess." Jack approached and laid a hand on his fiancée's arm, his broad smile an indicator he'd not heard their conversation.

The easy comfort was a good thing to see, not to mention a long time coming. Jack's first wife, Molly, had passed away several years back from cancer and it was only the previous winter Jack and Jessica had found their way to each other.

"What's up, babe?"

She shot Roman one final look that could have fried his shoes before turning toward Jack. "Nothing. Absolutely nothing. I need to go get set up at home."

She gave Jack a quick kiss before grabbing the bag of ice and stalking off in the same path Avery had taken. Jack's eyes followed her, his jaw slack with surprise. "What the hell did you say to her?"

"Nothing, Jack."

"She doesn't get mad like that unless we're talking paint colors. Seriously, what the hell happened?"

"I just asked where Avery went and she went off on me about not being jealous over Ronnie's interest."

"Are you?"

"Fuck, Jack." Roman took a few steps back from the crowd that had gathered around the horseshoes. Although he didn't think the assembled crowd was all that interested in his raging hormones, you couldn't be too sure in Indigo. "I don't know."

"She's entitled to live her life. And she's done more than enough waiting around for you."

"Has she?"

Jack screwed up his face, lines forming on his forehead as he scratched at his cheek. "*Waiting*'s not necessarily the right word, but she's been in some weird holding pattern. Her mom took a lot out of her and then the grief afterward. It's like it's finally her turn, you know?"

"Is this your professional opinion, Dr. Rafferty?"

Jack did grin at that. "Molly had her thoughts and now Jess does, too. Maybe I've just gotten more vocal about sharing my opinions. Especially the ones that matter."

"Do you think they're right?"

"Look. What do I know? I spent so much time, almost too much time, ignoring the wonderful opportunity right in front of me."

"So you're saying Avery shouldn't waste any more time."

"Yeah, I guess so. Avery's a great girl. She deserves better than to be stuck here if she'd like something else."

"Stuck here?"

The assessment caught Roman up short. Of all the things he'd ever imagined, he'd never thought of Avery as stuck in Indigo. She was a part of things.

In his mind, despite his family being here, Indigo was defined by Avery.

Did she really want something else?

Roman was still fuming on the idea of Avery going anywhere as he walked back into the hotel to get ready for his poker night. He'd picked up a bouquet at Tasty's as a peace offering to Jess. The fact the man carried flowers in a bait shop was almost too strange for Roman to wrap his head around, but he was glad there was someplace in town to get flowers, and the yellow roses were surprisingly fresh-looking.

"Well, well, who are those for?"

Roman saw his mother's eyes light up as he crossed the lobby toward her. He leaned over the counter and pressed a kiss to her cheek. "Jess."

"Oh?"

He saw the confusion stamp itself in his mother's expression and avoided the full truth in favor of something more polite. "She's hostessing poker night."

He laid the flowers gently on the counter before turning toward Susan. "Has it been busy in here? I thought everyone was outside?"

"It's quiet, but there is the occasional person walking through. We've all been taking turns at the counter so we don't have to miss too many of the festivities outside. Most of the guests are there so it's not too bad."

"It's nice for Sloan and Walker."

"It is." His mother glanced up from the printout she was reading. "It could be nice for you and Avery, too."

"Mom. Come on. You too?"

"You know I'm your biggest champion. Yours and Avery's."

"It's not that easy."

"Oh, I don't know. It's not all that hard."

A helpless frustration gripped him all over again. "Why does everyone seem to think we should pick up where we left off?"

"Don't you want to?"

"It doesn't matter what I want."

Her gaze grew sharp at that and she laid the piece of paper on the counter. "Why not? You're not entitled to happiness?"

"I didn't treat her the way she deserved. I can't just show up and expect to be forgiven."

"Oh, baby." She leaned forward, her hand resting on his cheek. "That's what forgiveness is all about."

"Well not in this case." He pulled back. "She's got a life—and she's entitled to it. I wasn't even here for her when her mother died."

"Roman?"

He glanced around the lobby, confirming it was empty, before saying the words that burned in his chest with the bitterest acid. "I wasn't, Mom. Forget the rest of the time I wasn't here and she was dealing with Alicia all by herself, I didn't come for the end."

"I told her you expressed your sympathy."

"It's not the same."

"Did you ever think maybe she couldn't have handled having you here then?"

"What?"

"Roman. There was a reason I kept a lot of it from you."

He stared at his mother, the stark reality of her words lancing through him. "You what?"

"You didn't need all the details."

"She was struggling with this all by herself."

"No, she wasn't. She had me and your grandmother. She had Jonas to help out for most of it. What good would it have done to tell you about it?"

Roman shook his head, desperate to reconcile his

mother's words with what he knew to be an incredibly caring woman. "How could you have done that to me? To Avery?"

"It's fine, Roman. She's doing well and she's past the biggest part of the pain. What could you have done?"

"You should have told me everything. Why do you keep doing this?"

"Doing what?"

"Pretending like nothing's wrong."

The soft lines that bracketed her mouth faded as her lips thinned into a straight line. "I do no such thing."

"You do. You started it after Dad died but you've kept it up. Like you can't tell me anything bad when I'm so far away. Bad shit happens, Mom."

"I'm not sure where this is coming from but I'm not interested in a lecture, young man. I made the decisions I felt were right."

"I'm an adult."

"An adult with a life and responsibilities four thousand miles away. You don't need bad news from me."

The urge to pick a fight—or at least try to talk some sense into her—was huge, but Roman had no idea what to do about it. He knew that stubborn set to her jaw—had worn it more than once himself.

Add on the underlying truth—that he never pressed her or tried to dive beneath the surface of any of her comments—and he knew he had a role in her behavior.

A rather sizable role.

"I need to go get ready."

"Have fun at poker night. Say hi to everyone for me."

"I'll do that."

It was a long while later before Roman felt his shoulders relax and the subtle headache that hovered behind his eyes fade. What he couldn't dismiss quite as easily was the raw and bitter knowledge that he'd enabled his mother's behavior.

Chapter Nine

"Hello, beautiful."

The cocky smile winked at her from her computer screen and Avery smiled back, feeling the dark mood that had ridden her shoulders all day fading in the reflected light of warm blue eyes. "Hello, Declan. Ever the sweet-talking Irishman, I see."

"It's not sweet-talk when it's true." A brogue coated his words, and Avery thought—not for the first time—that Declan O'Mara was hell on wheels for the female population.

So why in the hell couldn't she seem to feel anything more than a mildly passing interest in the man?

First Ronnie and now Declan. Was there any hope for her?

"How was the wedding?"

"Wonderful and beautiful and a tiny bit sad, all at the same time."

"Major life events have a way of being all those things."

She mentally added sweetly pragmatic to his impressive list of attributes.

"How's Lena?"

"Pining for her dear, cold Alaskan wilderness and wondering how long it will take her to save enough money to get back."

"She and I should set up a swap again. Susan loved her and is ready to canonize her as the patron saint of the hospitality industry."

"I thought you held that title."

"Nah." Avery waved a hand, smiling again in spite of herself. "I'm too bitchy to ever get the word *saint* before my name."

"That's true. Martin Murphy is still complaining that you yelled at him for parking his car in front of our entrance the night of your going-away *ceili*."

"I nicely asked him to move it three times before I yelled."

"A fact I've reminded him of on more than one occasion."

"I'm sorry if he's still upset."

"When he does bring it up, I gently suggest he remember how delightful your ass looked when you walked away after yelling at him and he gets a sweet, misty look in the eye." Declan looked thoughtful before that cocky expression took hold of his features once more. "Maybe that's why he brings the incident up so often."

"I knew those choirboy looks of yours were all for show."

"Of course they are. However, being a choirboy did get me some behind-the-scenes action in the choir loft with my fellow choir girls so it wasn't a total waste of time."

He sighed with a great deal of drama and panache before gobsmacking her with his next comment.

"So what has the clouds in those beautiful eyes of yours?"

"There aren't any clouds, Declan."

"Then I won't embarrass you by saying there are circles underneath them, too, indicating lack of sleep or a crying jag or both."

"You're evil."

"No, I'm a friend and you look like you need one." Any hint of teasing was gone, replaced with the face of someone who genuinely cared.

"My past has caught up with me."

"Mine does that regularly." His expression was wry as he added, "Roman? He's causing you trouble?"

"His being here is trouble."

"Ah." The dramatic flair was back as Declan clutched his hands to his breast. "I knew the wanker would have me beat in the 'I'd like to see Avery naked department.'"

"He hasn't seen me naked."

"Yet."

"Ever again." The words floated up with ease, but her heart gave a defiant lurch even as her mind screamed, *Wanna bet?*

"It's not that easy, love."

"It should be."

"And weddings should be nothing but happy, but they aren't." He leaned forward and Avery watched as his broad shoulders filled the screen, his blue-eyed gaze zeroing in on her through the webcam. "Joy doesn't come our way all that often, Avery. Believe me, I know."

The earnest words—and the slight hitch in his voice—had her heart plummeting. "Declan. I . . . I'm sorry."

"And you shouldn't be. I've broken my fair share of hearts. It's about time I got the treatment in reverse. Might make me a more decent fellow, come to think of it."

She shook her head. She'd suspected his feelings—had even tried returning them—but hadn't thought they had any real depth or staying power to them.

"Now. What are you going to do about it?"

"About what?"

"Getting naked with Roman."

"Declan!" Avery wagged a finger at him and realized how odd that must look coming through a webcam. "I'm not getting naked with Roman."

"Then put that luscious body to use and come back to Ireland and be with me." His face turned serious, the smile vanishing as if it had never been. "You're too vibrant for this, Avery Marks. Too wonderful to let life pass you by."

The same frustration that pounded her that morning with angry boot kicks had dulled to a steady throb in her stomach. "There's nothing to be done about it. He's here for longer than usual, but he's not staying. This isn't his home any longer, no matter how the entire town feels about him. And even if he were staying, why does everyone think we should fall right back into each other? I don't."

"Because you can't stay apart."

"It's not that easy."

"Is that pride talking?" Once again, those blue eyes penetrated the distance with disarming acuity.

"No."

"You sure?"

"It's not pride, Dec. It's self-preservation."

He sat back in his chair, the intense moment over even though he maintained a thoughtful air, seated there in his small office. She saw the glass of whiskey at his elbow and knew his large Irish wolfhound, Sampson, was likely snoring at his side.

It was just so homey, Avery thought as she waited for him to speak. Her entire experience in Ireland had been like that, from the very first day of her arrival. Warm, welcoming and homey.

"Pride's one of the seven deadly sins for a reason."

"Well so is lust. And those are the only two emotions I seem to have around the man."

"While I may want to beat his face in, I know your feelings for this Roman fellow run deeper than that. I'd wager it's likely because he deserves it. Maybe you need to stop focusing on what was in the past."

"What's past is prologue."

"Thanks, Shakespeare."

"We can't change what comes before."

Dec sat forward once more, his eyes fierce with emotion. "But we still have the power to change what will be."

Roman parked his car in front of Jack and Jess's house, still smarting from the monumentally shitty day. He was looking forward to poker night and a break from the thoughts that swirled like a tornado around his mind. He grabbed the bouquet he'd purchased earlier for Jess and headed for the door.

At least the conversation with Sophie about the hockey rink had gone well, so he couldn't chalk the day up as a total wash. She agreed with his assessment of what needed to be repaired and offered up some budget funds to aid in the fixes. She also supported his desire to get the community involved and graciously accepted his offer to pay for some of the building materials.

She also promised to spread the word, which, Roman knew, meant they'd have a slew of residents ready to go by this weekend. All he had to do was put in his order for supplies with Mick and Jack this evening and they'd pick up whatever he needed this week.

Although he couldn't quite shake the day from his shoulders, Roman did at least feel some sense of purpose as he walked up the front steps, the sun as bright in the sky at eight p.m. as it was at noon. Man, he had missed this.

Even after so many years away, not much fascinated him like the daylight in Alaska. Short and unfathomable in the winter and long and unending in the summer.

Yet another element that made his birthplace unique.

He knocked as he balanced a twelve-pack of beer under one arm and a bag of chips his mother had foisted on him and the flowers in the hand he used to knock.

The host for the evening opened the door with a broad smile, a cigar clamped in his mouth. "Come on in." Jack grabbed the beer as he closed the door behind them.

Roman heard the distinct notes of trash talk coming

from the back of the house and was glad he came. "Where did Jess get off to?"

"She's upstairs reading a book."

"Brave woman."

"And supremely awesome. She made enough food for us to eat for a week."

They stepped into the dining room and Roman eyed the plates of wrapped pigs-in-a-blanket on both ends of the table, and smiled before he popped one in his mouth. "Let me add my compliments on the awesome food." Roman held up the bouquet. "And maybe a request to talk to her for a few minutes?"

"I'll go get her."

Mick and Hooch, Bear, Mort Driver, Dr. Cloud and an eager-faced Tasty, who, Roman suspected, was Walker's stand-in tonight, all sat or stood around the table. The poker game had been going on for years, a throwback to the games Mick's grandfather used to host. The players changed week to week pending personal fortunes but their core group of Mick, Jack, Walker and Doc Cloud was pretty solid.

Jack reappeared, Jess at his side. "Roman?"

Roman excused himself from the crowd and followed Jess into the small living room near the front door. "These are for you."

"Thank you." Jess accepted the bouquet with a small smile. "Although I think there's someone else you should be giving these to, don't you?"

"Since you were the one to put up with my boorish behavior on the town square, I think you've a right to them, fair and square."

"Have you cooled down a bit?"

"Not much."

"Want to talk about it?"

The opportunity to say what he was thinking—to have someone listen to him who might not be as crazy-blind as his mother—was too good an opportunity to pass up.

"I know I left Indigo. And I know Avery's entitled to a life. A happy one. I just don't think it's with Ronnie."

Jess looked at him over the top of the yellow blooms, her lawyer's gaze direct. "And you don't think you'd say that about anyone who might have an interest in her?"

"Hell, I don't know. I just know Ronnie isn't the right guy."

She let out a small sigh before she nodded. "For what it's worth, I only tease her about it because he's handy. I don't think he's the right one, either."

"You don't?"

"No, I don't. Although my reasons are probably a hell of a lot different from yours."

Curiosity won out and the words were out before he could stop them. "What are your reasons?"

"I meant what I said earlier. Avery is a bright, vibrant woman and she deserves someone who loves her and cares about her. And I know she knows that, too. If she wanted Ronnie, she'd have been with him already."

"Oh."

A wicked grin lit up her face. "I told you my reasons were going to be different."

"So you did."

"So there's really only one other question."

When he just stared at her expectantly, he saw the

gleam in her eyes, a direct match for the grin. "What are you going to do to win her back?"

Roman was prevented from saying anything by the arrival of Jack in the living room. "Are we playing or what?"

"I'll see you later." Jess turned back at the entryway to the room. "But do me a favor. Think about what I said?"

"I will."

Roman followed Jack back toward the kitchen, grateful when the man handed him a beer and gestured to a seat. "Let's get this party started."

The game started with a series of lively insults and Roman pushed the conversation with Jess to the back of his mind. Focusing on the men gathered around the table, he thought how oddly similar the talk was to the locker room before a game. Verbal abuse and puffery had a surprisingly calming effect and he felt himself relax for the first time in days as the seven of them settled into a comfortable rhythm.

About an hour later, Bear threw down his cards in disgust and picked up his beer. "Fold."

"You out again, big man?" Jack smiled around his cigar as he pulled a pile of chips his way.

"Deal me out of the next one. I'm going to go rustle up some of Jess's pizza."

Roman watched Bear walk off, his heavy lumber a suitable representation of his name, when he thought about his conversation earlier with Sophie.

"I've got a favor to ask of all of you."

Five pairs of eyes snapped to interested attention and Bear stepped back in from the kitchen. "What's up?"

"I'm helping out the kids for a few weeks, running them through some training drills since their coach took off."

"That coach was an asshole," Tasty muttered under his breath. His comment was punctuated by a few head nods around the table.

"And the rink's in pretty bad shape. I've got Sophie's permission to make some repairs and I'd like to get a group of us together to fix it up."

"Sure thing." Bear nodded before heading back into the kitchen.

A chorus of "Yep," "Anything you need" and "Of course" echoed around the table, and Roman fought the irrational irritation that floated up at their quick agreement.

If they were so damned agreeable, why the hell hadn't anyone fixed it sooner?

On an inward sigh, he held back his frustration. No use in pissing all over the people who'd just agreed to help, but it still bugged him.

It had never set well with him—still didn't—but he'd gotten used to the fact that people fell over themselves when he asked for things. In the realm of his profession, he understood it, even used it to his advantage. He was a well-respected leader on the team and could motivate, manage and push the team to do better.

But here? In Indigo? He couldn't understand why it took his comments to rally people to do something.

"You in, buddy?" Mick's voice penetrated his thoughts and Roman looked up from his cards and threw a few chips into the pot. He didn't miss the glint in Mick's eyes—the one that suggested he knew exactly what was going through Roman's head—but he simply nodded once the bet was made.

Roman played his cards and tried to force the negative thoughts from his mind. But it didn't escape his notice that the poker night he needed so badly wasn't nearly as much fun as he thought it would be.

Declan's words still rang in her ears a few hours later as Avery moved from one room of her apartment to the next. The bold colors she'd decorated with—a bright palette that usually comforted her and had her feeling at home—instead had her feeling closed in and restless.

Why couldn't he have been the one?

He was interested and attentive and he'd embraced her ideas for his bed-and-breakfast in the few months she was there.

She'd also gained a friend, she knew. A good friend who wanted the best for her.

A friend who had a point, even as she wanted to bash his gorgeous face in for how damned reasonable he was being.

She and Roman *did* have a history. And she *was* attracted to him. It didn't mean either should be acted on.

So get over it, Marks, and get on with your life.

On a soft sigh, she resumed her pacing. A glance out her window indicated just how late it was. She could still see light, but she knew without looking at the clock it was after midnight.

Although sick of her own company, she didn't want to call Grier and disturb her. And they'd closed the bar so there wasn't even any company to be found there.

She briefly flirted with the idea of going down to use

the gym, but she had no motivation to get in a run at this time of night. The thought of exercise did give her an idea as her thoughts drifted to the hotel's workout facility and she knew what might help.

Snagging her keys and a bottle of water from her fridge, she headed for the sauna.

A short while later, she had a towel wrapped tightly around her, the heat flowing over her in lovely, languid bursts. She allowed her thoughts to drift with the heat, landing wherever they chose.

Which was why, when a memory of her and Roman the summer before he left filled her mind's eye, she allowed it to take root and flourish.

"You were quiet at dinner."

"Not much to say," she said, shrugging. There was never much to say when her mother was on a bender.

"You don't have to bear this alone, Avery."

"No one else can do it for me, Roman." She ran a hand through his thick, dark hair, enjoying the simple feel of the strands and the heavy weight of his head in her lap. A light breeze ruffled the grass around them and she looked up, grateful no one else in town had any sense how wonderfully private the ground behind the bleachers was at the town rink.

"That can't be true. My grandmother would help if you asked."

"No." She shook her head and fought the panic that rose up in her at the idea of telling Julia Forsyth about her mother. "Just no."

It had taken her a long time to talk to him about her mother and the increasing concerns she had that Alicia had gone from being someone who drank too much to someone who was a drunk. The pitying looks she got in town had increased over the past few months as well, and she'd had to call their neighbor, Jonas, more than a few times for his help in getting her mom home.

"There has to be a place you can get her into for help. For treatment. There are facilities for these things."

"Facilities that require large payments to make you well. We're lucky we have insurance."

"There has to be a way."

She didn't want to talk about it. She didn't want to tell him there wasn't a way—or at least not one she'd been able to find.

And she didn't want to waste one more precious moment with him talking about a problem that she couldn't fix or wish away or make better.

Just like his leaving.

He downplayed it, but she knew it was coming. Knew the number of scouts who'd been up to visit their small town had increased.

Aside from the town gossip whenever an unfamiliar face presented itself in Indigo, she saw them when she worked shifts at the hotel. Saw their credit cards and the names of their employers emblazoned on those cards. Red Wings and Islanders, Rangers, Oilers and Metros.

The NHL wanted him and it was only a matter of time before he left.

With a sudden desperation she fought daily to hide, she bent down and pressed her lips to his. This crazy need she had for him wouldn't be sated no matter how much time they spent together.

Yet the more time they spent together, the more powerful it grew.

He responded immediately, his tongue slipping between

her lips in a languid slide that never failed to turn her insides over on top of themselves.

When had he become so necessary to her?

Maybe he always had been.

He lifted his head from her lap and rolled next to her. Lying on his back, he settled her above him, one large hand at her hip while with the other he teased the sensitive skin of her stomach with his index finger.

"You're beautiful."

"You sweet talker."

His compliments always caught her by surprise—the honest look in his eye when he spoke them even more. She was embarrassed by the attention. By the raw emotion she saw in his dark green gaze.

"It's the truth." His hand snaked up and wrapped around her neck, and with gentle pressure he pulled her down until their lips met. "To me you are perfect."

Love burst in her chest, so hard—so fierce—she lost her breath as their lips met once more.

A hot tear hit her chest and Avery looked down, watching that lone drop slide toward the white cotton of her towel. With a quick brush of her finger, she dashed the other tears on her cheeks away.

She had so many memories of Roman, but that day had always stood out in her mind as the day things were different. Up until then, they'd spent their time in the carefree abandon of new love and youth. But that day, something had changed.

Maybe it was the realization that her mother wasn't going to get any better. Or the even harsher realization that he'd be leaving sooner rather than later, but things had been different after that.

Quieter and more intense.

And the moments they'd spent together in the months before he left had been full of a strange awareness that had bonded them irrevocably together.

She could still smell the sweet scent of the grass that day behind the bleachers. Could still see the vivid green of Roman's eyes as his fingers played over her body. Those long fingers, so strong and so clever, had educated her about herself.

About the sensual power that lived in her own skin.

For years, she'd fought using her memories of Roman as the fuel for her own pleasure. She was well able to take her release at her own hands, but she also knew the act would seem empty and hollow if accompanied by long-ago visions of him.

Maybe it was the tears or the heady frustration at having him back in Indigo, but for the first time in nearly fourteen years, she allowed him into her thoughts as her fingers navigated the flat length of her belly, lower into the soft folds at the apex of her thighs.

With no concern she'd be discovered—the relative emptiness of the hotel and the lock on the door left her mind at ease—she allowed her own fingers to explore as she lay back on the hard expanse of wooden bench underneath her.

Hot images flashed through her mind, her body responding with the exquisite memory of his large chest covering hers, the thick length of him as he filled and stretched her.

A low moan rose up in her throat as the slickness at her core heated even further, a telltale tightening beginning deep in her womb.

As the memories intertwined with the increasing demands of her body, she whispered his name as she fell. "Roman."

Roman passed through the quiet lobby of the Indigo, the muted light of the midnight sun still streaming through the front windows. With the sun's position low in the sky, the lobby reflected a beautiful mix of golds and reds that usually brought him a quiet sense of calm.

Tonight, all he felt was irritated and alone.

He'd tried desperately to shake off his annoyance as the poker game wore on, but after losing three hands in a row, finally acknowledged his mind wasn't on his cards and he was better off just throwing in his hand and turning in for the night.

He used the convenient excuse that a herd of teenage boys was waiting for him the following morning to run practice drills and no one paid him any mind.

Especially since he left his money behind.

He stalked down the hall toward the apartment he used in the back of the hotel and knew he wasn't going to find any rest there, either. His eyes alighted on the hotel's extensive spa area as he passed and a dim light reflecting from the end of the corridor in the spa wing caught his attention.

Someone had left the lights on in the sauna. With a resigned sigh, Roman headed down to turn everything off.

His mind still filled with the overwhelming dissatisfaction of the evening, he tumbled against the door and nearly smashed his bad eye against the doorframe, not expecting the resistance.

Who the hell locked the door with the lights still on?

With a curse, he fumbled for his keys and unlocked the door, a rush of heat hitting him in the face as he heard a sharp intake of breath and a soft, distinctive moan.

The hazy air coupled with the bright glint of a towel caught him up short, but it was the position in which he found Avery that had every ounce of blood draining from his body, rooting him to the spot.

She was a vision.

Her back arched on the wooden bench of the sauna as her hand worked the flesh between her thighs. A towel covered her fully but he didn't need to see her naked body to know what beautiful secrets hid beneath her fingers.

And as she let out one final cry of pleasure, the heavy key ring in his hands fell to the floor with a hard, jingling thud.

Her eyes opened at the noise and she screamed, before scrambling up to a sitting position.

"What!"

She reached for the towel with one hand while another snaked out to the stack nearby and grabbed a second, folded one, which she slapped against her lap.

"What the fuck are you doing in here?"

He still didn't say anything, the image of her in the throes of taking her pleasure forcing him mute.

"Roman?" She stood up and stalked toward him. "What the hell are you doing skulking around in here like some pervert?"

The word caught him up short and pulled him from the silence that gripped his throat. "I'm not a pervert.

And what the hell are you doing in here? Doing . . . that."

"I'm. I'm. Well, what are you doing in here? I asked you first."

"The light was on and I came down to shut it off."

"Oh."

"And then you—" He broke off, the image of what he'd witnessed moments before hardening his body and removing any sense of decorum or control or thought from his mind.

The urge to take—to devour and plunder—was strong as they stared at each other across the heated room.

Before he could summon a thought, she moved, whip quick, and his arms filled with her.

Without giving her time to reconsider, he wrapped his arms around her, walking them backward toward the door. His tongue slipped through her lips and a growl of satisfaction filled his throat at her ready acquiescence. He hit the heavy wood of the door with his back and he paid it no attention as his mouth devoured hers.

"Roman," she whispered against his lips, her hands against his chest, before she allowed her head to fall back.

"Roman."

The whisper against his lips was all he needed.

With his hold on her still iron-tight, he turned so that her back was against the door and then he plundered.

Lifting one hand he flicked off the towel while the other moved on an unerring course toward the slick, hot skin she'd just pleasured. A hard moan met his ear and it only served to heighten his need as he drove one finger, then another, into the folds of her body.

Her arms tightened around him and her head rested against the door, turning back and forth as they both rode the madness. The tight channel around his fingers clenched as her breath hitched and he worked her flesh harder, satisfied when the telltale quivers began, timed with the hard moan that escaped her lips.

Manic with desire for her, he kept up the merciless assault with his fingers while he bent his head to take one hard nipple into his mouth. He used his tongue to draw her in with a ruthless, demanding suction, then shifted to provide the same attention to her other nipple.

The hard, sweet sound of her pleasure rose up in a heavy cry and Roman moved his mouth back to hers, taking it in as she screamed.

Avery felt the release through every single muscle she possessed, the rapid-fire exertion of two orgasms leaving her no strength to do anything but cling to Roman like a rag doll.

What the hell had just happened?

Even as she wondered at it—and the embarrassment at being discovered by him—she realized she didn't want the pleasure all to herself. She also realized he'd not stopped kissing her. From her mouth to her neck, then following a path back up to her ear, he never moved away from her.

Never gave her the room to move away from him. And further, she realized that she didn't want to move away.

With shaking hands, she drew on her reserves of strength and tested her ability to stand and hold her own weight. When her quivering thighs didn't dissolve into a pool of oatmeal, she pressed her back against the wooden door of the sauna and turned the tables.

Her hand flashed to the button of his jeans and she had it undone and her hands inside his briefs before he could stop her. His hard cock filled her palm and she gloried in the sense memories that ran through her mind as she traced the remembered length of him.

His grip on her shoulders tightened as he dropped his forehead to hers.

"Ave."

"So you *can* speak," she whispered against his chin as she nipped his five o'clock shadow with her lips while increasing her speed and grip against his thick flesh.

"Not for long," he whispered as his jaw hardened, his eyes half-closed at the exquisite pleasure her touch imparted.

"Come for me."

He thrust his body into her hand, matching the rhythm she set with his hips. She drew him through his paces, stroke for stroke, determined to turn him as inside-out as her. On a heavy groan, she felt the jerk of his body as he took his release.

She kept up the pressure, the remembrance of how he'd taught her to pleasure him years ago as easy as breathing, and used her palm to ride him through his orgasm.

Only after he'd finished did she lift her lips to his, their breath mingling in the dry, heated air.

"It's been a long time since I've done that," she whispered, a satisfied giggle rumbling in her chest.

His lips spread into a large grin as he pressed a quick kiss on her. "I think the last time I came on a hand job was when we were in the eleventh grade."

"Sweet memories."

They were, she realized. Incredibly sweet memories.

She thought back to the innocence they'd shared and the freedom they'd enjoyed learning about each other and about themselves. What felt good, what made the other feel good. All without the adult pressures that now came with sex.

It had been an unexpected joy and she knew she'd been gifted with an exceptional partner.

"Do you do that often?"

They still hadn't moved. Her back was flush against the door and their bodies pressed against each other.

"Give hand jobs in the sauna?"

"Um, I meant, your own pleasure."

While she suspected it was unintended, his question effectively ended the spell of intimacy between them and she shifted from his embrace, slipping away to put some distance between them. Avery bent to pick up her towel, wrapping it around her breasts and tucking the free end in once more. "A single gal's gotta find a way."

He fixed his jeans, rearranging himself and pulling up the zipper. He kept his eyes averted but she could have scripted his next words. "You ever find a way with someone else? I know you've dated."

"Yeah." She walked over and picked up the shorts and T-shirt she'd worn downstairs. "From time to time."

"Oh."

"Don't sound so surprised, Roman. I'm sure as the hockey god of New York, you get your fair share of hand jobs, not to mention any other job you can think of."

"It's not like that."

"You haven't had sex since you left Indigo?"

"I didn't say that." She saw the mulish expression settle over his face. "I just don't understand why everyone thinks professional athlete is synonymous with male whore."

"Maybe because it usually is."

"Well, then I'm not usual. I don't sleep around indiscriminately."

"That's very refreshing."

She dragged the T-shirt over her head and was reaching for the shorts when he stopped her, his hand on her arm. "I'm sorry. I shouldn't have asked you that. I had no right."

"Not by a long shot."

Before he could respond, she was out the heavy wooden door that swung gently closed in her wake.

Chapter Ten

A wall of sound echoed off the back of Roman's head as he drove Chooch's Suburban the thirty-minute trek to Talkeetna. He had seven teenagers in his car, and Mick had volunteered to take the other seven in the large SUV they kept out at the airstrip.

The cacophony of heavy laughter, the discussion of the Metros' odds next year and the general joviality of teenage boys was lost on him as he relived the night before in his mind.

Over and over.

Like a game replay shown from ten different angles, every time he thought of those moments with Avery he remembered something different.

The sweet, musky scent of her skin.

The expression of ecstasy on her face as her orgasm overtook her.

The feel of her hands on his cock, driving him to madness.

They were some of the hottest moments of his life. And then he'd gone and fucked it up by asking her if she'd slept with anyone else.

Classic caveman move.

"You okay, Mr. Forsyth?"

Roman turned at the sound of his name, grateful for something to get his mind off the torturous images. "Sure, Mike. Just thinking."

"About how many drills you're going to put us through."

He smiled at the kid's earnest voice and made a show of tilting his head slightly. He didn't dare turn his head far enough to look at the boy in the seat next to him and take his eyes off the road, and inwardly cursed at the lack of peripheral vision that clearly wasn't going to get any better. "I'm not quite ready to torture you all on the first day. I'll save that for after you get a few days of practice in."

"You're going to spend a few days with us?"

"Sure. I promised I'd do at least a few weeks of drills. Give you all a routine and make up a workout schedule so you can keep with it after I'm gone."

"We haven't had a lot of good practices since the coach left."

"So I've heard."

Mike's grin was broad and lopsided. "I'm not sure what he expected, but winter up here wasn't it."

"It can be a bit much if you're not used to it."

"Are you glad you left?"

"I'm glad I got the opportunity I did. It was never about leaving Indigo but about living my dream."

The raucous sounds of the car had quieted as he and Mike spoke, and it was only when one of the boys piped up from the back—he thought it was a junior named Aaron—that Roman realized they were all deeply interested in what he was saying.

"What was it like? Leaving for the NHL?"

"Fun. Exciting. And scary as hell."

"Scary? Why?"

"It took my game to an entirely different level. I still remember my first month. I was convinced they'd send me home any day and I spent more time on my butt than upright on the ice."

"But you're the MVP," another boy hollered from the back.

"Well, I had to be a rookie first and take my lumps and learn how to play in the big leagues."

Roman smiled at the simple innocence of the boys—that somehow his ability on skates had kept him from getting his ass whipped by guys who were bigger, faster and a hell of a lot more experienced than he was.

"But you're the luckiest guy in the NHL. You've made some of the hardest shots in the history of the game."

Roman grinned at that. "I'll never turn down a little luck, but it's amazing how much hard work has something to do with it. Do you know how many times a day I practice those shots?"

Multiple voices rose up, each breathless with curiosity. "How many?"

"After practice is over, I spend at least another hour, maybe two, working on my shooting."

The van quieted before a shy kid they called Stink piped up from the back. "But you still have to believe in luck, too. Don't you?"

Roman had never bought in to the well-documented superstitions of his teammates. He'd take hard work over a run of good or bad luck any day as the true road to success. But he wasn't completely immune.

Shifting his seat belt, he pulled the thin leather cord from around his neck. A small, platinum horseshoe—no bigger than his thumb—hung from the center. He'd gone through several cords since Avery had given him the charm for his sixteenth birthday but had never worn anything else around his neck except for the horseshoe.

To this day, he had no idea how she'd saved for what had to be an expensive item at the time. He still remembered what she'd cheekily written in the card.

Even though you don't need any luck, it's always nice to have backup.

"I do wear this every time I play."

Except for the day he got injured, he knew. The cord had broken that morning in the shower and he didn't have an extra one to restring the horseshoe. It still struck him as strange that the two were connected, but like those superstitions he fought so hard to ignore, he had refused to dwell on it.

The shouts of "I've got one of those!" or "I carry this!" shifted the conversation momentarily and he was prevented from saying anything more.

As the comments quieted down, he couldn't resist imparting whatever wisdom he could. "I still say hard work trumps luck every time."

Roman saw a few of the boys nodding as he looked at the crew in his rearview mirror. He wasn't sure a few days together would make that big a difference, but if he could leave them with the understanding that they had a lot of influence on how well they ultimately performed by being dedicated to their goals, he'd know they had been left with something tangible.

Mike piped up again from the seat next to him. "What's it like?"

Roman risked a full glance at the boy as he turned slowly into the parking lot of the rink. "What's what like?"

"The big leagues? Playing on a championship team in front of all those people?"

"It's pretty great."

"That's it?"

"What do you mean, that's it? What do you think it would be like?"

The kid blushed a ripe red, but didn't hold back with his answer. "Sex, an ice-cream sundae and Christmas morning all rolled into one."

"That's not a half bad description, Mike." Roman pulled into a spot and turned off the engine. "Not bad at all."

Mick waved at him from the other van and Roman jumped out to start unloading equipment. He wasn't surprised when his old friend rambled over shaking his head.

"Did we talk that much?"

"Probably."

"I thought we just grunted."

"Nah, we did actually know words." Roman grabbed several hockey sticks and his duffle from the back of the van, then turned to face the departing gaggle of gangly teenagers.

"They're something else."

"Tell me about it. We were barely out of Indigo before someone got up enough courage to tell me he thought Grier was one hot woman. For an older lady and all."

"Mine told me playing in the big leagues had to be equal to sex, ice-cream sundaes and Christmas morning all rolled into one."

"You never told me that."

"And flying's not the same?"

"Damn straight." Mick pointed toward the building. "You ready to go get your clock cleaned for the next three hours?"

Roman thought about the lead weight that had ridden his chest since the night before. "A little workout is just what the doctor ordered. You playing?"

"I might put on skates, but only as ref."

"Have you turned into a chickenshit in the last fifteen years?"

"I was always the worst skater out of the three of us."

"Well, you've got a hot woman now. Get a few bruises and maybe she'll kiss and make them all better."

Mick slapped him on the back. "Good point. Let me grab my gear."

An hour later, Mick slapped him once more, his breathing heavy as he clutched the boards with his free hand. "They've got more energy than an entire pack of Chooch and Hooch's dogs."

"And you're an old man." Roman couldn't resist ribbing his friend. "You do have a year on me."

"Damn." Mick leaned over and put his hands on his knees. "Had you asked me this morning if I was in good shape I'd have said yes. I'm going to keel over."

"Just work through the burn, buddy."

Mick turned his head and gave him the evil eye. "Fuck you."

Roman did a fancy backward skate to add insult to injury. "Not my fault you're flat-footed on ice."

"See if I help your ass any more this week."

Several of the boys skated over, water bottles in hand. "What are we doing next?"

Roman pointed to the cones he had set up around the ice. "We're going to practice footwork. You need puck control and you need speed, but most important of all is you need to skate better than you walk."

"This is Alaska, Mr. Forsyth. We were born on skates."

"We'll see about that." Roman picked up the whistle from around his neck and blew a few times. "Break's over!"

The kids scrambled around them and Roman shot a wry look at Mick as he skated backward a few feet to give the herd of teens room.

With quick instructions he gave them the ins and outs of the drill. They had to skate as fast as they could around the orange cones, and they also had to do their level best to knock one another over. The immediate guffaws and trash talk warmed Roman's heart and he told them where to line up.

"This is better than racing Miss Avery through town."

"What?" Intrigued, Roman skated next to the boy, Brock, who'd made the comment.

"Miss Avery from the hotel. She runs drills with us through town. She's hard, too. And kicks our butts most of the time."

"Avery runs with you guys?"

"Yep."

"How often?"

"Couple times a week, at least." Brock shrugged, then skated toward the wriggling line made by the rest of the team.

Roman skated backward so he'd be out of the line of fire, then blew on his whistle.

As the boys took off, bounding around and off one another like oversized puppies, he couldn't shake the image of Avery in running gear, the same gaggle of kids trailing behind her.

Likely staring at her ass.

Avery stared at her clipboard as she did her liquor inventory and reread the same column of numbers three times.

Did they need eight bottles of vodka or ten? And did they really go through five cases of wine last week?

With a frustrated oath, she threw the clipboard on top of the bar and decided to focus on something that required fewer brain cells.

It was obvious Roman killed too many of them the night before.

God, what was she thinking? Why had she let it go that far? And how could it have been even better with him than she remembered?

They hadn't tortured each other with penetration less sex since they were in high school, but oh, she remembered it well. It had taken well over a year before she'd been willing to give in and have actual intercourse with him, but all the heavy petting they could think of had been fair game.

Funny that's how they'd get reacquainted with each other.

It was sort of sweet.

And a really bad idea in the light of day.

She grabbed a towel and spray bottle and began to clean down the bar. With her current level of concentration, she'd be lucky if she ordered even half their inventory correctly. Jack didn't need the order until tomorrow anyway—she'd deal with it later.

The simple, soothing motion of cleaning the bar calmed her and she allowed her gaze to wander with her thoughts as she roamed around the room. She stopped when she got to the large, colorful glass sculpture that bookended the far side of the lobby.

It had been one of Roman's first gifts—a Chihuly glass sculpture she'd later learned he'd purchased at one of the major auction houses in New York. The piece never failed to lighten her spirits, its bright swoops and swirls of color leaving the impression of active motion, even as it stood stock-still against the wall.

Although nothing had ever been mentioned—the sculpture had come with a simple card, addressed to his mother—Avery knew her love of the artist had influenced the purchase. She'd talked of an article she'd seen on Chihuly's work when they put together a high school art project, and she knew to the bottom of her toes it had left an impression on him.

A friendly hello echoed from the front of the lobby and she turned her attention toward Grier's jaunty wave.

"You look busy."

"I got bored doing inventory." The lie tripped easily off her tongue but try as she might, she didn't want to get into a discussion of the evening before.

"I can understand that. Although please tell me you are putting more wine on the list."

"Of course." Avery gestured for the length of bar. "Come join me."

"Good idea." Grier pulled out one of the bar chairs and sat down. "Anything I can help you with?"

"You're chipper today."

"I'm hangover-free and I successfully campaigned— and won—the battle to get Chooch and Hooch to start doing quarterly tax payments."

"How'd you manage that?"

"I told them they'd have to do their own taxes next year if they didn't make it a little easier on me." She nodded with a satisfied smile. "That seemed to be more than enough of a threat."

Avery knew what a big victory this really was. Grier had spent a week the previous January working through the older couple's tax returns and nearly went cross-eyed in the process.

"They adore you."

"Yes, well their madness helped cement my business here in Indigo so I really shouldn't complain. But damn it, five boxes of receipts was nearly my undoing."

"I think I saw tears of joy roll down Hooch's face when he left those receipts with you, dumped all over the conference room table."

Grier visibly shuddered. "Don't remind me."

"So it was that easy to convince them to change their

ways?" Avery threw the rag down on the table and reached under the bar for a bag of pretzels. She filled up a small bowl and set it between them.

"Roman borrowed their car to take the kids up to Talkeetna for their hockey practice. I drove myself over to their place and cornered them, making up a royal sob story about how busy I was going to be for the next several months planning the wedding."

"Nice battle tactic."

"Thanks." Grier glanced around the bar in a move so furtive Avery thought a few mobsters might walk in wearing fedoras. "I have a few more up my sleeve."

"Who else are you trying to get on an accounting plan?"

"I was actually thinking about you."

"Me?" Avery nearly choked on a mouthful of pretzel. "I don't need an accounting plan."

"No, but you do need a love plan."

"Excuse me?"

"Mick told me you and Roman had a few tense moments yesterday morning at the diner."

Moments?

Hell, if the time at the diner consisted of "moments," she wasn't even sure how to define what happened in the sauna. "He hurt himself on his run and I tried to put a few napkins on the cut to stop the bleeding. No big deal."

"You sure that was all?"

"Yeah, I'm sure. We had a nice conversation, that's it. What did Mick get his panties all in a wad over?"

"It wasn't like that. He simply mentioned how you two seem to dance around each other."

"We're not fucking dogs, Grier." Avery heard the tension in her voice and fought to hold it back, but it stung a bit. "And what's Mick doing running back and gossiping like Myrtle Driver?"

"Ouch. Okay." Grier held up her hands. "Fair."

Avery smiled at that and the tension gripping her stomach uncurled a few degrees. "You know I'm going to give him a hard time about it when I see him."

"Fine. We earned it. Him for saying anything and me for running my mouth about him saying anything."

Grier glanced around the lobby, and if Avery still hadn't been so wound up from the night before, she might have laughed at her friend's decided lack of subtlety.

"But since we're talking about it, you sure that's all? Because then you went over to the hockey rink, right?"

"Yes, Lois Lane. Anything else you need for your report?"

Grier picked up the discarded rag and Avery felt the heavy splat as it hit her collarbone. "That can't be all that happened. You had breakfast and went to the hockey rink."

"It is all."

"So nothing happened?"

"Define 'happened.'" Avery felt a light heat creep up her neck and took a deep breath, hoping she could fight off the blush. Nothing might have *happened* at the rink but it sure as hell *happened* last night.

"I don't know. Something."

"We had a fight, but so what else is new?"

"About what?"

Although the urge to keep all of it inside was strong,

she was going to burst if she didn't talk to someone. "We had a fight about my mom."

At Grier's concerned look, Avery pushed on. "He started in about how sorry he was and I just didn't want to hear it."

"I'm sure he was sorry."

"He probably was. Is. But it doesn't change the fact that he wasn't here for it. He hasn't been here when I needed him. It felt like he threw our friendship away. And no matter how many ways I slice it, it hurts."

"What did he say?"

"Just that his mom had told him how bad things were."

"Were they? Bad, I mean? Like apocalyptically so?"

"My mother's battle with the bottle was the zombie apocalypse."

"Oh." Grier nodded and reached for a pretzel.

"I thought about it a lot while I was in Ireland. I'm not sure if it was the change of scenery or just the sheer distance, but I did a lot of thinking and praying and trying to figure it out."

"What did you decide?"

"I think I've made peace with it. And I've stopped looking at her choices as something she did to me. I think that's made a huge difference."

Grier nodded and reached out, her warm grip solid and reassuring. "That's awfully wise and forward thinking of you."

"It was time to let it go. And while it makes me sad, I'm also relieved. If she were still here I couldn't have done Ireland. And I probably couldn't have spent the time with you and Sloan over the last several months, either. She was a burden for most of my life and I've damn near gotten to the point where I can say that without wincing."

"I'm glad. You did right by her and you're entitled to a fresh start."

"Thanks."

"Unless you wanted a fresh second-time-around."

"Grier!"

"I'm just saying."

"You're always just saying."

Although she didn't want to end their conversation, the need for a few moments of peace rode her, and Avery's gaze caught on the cappuccino maker behind the bar. "I completely missed my coffee this morning. Want me to fix up some cappuccinos? I'm not nearly as proficient as the Jitters, but I've got some caramel sauce in the fridge I can add to liven them up."

Grier nodded, and in the silent gesture Avery knew she saw understanding. "Sounds good."

A few minutes later, Avery set two steaming, frothy, whipped-cream-topped mugs down on one of the tables in the lobby. "Here's to a sip of heaven."

"And to your mom." Grier clinked their mugs.

Avery took a sip and closed her eyes as rich caramel flavor burst on her tongue. Grier's thought to toast her mother had a tight ball welling in her throat and hot tears pricked the backs of her eyes.

"I'm sorry. I didn't mean to make you sad."

Avery opened her eyes. "No. It was actually a lovely thought. Thank you."

"You're welcome."

Grier blew on her coffee and took another sip and Avery deliberately waited until Grier had swallowed before saying, "Roman and I got it on in the sauna last night."

"You what?"

The slight daze that covered Grier's face from the sugar rush of the caramel and whipped cream cleared at the rapid—and scintillating—change in subject. "You did what?"

"Um, well."

"Don't *um* me." Grier carefully set her coffee down on the table before turning. "What happened?"

"We sort of reenacted some of our earliest relationship memories."

When Grier didn't say anything, just looked sort of puzzled, Avery clarified. "We used our hands on each other."

"Oh." The confusion lifted as Grier's eyes widened. "How was it?"

"Shockingly satisfying, even while it wasn't, if you know what I mean."

"It's sort of sweet."

"That's what I thought."

"Damn, but that sauna gets some action."

Avery couldn't help but smile. She knew Grier and Mick had put it to good use themselves the previous winter. Although she'd never gotten an explicit accounting of the evening—nor did she want one—she knew it had been the start of a physical relationship between the two of them.

"It was fairly unexpected."

"The best encounters usually are." Grier lifted her mug and took another frothy sip. "Are you happy with the decision?"

"I'm not exactly sorry about it."

"Good."

"Did you turn off the cameras?"

"Of course I did." Avery laughed as Grier's large gray eyes widened over the rim of her mug. "But, true to form for both of us, it didn't end all that well."

"What did he do?"

"How do you know it was him?"

"Because you're my friend and you're sitting here giving me juicy details. You're an angel walking this earth, capable of doing no wrong and living a life of quiet perfection."

"Wow. I'll have to remember that. But in this case, I actually do think he was the asshat. He asked me if there'd been anyone else."

Grier's eyebrows rose so far they were nearly swallowed by her forehead. "Before or after?"

"After, of course. We were breathing hard and sort of feeling that lovely glow and he asked that question."

"Surely he doesn't think you've spent nearly fourteen years in celibate solitude."

"I don't think so, but he certainly got in touch with his inner caveman and felt the need to ask me."

"Moron." Grier shook her head as she licked a small spot of caramel off the rim of her mug.

"Yes."

"Well, putting the He-Man-gene-slash-character flaw aside, there's really only one question, to my mind."

"And that is?"

"When are you doing it again?"

*　　　*　　　*

If four hours with fourteen teenage boys was a lesson in humility and perseverance, two seemingly tipsy women in the lobby of the Indigo Blue was the icing on the cake.

"Would you get a load of the two of them?" Mick pointed to Grier and Avery where they huddled in hunched-over laughter at one of the conversation tables.

"Are they drunk?"

"It appears so."

"I only see coffee mugs."

"Did they put shots in them?" Mick shook his head as he crossed the room, and Roman followed, hesitant as to what sort of reception he was going to get from Avery after the way they'd left things the night before.

"Hello, baby." Grier waved a hand at Mick before pulling him close for a big kiss.

"Are you drunk?"

Grier had the good sense to look offended as she swatted Mick on the ass. "We most certainly are not. We may, however, sink into diabetic comas in the very near future."

Avery pointed toward the bar. "You two look like you've been through the war. Want a few beers?"

Roman walked up to the table, careful to take the empty seat that allowed him to keep his bad side away from the conversation. "The sugar rush actually looks like it's got some merit." Roman pointed toward the empty mugs, intrigued when he saw the remains of caramel and whipped cream.

A funny look came over Avery's face before she stood up. "I've got another idea."

A few minutes later, Avery returned, bottle in hand.

As soon as he saw it, Roman understood. He turned toward Avery and didn't care if his mouth gaped open like the fish Doc Cloud liked to go after in the river. "You still have it?"

"I save it for special occasions."

"What qualifies as special?"

Complete silence descended between Grier and Avery, and the answer hit Roman square in the chest.

All—or at least part—of the previous evening had been recounted right here in the bar.

"We were enjoying each other's company." Avery smiled as she said it but he didn't miss the shot of mischief that wove through the dark depths of her eyes. "And I'd like to share a glass of some really excellent wine with my friends."

Grier leaned forward and nearly fell out of her chair. "Is that what I think it is?"

"Yep."

"Oh my God." Grier's voice was a reverent whisper as she reached for the bottle. "Where did you get it?"

Roman felt Avery's gaze land squarely on him before she shot him her usual, sassy retort. "Where do you think?"

Grier turned on him. "Okay. Where did you get this?"

What he'd initially done as something he'd hoped would make Avery happy had a rush of heat creeping up his neck. "A wine auction."

"Wow, Roman. You're a Renaissance man." Grier patted him on the forearm. "I wholeheartedly approve."

Glad the moment had passed, Roman tapped the bottle. "Avery. How much of it do you have left?"

"Nearly all of it. I split the case with your grandmother because your mom didn't want any. I've only had one bottle before this."

"You've really got four more of these?" It was Grier's turn to gape, her mouth hanging down.

"Yep."

"It was given as a gift." Roman couldn't hold back the words. "To be enjoyed."

"Oh, we're going to enjoy it." The teasing note dropped from Avery's voice. "Sharing with friends will be more than worth the wait. Let's get it open and breathing and you guys can tell us how the first practice went."

"I'm not sure there's enough liquor to numb the effects of the day." Roman smiled, rapidly warming to the idea of sharing a superb bottle of wine with friends. "But it's well worth a try."

He watched Avery's hips sway as she crossed the lobby to retrieve glasses, and he couldn't think of anyone he'd rather share a glass with more.

Chapter Eleven

Roman popped the cork as Avery set down the wineglasses.

"So come on and tell us. How did it go today?" Grier crossed back to their table, a fresh bowl of pretzels in hand.

"The kids have some skills and they're good students. They ran every drill I gave them and kept asking for more."

"That Mike's a great player." Mick took the glass Avery handed him. "He stands out."

"He's a sweet kid, too." Avery smiled at the image of gangly arms and legs she always associated with the oversized teenager.

"Which one is he?" Grier asked.

"Ronnie's younger brother."

"Yep. I know who you mean."

Roman's back stiffened at the mention of Ronnie but he didn't say anything. "The kid has a future if he works at it. At a minimum, he should get a college scholarship out of it."

"Those kids were in heaven today," Mick said. "Our

Roman's words dripped with gold as far as they were concerned."

"I just gave them some structure. It's up to them what they ultimately do with it."

"It's a good thing you're doing." Avery smiled at him and handed him the last glass.

"He's really good with them, too. Gets down on their level."

"It's really no big deal." Roman lifted a couple of glasses for the pour and Avery thought it was cute how he almost squirmed in his seat at the compliment.

"Oh come on, you know how important it is. You talked about Wayne Gretzky for three months after you met him at that hockey camp in Seattle."

He added a tapping foot to the existing discomfort as his green gaze whipped to hers. "That was different."

"No, it's not. To them, you're Wayne."

For some reason, despite it being their typical behavior, she couldn't muster the urge to tease or bait or argue with him. Instead, at the moment all she could picture was Roman running drills on the ice with a group of hero-worshipping boys.

It touched her.

And showcased a facet she hadn't expected to see.

On the rare occasions he did come home, he was cordial and pleasant to everyone. But this was different somehow. He'd not only given these boys a memory they wouldn't forget, but he'd also possibly given one or two of them the push they needed to work to meet their own goals.

"We need a toast." Grier lifted her glass, gesturing

toward Roman. "And since you provided this most lovely of lovelies, you should have the honors."

Avery watched as Roman raised his glass, his smile broad as he focused on the rich red of the Petrus before turning his gaze on Mick first, then her. "To friends. The old ones who have been around long enough to remember the thrill of skating on muscles that don't ache." He turned toward Grier. "And to new friends. Who don't care how achy your muscles are so long as the wine keeps flowing."

A chorus of "Hear, hear"s went up as they clinked. Avery took a sip of the wine and closed her eyes. "Oh wow, is that amazing."

"I'll second that," Grier added around her own reverent sigh.

"You can say whatever you want about my influence, Avery, but the way I hear it, you're the one the boys have a case of heroine worship for," Roman said.

Grier's half-lidded eyes popped wide at the prospect of news, and Avery shot Roman a dark look at the artful shift in the scrutiny from him to her. "What's this?"

"She runs drills with the team."

"I run with them through town. They're good motivators." At the collective question she saw on everyone's face, Avery explained.

"The boys don't want to be beat by a girl and I'm just competitive enough to want to kick their asses. So we go running through town and see who's got the most stamina."

"I wouldn't bet against you," Roman said, his groan audible. "You kicked everyone's ass in high school for distance."

"Slow and steady wins the race." Avery couldn't resist adding the tease. "I don't aim to be the fastest, I just hang in there the longest."

"Every damn time," Mick grumbled. "No matter how the rest of us tried to pace ourselves, Ms. Marks over here was the last man standing."

"Which is why she's got such a killer pair of legs, no doubt." Grier winked as she took another sip of her wine.

"Which is also why she's coming with me tomorrow."

"Coming where?" She sat up straighter and looked at Roman. "I've got to work tomorrow. I still have to get inventory done and a stack of paperwork that went ignored during the wedding festivities."

"I will beg and plead with my mother if necessary, but you're joining me. Mick can't help and I'm not facing all of them alone."

"They'll listen to you."

"Nope. They'll listen to you. I just have to stand there and look pretty."

Avery rolled her eyes at that. "Well, I look pretty *and* I can kick their butts."

"Which is exactly why you're coming."

Roman's grin was victorious and Avery could only sigh at his artful dodge of an afternoon alone with the kids.

Their quiet foursome broke up as the happy-hour crowd drifted into the hotel, and Roman had watched with some regret as Avery got up to work the bar. The crowd was steady and it filled him with pride to see what a successful business his mom—with Avery's obvious help—had built here in town.

But he still wished they could have had a few more quiet moments, just enjoying the time as friends.

The heavy throb of voices deep in conversation hummed around him, and his thoughts drifted to what the Indigo Blue had meant to his family.

His father had died young, just like his grandfather, and his mom had been aimless for a few years as she tried to pick up the pieces. He and his sister had been too young to fully understand at the time, but it was after his grandmother had decided to invest in the hotel that Roman saw a change in his mom.

She'd had purpose again. An outlet.

And in the process she became the hub of their very small town.

Susan Forsyth knew how to talk to people and how to make them feel welcome and she'd created a place people enjoyed coming to over and over again.

"What are you doing back here?" Avery's eyes widened as he pulled a few beers from the fridge behind the bar and flipped off the caps with practiced ease.

"I know how to work the bar and you look like you need help."

She pointed to the cash register. "You know the inventory system?"

"I can figure it out."

"It's hard."

He leaned over the flat screen, tapped a few colorful squares, and keyed in the beers on Bear and Skate's tab. The cost tallied up and added to the bottom line and Avery nodded in satisfaction.

"You've got it."

"I know."

He walked the beers over, a broad smile on his face, then snagged three more orders as he wove his way back through the crowded lobby bar.

A few people asked him questions and a couple of parents thanked him for his help with the hockey team. He used each stop to pump everyone up for the weekend and got a lot more folks signed on for the rink construction project.

He was back behind the bar and midway through filling an order when the familiar scent of Chanel wafted toward him. He looked up from pouring a refill of Chardonnay, straight into the smiling face of his grandmother. "You're a man of surprising talents."

"I can do more than chase a puck around a rink."

"Of that, I have no doubt, dear, but I never thought making fuzzy navels was part of your repertoire. I'm impressed."

"You want your navel fuzzied or your tonic vodkaed, I'm your man."

"How about a glass of that Chardonnay and we'll call it even."

"You've got a deal."

He reached for a wineglass, the fresh row of clean ones exactly where Avery had placed them on the bar. As his hand snaked out, he misjudged the distance through the darkness of his peripheral vision. Before he could react or correct his mistake, the entire row went flying, crashing to the floor next to him.

"Shit."

The loud crash of glasses stopped all conversation in

the room and he cursed inwardly at the stupidity. He'd been moving quickly and had simply forgotten to back up a step so he could work around the issues with his vision.

Now he was facing down a room full of expectant stares, his grandmother's the sharpest.

"Are you all right?"

Avery moved up behind him, her hand on his shoulder as she squeezed through the narrow space between his back and the wall of liquor behind him. "I'll get a dustpan."

A blaze of irrational anger shot off sparks inside his chest and he grabbed for her waist and bodily moved her to the side. "I'll get it. Stay away from it so you don't get cut."

"It . . . it's fine. It happens."

"I got it."

He stalked off, already feeling like an asshole for acting like one but couldn't stop the rush of anger that beat through him.

This was his third mistake in as many days. All his efforts to hide his injury would be for nothing if he kept tripping up and doing clumsy things. He was one of the NHL's top scorers for fuck's sake. He could thread the needle, driving down the ice and scoring with the narrowest windows of opportunity.

And it was all slipping away.

"You okay?" Avery's voice was quiet as she spoke from behind him in the utility closet.

"I told you I was fine. It's my mistake and I'll clean it up. The last thing you needed was me making a clumsy mess tonight. This place is hopping."

"It's no big deal. We break glasses all the time."

"It was stupid."

"Really, Roman. It's no problem."

"Damn it, Avery! I'll take care of it. First the damn knee the other day and now this. Quit coddling me."

"I'm not—" She broke off, and he didn't need the full range of his vision to see she was hurt.

He gentled his voice. "Just give me a minute. That's all."

She'd given him more than a few minutes after the incident with the glasses. In fact, Avery had steered clear all night, talking to him only when she needed to give him an order or ask for his help to snag something from the supply closet.

The last of their patrons had left fifteen minutes before and the large lobby was eerily silent, broken only by the sound of clinking glasses. Roman turned away from busing his last table to see Avery wiping down the bar.

"I'm sorry about before."

She shrugged, her strokes over the bar long and even. "It's nothing."

He set his last tray of glasses on the still dirty end before coming around the backside to finish cleaning them up. "I was embarrassed and you were only trying to be nice."

His gaze alighted on the empty bottle they'd shared earlier. Avery had rinsed it and stowed it on a small shelf near the bar. It touched him—the idea that she would hang on to it—and the urge to tell her about his vision hit him so hard the words were nearly out of his mouth before he pulled them back.

His coach didn't even know the depth of the problem.

He *had* to keep this one to himself.

"Busy night."

"Your mom does a good business."

"You certainly seem to have something to do with that." Roman flipped open the door to the dishwasher and started loading what was left of the glasses.

"I enjoy it. The whole trip to Ireland wasn't about just going somewhere. I like hospitality. Seeing people enjoy themselves and knowing I had a hand in that."

"You're good at it and you always have been. People raved about the prom the year you were the committee chair. And you did single-handedly coordinate travel for all of Sloan and Walker's guests."

"People like when things run smoothly. I've had a lot of years to practice thinking several steps ahead."

Roman put the last glass in and closed the door of the dishwasher and turned toward her. He knew she spoke of her mother and, just like his bad eye, he wanted to talk to her about it.

Wanted to understand what she went through.

"I made a mess of it the other morning, but I am sorry for your mom's passing. And all that came before it."

He waited for her angry reaction and was pleased when a smile softened her face instead. "Thank you."

"I'm also sorry for the inappropriate things I said to you last night. After." The words felt stale on his tongue but he kept going, unwilling to shortchange her from the apology she deserved. "You're a beautiful, amazing woman and I want you to have a full and happy life. I had no right to ask you about the intimate details of it."

Roman's words echoed in her ear and she was touched. Although she didn't want to repeat herself, she had no other answer than "Thank you."

He picked up another rag and finished wiping off his end. "Do you want to talk about it? Your mom, I mean."

"There's not a whole lot to say. You know her background. What she was like."

"She loved you."

Avery thought about the long years of living with Alicia Marks. A woman who could smile with the quickest of ease, yet who never managed to get rid of the disappointment that lay banked behind her eyes.

"That's probably the only thing that made it bearable."

"I think it's hard. When our loved ones can't be who we need them to be."

"Who's wrong in that case? Us or them?"

He walked around the bar and took one of the high barstools, a fresh glass of club soda in hand. "I think it's less about right or wrong and more a matter of acceptance."

Avery glanced down at the rag in her hand and the top of the familiar, scarred wooden bar. She'd cleaned it so many times over the years she knew every seam and divot. She looked up and caught his gaze, unwilling to say what she needed to facing the bar.

"That was the hardest part."

"Watching her unable to change?"

"No." Avery swallowed hard. "Not being able to get over you. All I could think was that I was repeating her mistakes. Making the same choices, unwilling to move on after the grief of losing a relationship."

"It's not the same."

She shook her head. "No, it's actually quite similar."

"No, Ave, it's not. I didn't leave you pregnant and alone. And I certainly kept up with you. Your father was never a part of your life and he wasn't a partner to your mother. They didn't have what we had."

"It doesn't change the fact that you've been gone a long time."

She saw the frustration cross his face in harsh lines and tried to defuse the situation.

"It's not meant as an insult, Roman. I know what we had was a powerful thing, especially at the age we had it. But it doesn't change the fact that it has haunted me."

"It's haunted me, too."

Her gaze was drawn to his large hands where they were splayed on the countertop, and she marveled at how the tips of his fingers pressed into the wood. "You got the adventure."

"I know I did. It doesn't change the fact that I missed you terribly." His fingers moved into a light tap on the bar and she guessed he didn't even realize he made the gesture. "It took me over a year to be with anyone."

A sharp spear of pain lit up her abdomen at his words. "What?"

"Years ago. When I went to New York. It was over a year before I slept with anyone."

"Oh."

Although the image of him sleeping with anyone was uncomfortable, the knowledge that he didn't simply leap into bed with the first available rink bunny was touching.

"I meant what I said yesterday. I'm not a man-whore athlete. And I haven't been with that many women. Haven't wanted to be, either. But that first relationship was tough."

"We grew up and went in different directions."

"We did. And even though we did, I just thought you should know that."

"Thank you."

"Hat trick." He glanced up from his drink and there was a smile in his eyes. "That's the third time you said 'thank you.'"

She smiled in return at the sweet little memory his words evoked. They'd teased each other as kids whenever one of them said something three times. "So it is."

"So speaking of adventures. How was Ireland?"

The image of misty mornings and rolling green hills immediately filled her mind's eye and she returned his smile with a broad one of her own.

"Take whatever magnificent image you have in mind about Ireland and fine-tune it. Do you have it?" When he nodded, she added, "Now understand you're still only about halfway to right. It's a glorious place."

"You loved it."

"I did."

"And the woman who changed places with you?"

"Lena."

Roman nodded. "I didn't think my mom would be as open to her as she was, but she couldn't stop singing her praises. I know she hopes Lena will come back for a visit."

"She and her brother are fantastic. Her brother owns the hotel I went to."

"Is that Declan? He of the sexy voice every woman in Indigo's been talking about?"

She shot him a dark look as she tossed the wet rag into the small hamper they kept in a corner of the bar. "Do you really want to go there again, Caveman?"

"Not really."

"Then suffice it to say Declan O'Mara has many wonderful qualities. But King of my Heart isn't one of them."

"Poor bastard."

Avery came around the bar, unwilling to mar the lovely glow hovering between them. Rather than risk their conversation turning sour, she gave him a quick kiss on the cheek instead before leaving for the night.

"Damn straight."

If she felt the heat of his cheek on her lips long after she'd returned to her room, she decided it was a fair exchange for the joy to be found in a quiet conversation with one of her oldest friends.

Chapter Twelve

"*A*re you really going to get your asses kicked by a girl?" Avery hollered over her shoulder, one of her most favorite insults. She usually saved it for mile four of their run, but the team was dragging and she pulled it out after their third lap around town.

"We're keeping up, Miz Avery!" one of the boys hollered as he extended his legs to pass by her.

Tasty waved at them from his shop as they all passed, and she saw him shake his head as the boys tumbled past her like a pack of oversized puppies.

"You're quite the slave driver." Roman whispered it as he paced alongside her.

"They love it."

"They also love your very fine ass and runway legs. Which is no doubt the reason why they run behind you."

She turned to him, her mouth hanging open. "That's not true."

"It's completely true. I heard Mike whisper it to Scott."

"That dog."

"Oh, cut the kid a break. He's as smitten with you as his older brother."

"You know about that?"

"Everyone knows about it. Half of Alaska knows about it. They talk about it in the bars down in Anchorage. Just how smitten Ronnie the bartender is for Avery the hot hotel proprietor."

"You're a jerk." She pushed him, satisfied when the shove was enough to break up his steady, even pace.

He shrugged and lifted his hands out to the side. "I'm honest."

"Besides, how would you know the gossip in town?"

"Ronnie's been in love with you since he was a kid."

Avery recalled a conversation she'd had the previous winter with Grier and Jess. "Yeah, well, he won't make a move because of you."

"What do I have to do with it?"

"You tell me. The way I hear it, you've put the fear of God in him."

"I did no such thing."

Avery caught the way he averted his eyes when he said that last bit and she pushed harder. "What did you say to him?"

"Nothing. I haven't even seen the guy since I've been home."

"Roman Andrew Forsyth. At any time in the past, have you said or implied anything to Ronnie?"

Roman kept his gaze straight ahead as they moved into the fourth mile of their run. "I might have suggested to him on a visit home a few years ago that he seemed awfully fond of his hands."

"And?"

"And nothing. He works with his hands, making all those drinks, flipping beer caps off, that sort of thing."

"What the hell have you been learning in New York? You're like Tony Soprano or something!"

He shrugged but still wouldn't meet her eyes. "It was nothing."

"It wasn't your place."

"Look, I saved you a hassle."

"How so?"

He did turn at this, his height advantage causing her to have to look up to meet his gaze. "If he really wanted you, a few comments from me shouldn't have deterred him."

Then Roman ran off, hollering at the boys to speed it up as they raced toward the finish at the entrance to town.

As she followed behind, Avery couldn't completely fault him for his logic.

Roman shouted out orders like a drill sergeant. Most of the boys were in pairs around the gym at the Indigo Blue and he sent the last few off to their positions.

"Charlie. Greg. Get over there and spot Steven." Roman pointed to the free weights. "Mike and Stink, go take the rowing machines."

Avery shook her head as she put her hands on her hips. "Stink really needs a new nickname."

"Have you smelled the kid?" Roman whispered as everyone took their places.

"I thought you were immune to hockey funk?"

Roman eyed her after he was satisfied each of the boys was doing his reps properly. "There's funk and then there's funk. He's got the latter."

"I'll talk to his mother. I think he just needs some

new gear. The grandmothers make an annual donation to the team scholarship fund. Maybe we can get him fixed up with some new stuff."

Roman filed away the news of his grandmother's generosity—not a surprise, but something he'd like to remember to thank her for all the same—and focused back on the boys.

"They've got a lot of talent."

"They do. What they need is a coach who'll stay put for the long haul."

Roman had been thinking that very thing. "I do know a guy. I have no idea if he'd even consider taking the job, but he is worth talking to."

"Who is it?"

"A guy I played with early in my career. He got out after an injury. Moved down to the minors for a few years and then has bummed around from coaching job to coaching job. He's good, just a little restless, and the minors aren't always the most dependable. Teams get relocated or local towns lose interest after the novelty wears off."

"Restless is going to be a hard sell. The town wants someone to come and make a commitment."

"He'll at least commit to an entire season, unlike the last guy. Besides, that's a bit of a shortsighted expectation, don't you think? I mean, this is a hard life here. A good life, but a hard one. No one knows how they'll handle it until they actually live here."

Roman knew he didn't have a full right to criticize every little thing happening in Indigo, but he did have a right to an opinion.

"Fair point. It's not for everyone." She cracked a

broad smile. "I still say Sloan and Grier are in for a big surprise when the glow of sex wears off and they realize they're smack in the middle of nowhere."

"You don't think they can handle it?"

She grew more serious, the question obviously one she'd thought of herself as well. "No, it's not a matter of handling it or not. But I do think they're going to have an adjustment all the same."

"They probably will. I had one in reverse going to New York."

"Really?"

"Hell, yeah. Here I was, in the middle of one of the largest cities in the world. I was a nobody on the team, getting my butt kicked on an hourly basis, and I was scared sh—spitless." He caught himself just in time and censored his language in the event the boys were paying more attention than he gave them credit for. "And I missed my home."

"Well, it figures." She moved up into his personal space.

"What does?"

Her skin was still flushed from the run through town and her cheeks had a pink vitality to them that tugged at his insides. She was so close he could see the dark ring of blue that rimmed the edge of her dark irises.

"Maybe if you were getting laid you'd have enjoyed yourself a bit more."

And maybe he should have faced the kids alone today, he realized with a start.

Spending the morning with a teasing, sweaty, happy-go-lucky Avery was wreaking havoc with his libido. Add to it the embarrassment of potentially being caught—the thin workout shorts he wore would do nothing to hide a raging hard-on—and he cursed himself a million times the fool.

Before he could curse himself any further, a shout from the corner pulled him from the moment and he headed for the fight brewing in front of the weight rack. Stink was surrounded by two boys and it didn't take much to figure out who was the instigator.

Roman had had his eye on the two kids on the team with the weakest skills. Both had been overly aggressive with the hitting while on drills the day before, and he had a suspicion that if there were holes in the team's camaraderie, it came from them.

The two of them had Stink against the rack of weights and a clearly menacing aura had descended over the interaction.

"Problem, gentlemen?"

"Stink over here is bothering the rest of us."

Roman glanced quickly at the boy but didn't react to the statement. A misplaced word and the kid would have it even harder. "How so, Will? I put him on the rowing machine to work his cardio for a bit. I haven't called for a rotation yet."

"He stinks, Coach." Will's partner, Zach, wasn't quite as hot under the collar.

Working to keep it light, Roman offered up what he thought of as his Hollywood smile. "For the record, you all stink. It's called a workout for a reason."

The room had quieted and he got a good round of guffaws at that one.

"Not like this."

So Zach was the mouthpiece. Dropping his hands to his hips, Roman took a few steps forward, leveraging all of the menace six foot four inches could provide. "If you're not enjoying yourselves, then maybe you should leave practice early."

"But it's him, Coach." Will added a shoulder shove at Stink for good measure.

The move was enough to pull a clearly agitated Stink into the fight and bedlam broke out immediately. The force of Stink's movements and Zach's block had them tumbling away from the rack of weights, into Roman.

He stumbled backward, his footing off as he jammed his leg against one of the machines. He lost his balance, his own arms waving to right himself when he heard Avery's soft cry as he fell into her.

A few of the other boys ran up, pulling Will and Stink away from each other, but in the midst of the melee, Roman wasn't able to move off Avery all that quickly.

"Avery. Are you all right?"

"Damn it, but you're heavy."

"Well, yeah. I didn't even know you were behind me." He dragged himself off her, rolling back over to grab her hand to pull her to a sitting position. As he did, he immediately caught sight of the red splotch next to her eye.

"You're hurt." Roman reached out, cupping her cheek in his hand and running his thumb over the red mark.

"I grazed it on the bench of the machine on the way down." She smiled ruefully as his thumb ran over the rim of her eye socket. "At least it was padded."

"I don't care."

The hum of excitement that had gripped the room fell silent as Roman stood and bent down to help Avery up. The adrenaline that was rapidly fading—along with the knowledge he was about to mete out punishment—had the boys waiting in quiet anticipation.

"Practice is over. And since this is such an excellent example of your teamwork, I don't want to see Zach, Will or Stink until Friday's practice. Take a few days and cool off."

Cries of "But Coach!" and "Not fair!" rose up from Will and Zach, and it didn't escape Roman's notice that Stink was noticeably quiet.

"Since Avery got caught in the cross fire, let's call it a day." With a pointed look at Zach and Will, he added, "I'll see the rest of you tomorrow."

Stink was already out of the room, his shoulders hunched as he slammed through the door to the gym. The other boys filed out shortly after, and Roman turned back, anxious to see to Avery.

"Are you sure you're all right?"

"I'm fine, Roman. I think Stink's the one you need to worry about. He's a lot more bruised than I am."

"If I call him out or favor him, the kids'll only make it harder on him."

"I know."

He crossed the room and grabbed a cold water from the small fridge that sat in the corner. Walking back to Avery, he handed it to her. "Press that to your eye for a few minutes. You're going to have a shiner all the same."

"I'll consider it a badge of honor."

"It pisses me off. They're a group of boys who should know better." He took her by the shoulders and led her to one of the weight benches. "Sit down for a few minutes."

"And they've got hot heads and the tempers of young men."

"You could have gotten really hurt. Hell, scratch that. You *were* hurt."

Roman was surprised at the quick and ready anger that still simmered under his skin. He knew she was okay—the bruise was minor and she'd get a few good stories out of it around town. He also wasn't sad to have a reason to get Will and Zach out of the team environment for a few days so he could assess what the team looked like without them.

But things with Stink bothered him.

"You've gotten awfully clumsy since the last time I saw you."

Avery's words were quiet but she could have screamed them, they echoed so loudly through his head.

"I'm fine."

"You sure? You've tripped a lot and that was quite a fall you took against the machines. Didn't you see them as you went down?"

"I was sort of focused on the gaggle of teenage testosterone getting ready to explode."

She cocked her head, the motion oddly charming with the water bottle still pressed to her eye. "So what's the excuse for last night with the glasses? Or the other day on your run?"

Panic balled up in his gut, reaching up to tighten his chest with hard squeezes that matched the pounding of his heart. Despite the immediate reaction, Roman fought to keep his voice level.

He would not discuss this. Would not admit there was anything wrong. Because it damn well wasn't anything he couldn't handle.

"I'm a tall man. Believe me, I trip more than I'd like to admit."

"Don't bullshit me, Roman. You're so fucking graceful the ballet would take you."

"What do you want me to tell you? That I feel good about the fact that I almost got my ass kicked by a bunch of kids?"

She dropped the water bottle and stood. "And the run? And the wineglasses? You're going to sit there and tell me they're nothing?"

"You said yourself glasses get broken all the time. I just had the bad luck to swipe out an entire row."

The doubt persisted, plastered all over her face in twin lines of skepticism and annoyance, but she backed down.

Sort of.

"You'd tell me if something was wrong, wouldn't you?"

Frustration of his own crawled through his veins like a poison. He'd lived with it since his injury the previous season, the self-doubt and fear coiled and hissing at him like a snake.

Unwilling to give it any more power, and anxious for a way to change the subject, he went on the offensive. Closing the narrow gap between them, Roman moved back into her personal space, pleased when that light flush rose once more in her cheeks.

Even better, instead of the flush of exertion, this blush of pink smacked of something far more interesting and enticing.

Arousal.

"Are you sure you're okay?" He ran a finger along her cheek, brushing lightly against her cheekbone. Her skin was still cool from the water bottle and Roman marveled at the difference between her cool flesh and the body heat he felt emanating against his chest.

"I'm fine."

He bent his head and pressed his lips against her cheek. "Maybe you need a few kisses to make it all better."

"Roman."

He heard his name come out on a sigh and it only encouraged him to maintain his strategic assault. With exquisite gentleness so as not to press too hard against the bruise, he ran his lips across the remaining expanse of her cheek, then added suction as he moved to her earlobe. Pressing a kiss to the shell of her ear, he whispered back.

"Such beautiful skin. It's a terrible thing to mar it."

He placed one hand at the base of her neck, gratified when he felt the tension in her body loosen as her head fell back. He continued to tease her ear with his lips and she tilted to give him better access when he moved down to the graceful arch of her neck.

"Roman." When he only continued pressing kisses to her neck, she raised her voice in a heartier whisper. *"Roman."*

"Mmmm?"

"One of the boys might come back."

"So that's the only reason you won't kiss me back?"

"No."

He lifted his head and placed his hands on either side of her neck. "Yes."

Without giving her time to come up with any additional excuses, he pressed his lips to hers and slid his tongue through the seam.

A delicious familiarity gripped him as the taste that was uniquely Avery met his taste buds—a mixture of the sweet flavor of her sports drink and something darker and more intense, like the fine wines she loved. Whatever hesitation she might have had wasn't in evidence as she kissed him back. Her arms wrapped around his waist and he felt the light tease of her fingers where she ran them along the base of his spine.

The thought vaguely crossed his mind that the woman in his arms was the same as he remembered, yet distinctly different somehow.

Where their time together as teenagers had been a mixture of tentative exploration and an innocent give-and-take, the woman in his arms had the cultured notes of experience and self-confidence in the artful way she kissed him back.

It was heady and Roman found himself pulled by the undertow as the fever to brand her with his body increasingly took over all rational thought.

"Roman. We can't do this."

"Actually, we can."

The clear notes of regret stamped themselves in her dark eyes, their pupils blown wide with need as she stepped back. "No, we can't."

"Why are you pulling away?"

"Because I can't think when you're close to me like this."

"Thinking is overrated."

"Maybe so, but I'm not interested in making a mistake I can't undo."

Her words hit him with the force of an arrow. "I wasn't aware we were a mistake."

"We will be if we rush into things." She took another few steps away. "I care about you. I always have. And I'm not going to make a decision with my hormones."

"So you are willing to consider there's something there?"

"Oh, Roman." She shook her head, a gentle smile hovering at her lips. "There's always been something there. For God's sake, I used to give you my cookies at lunch when we were six."

"You told me you didn't like them."

"I was subjugating my desires for a man, even then."

A heavy bark of laughter welled up in his chest. "You were what?"

"I used to have my mom pack extras every day. And I was adamant that I had to have Oreos."

"So you could give them to me."

"Yep."

"I don't believe it."

She shrugged. "They made you happy. So they made me happy."

The quietly spoken words had the same effect as the last arrow to the chest, only this one spread a funny sort of warmth through his limbs upon impact.

"So when I tell you I don't want to make a decision

with my hormones, understand that's not meant to be an insult. You mean more than a roll around the gym."

"I was expecting we could use a bed."

"It's not the right time." She stepped forward and pressed a kiss to his cheek. "But you're lovely for asking."

He felt the soft press of her lips and knew there was a thread of truth in her words, especially if he put the raging needs of his body aside for the briefest of moments to listen to his brain.

Those long, coltish legs carried her to the door of the gym and he watched her take every step, imagining the feel of them wrapped around his waist. Maybe it was the vision or the subtle calm of her voice when she turned back to look at him.

"You coming?"

"Where are you going?"

"I thought I'd fix myself a post-workout treat of milk and Oreos. You're welcome to join me."

Roman didn't wait to be asked twice.

Julia took a seat on the hard marble bench in front of what the town fondly referred to as the Love Monument.

She simply thought of it as her refuge.

The monument had been her gift to her late husband's memory. She still remembered the day she lost him in vivid detail, the harsh shock of being a widow in her midthirties something she'd feared she would never recover from.

Her friends had seen her through, along with the son and daughter she adored, and slowly the joys of life had come back to her. And it had been Mary, in a late-night sob session a year after Andrew had passed, who had come up with the idea of a monument.

Something solid and lasting, she had said.

Mary had remembered a sculptor from Juneau that she and Charlie had seen on a vacation the previous year and gave Julia his name. With very little input, the man had managed to capture the exact essence of what she was looking for.

Heavy, curving lines that gave the impression of a man and a woman, folded in an embrace.

It was the lettering at the base, however, that had been all hers.

For those we aren't allowed to keep.

How true those words had been, especially when she lost her own son a little more than two decades later.

Once again, her girlfriends had been there, standing solidly beside her as she dealt with a grief that penetrated every single cell of her body with the most unbearable pain imaginable.

Mary and Sophie had been through everything with her. The most important moments of her life had been shared, dissected, remembered and treasured with the two best friends a woman could have.

So why couldn't she talk to them about Roman?

The thought nagged at her, and despite the slight feelings of guilt and the bigger puzzlement as to why she remained silent, she knew she couldn't share her concerns.

"Care for some company?"

Julia looked up to see Ken standing next to her, a hand lifted to shade his eyes from the afternoon sun.

"Of course." A light hitch caught her breath and she swallowed hard before adding, "Please. Join me."

His smile was warm as he settled himself next to her. "It's a beautiful day. You visiting with Andy?"

"I was thinking, more than anything." She hesitated for only a moment as his words registered. "And how do you know I visit with Andy when I come here?"

"It's too beautiful a spot not to."

"There's an odd simplicity in that."

He shrugged. "I'm a simple man."

"No, I don't think that's true. You only look simple and easygoing on the surface, but I think those still waters run very deep."

A distinct twinkle lit his gentle brown eyes. "I think that was a compliment."

"I certainly meant it as such."

"So if you're not really talking to Andy, and please tell him hi for me when you do talk next, what were you thinking about on this lovely afternoon?"

"My grandson."

"Ahhh." Ken shifted and settled his elbow on the back of the bench. "What has you worried?"

"He's hiding something."

"It's certainly not how he feels about Avery."

"No, not that."

Julia's gaze caught on the small bed of flowers that surrounded the base of the monument. The bright, pretty blooms winked gently in the breeze, their pinks and purples a jaunty wave to summer. "But I think something's wrong."

His years of practicing medicine kicked in and his face grew serious. "You think he's hurt?"

"I'm not sure."

With the ready admission that she felt silly even bringing it up, she recounted the broken glasses from the evening before. "And I can't put my finger on it, but something's off, Ken. I know it was only a few glasses. Anyone can make that mistake. But it was like he didn't even see them."

"Have you discussed it with Susan? Asked if she's noticed anything?"

A spurt of annoyance filled her chest. "All she sees is hearts, fireworks and grandbabies where Roman is concerned. And when Avery's in the mix, it's worse."

"She's not the only one."

"No. No, she's not." Julia played with the fringe on the light sweater she wore. "I think that's why I haven't been able to talk about this with Mary and Sophie. They're so focused on weddings and happy-ever-afters that they've stopped realizing not everyone gets one."

Her gaze drifted to the monument without any conscious effort. Before she could think on it, a light breeze whipped up and blew at her hair. She turned to look at Ken in an effort to blow back the strands waving around her face.

And caught sight of such a deep longing in his eyes she lost her breath.

The moment stretched out and she wondered at the light whisper of thought streaming through her mind.

She'd been alone for so long, she hadn't ever really expected she'd find anything with another man after losing Andrew. But as she stared into Ken Cloud's eyes, the strangest feeling—a subtle longing, really—urged her to consider not being quite so hasty.

And then the moment broke as he finally spoke, his tone solemn. "No, not everyone gets one."

That light breeze whispered around her shoulders once more and as it swirled, a funny impulse seized her. "I haven't taken my walk yet today. Would you care to join me?"

The empty look in his gaze vanished, replaced with something as bright as a beautiful summer day. "Yes."

He stood, his regal carriage gentlemanly as he extended a hand to help her up. "Where should we go?"

"There's a path along the river I enjoy."

"Sounds lovely."

The wind whispered over her shoulders once more as she and Ken walked away from the monument, and Julia couldn't shake the thought that Andrew approved.

Most heartily.

Chapter Thirteen

"You look like a woman contemplating sex."

Avery eyed Grier over the rim of her over-sized java mug, the surrounding buzz at the Jitters thankfully loud enough to cover Grier's bold pronouncement. "How do you know that?"

"Three reasons."

With a come-here hand wave, Avery sat back, ready to take it all in. "Bring them on."

"Exhibit one. You have an irritable glow."

"How is a glow irritable?"

"You're glowing 'cuz you're anticipating sex, but you're pissed about it. I've been there, girlfriend."

Avery decided to keep her thoughts to herself on point number one because the description was shockingly close to the truth. "Okay. What are your other reasons?"

"You're replacing the need for sex with chocolate."

"I am not."

"That mocha has about a billion calories in it and you usually just drink yours plain with skim milk."

Avery swirled the Twix stir-stick in the froth. "Chooch got me hooked on it. It's her Special."

"It hurts my teeth to look at it and you know that's saying a lot."

"I ran four miles with fourteen teenage boys. I earned it."

Grier tapped her forehead. "And you landed yourself a rather colorful shiner as well, so you can add medicinal to its properties."

"I like the way you think. And the shiner was an accident."

"Roman's still pissed about it. He was telling Mick about it earlier when he brought the truck back."

"There's nothing for him to be angry about. It was just boys being boys."

One lone eyebrow rose up over Grier's cool gray eyes. "I'm not going to dignify that with a response, especially since I heard it was the team's two little shits who instigated it."

"Will and Zach had their bully flags flying today."

"Assholes. I did Zach's parents' returns this past tax season and the kid stomped around the house like he was the damn prince of the castle."

"Neither Will nor Zach are very good and it pisses them off. I could have seen past it but when they started picking on Stink they went from annoying to something else."

"Stink. The one who—" Grier wrinkled her nose.

"Hockey funk."

"Yeah. That."

"Well, he's clean most of the time when he's not playing, I mean. The problem is his equipment's old and hockey players have freshness challenges on the best of days." Avery took a sip of her coffee as a sweet memory swamped her.

Roman used to race home after practice to clean up before they had a date. He'd scrub his skin bright pink, then go out in the cold. She could still remember the night he actually had ice in his hair because he'd gone out with it still wet.

"The equipment's expensive, too, isn't it?"

Grier's question pulled her from the image of Roman with crunchy hair, and Avery refocused on Stink. "He's a sweet kid and he loves hockey like it's his religion. He's always taken the ribbing pretty good-naturedly, but I think it's starting to get old."

"Having a cool nickname that shows you're a team sport is one thing. When the underlying reason's used to embarrass you, not so much."

"You haven't told me number three."

"Oh. That's easy." Grier reached for her own drink on a laugh. "You want to."

"Did you just chortle merrily before taking that sip?"

"I most certainly did not."

"You did."

"You're evading."

"I am."

"Because I'm right."

"Damn it."

Avery sighed, memories of the heated kisses in the gym earlier that day filling her mind's eye. They hadn't been far from her thoughts all afternoon and she'd barely gotten her inventory done on time to get the order out to Jack.

"Why are you right?"

"Um, because the man is crazy about you. Add on he's one of the most physically perfect specimens of manhood on the planet. Oh. And did I mention he's crazy about you?"

"It can't be anything, Grier."

"You know, someone gave me a hard time when I tried using that excuse a few months ago." Grier leaned forward and linked their hands. "It was the best piece of advice I've ever received."

"I can't go through it again, Grier. What if I give myself the permission to go back and he leaves again? He's not staying."

"No, he's not."

"I can't live through it again. Once was enough."

"You don't think you're different now?"

"I don't think he and I together are different. That's the problem."

"But you're older. Wiser."

"I don't know how to explain this in a way that makes even the slightest bit of sense." Avery took a fortifying sip of the lush, rich chocolate and allowed the sweetness a moment on her tongue before she started in.

"That's okay. I'll believe you, whatever you tell me."

Avery took one more sip for good measure, then began. "People talk about puppy love and first loves and teenage crushes. But what Roman and I had have—has always been different. Always."

"Describe it to me."

"He's just always been there. A part of me. And the time between us is special, somehow. I'm not big on the term *soul mate* because I think it diminishes the other relationships in our lives that matter, but he and I have that. Even when we were very small."

A distant memory whirled through her mind and she thought about it for a moment, allowing it to solidify.

"Once . . . I couldn't have been more than about eight. He was nine, and Mick and Walker ten. We were playing out around town the day after a snowstorm. It was after school let out and you know what it's like around here. Everyone's casual and easygoing and a bunch of kids running around the town square is just more of the perfect, Norman Rockwell thing we channel here sometimes."

"It's lovely. And homey."

"That, too."

It was funny, Avery thought, how a memory she hadn't had in well over a decade could come back so strong.

And so very vivid.

"So we were running around and carrying on and just having a great time and I started to run out toward Main Street. And without any warning, a car driving slowly down the street hit a patch and went sliding. The driver couldn't get control and all I could see was his face and I was literally frozen in place, the car bearing down on me."

"And Roman pulled you back?"

"Roman started running toward me before the car even lost control."

Avery saw the story register in Grier's gaze—saw her brow furrow as she tried to take it in.

"I asked him about it later. He walked me to my house, which he always did after we were done playing. I was still sort of freaked out by the whole thing and he was extra quiet. And I asked him how he knew the car was going to lose control."

"What did he say?"

"He said he knew something was wrong. He was nine, Grier. How does a kid know something like that?"

"I don't know."

"It's always been that way between us. We've just always been together. So in tune with each other."

"Then there's even more reason for you to act on these feelings. Not only do you have a connection emotionally, but you have a physical connection, too, and that's not to be undervalued."

A hard sob welled up in her throat, the hurt so immediate—so unexpected—she dragged a hand to her mouth to hold it in.

"Oh, Avery, I'm sorry. I'm sorry to keep pushing."

Avery shook her head. "No, don't you see, that's it? He was never just my boyfriend. He matters to me in the same way I need air to breathe. And he went away. I didn't simply lose my boyfriend. I lost my best friend when he left. And he was gone."

"Oh."

"That's what no one understands. They think how cute we are and how great it is that he's back and maybe he's finished sowing wild oats. But it's never been about that. The pain has never been about that." She hiccupped. "Or not entirely."

"You lost half of yourself."

"Which is why I can't go through it again."

*   *   *

Avery flipped through the latest *In Style* and abstractedly wondered what she'd look like with Charlize Theron's hair. The magazine was a mindless distraction from the day, and as she turned past Charlize and on to Reese Witherspoon, she let her mind wander back to the conversation she'd had with Grier at the Jitters.

After she got over the emotional hurdle of churning up all of her history with Roman, she realized it had actually felt rather therapeutic to get it out.

And God bless Grier, she was a good listener. She had also been through something similar enough to offer understanding and compassion without trying to add on a load of advice that wasn't helpful or wanted.

Of course, all the friendship or understanding couldn't change one major, glaring fact.

She *did* want to have sex with Roman.

There was little use in denying it to herself. The need for him vibrated under her skin like a hard, heavy drumbeat that wouldn't be silenced.

She was sick of fighting the attraction, but she was even sicker of the endless tension that had plagued their interactions with each other since the time he left Indigo.

The real question, to her mind, was, was she brave enough to go there again? And if they *did* go there, would he check out again when he inevitably went home?

The ringing of the phone interrupted her thoughts and she grabbed it, surprised when the caller asked specifically for her.

"Avery. This is Walt Singer." The man rattled off an impressive list of credentials along with his role in heading up one of the lead travel industry associations. "I'm incredibly sorry for the lateness of my call, but I'm in a terrible bind and your name just came to my attention. I figured it was early enough there I might catch you."

Intrigued, Avery reached for the computer and opened up a search box so she could look him up as he spoke. "Please. Go on."

"I'm running the travel conference that starts Monday in Anchorage and I've lost one of my speakers to a bad case of the flu. I understand you recently took part in an exchange program."

"I did."

"You'd be perfect. We're talking about ways to invigorate your career, how to create environments for employees that keep them motivated and happy, and how those things can build your business. Your experience would be perfect for the panel."

"I need to check with my boss."

"Let me get your e-mail information and I'll follow up with all the details. Your conference fee will be paid for if you'd like to stay for the duration, but if you could only do a day trip, that'd be fine as well."

Avery did a quick calculation as to who might be able to fill in for her. "I'm very interested, let me just do some checking in the morning and I'll get back to you."

"Wonderful."

They exchanged a few more pleasantries and were about to hang up when a thought hit her. "Walt. How'd you get my name?"

"A few places. You've got quite a good reputation in the Alaska hospitality community. But the exchange came to my attention from a Mr. Declan O'Mara. He and I have been working on a website project for the association and he's the representation from Ireland. He can't stop singing your praises."

"Oh, okay. Well. Thanks."

She hung up, somewhat shocked by the call yet buoyed by it as well. Her speaking skills were decent, and she did love what she did. Walt had also promised to send her the questions in advance, so she could prepare her thoughts.

It would also be great publicity for Indigo and the hotel.

As she went back to her magazine, she flipped back to the page on Charlize and wondered again about the haircut. And maybe the new suit she saw on page 232.

Roman fought the urge to squirm in his chair as his grandmother's steady gaze lasered in on him with unerring precision. "You've been busy since you've been back."

The standing invitation to dinner every time he came home was something he looked forward to, but this evening had the distinct overtones of the Spanish Inquisition instead of a leisurely family dinner.

"I have been. I'm enjoying the chance to coach the kids for a few weeks."

"And getting that rink fixed up."

"We start on Saturday."

"Everyone's getting excited about it. It's all anyone can talk about."

The slight edge of irritation that had ridden him

since he first saw the rink resurfaced and he knew Julia Forsyth was the one person he could unload it on.

"Why hasn't anyone fixed it before now?"

"No one's cared enough, I suppose."

"They sure care now."

"What you do matters to people. They love that you're from here and that you've made something of yourself."

"I'm a person, Gran. Just a person."

She winked at him. "Why not leave them to their delusions?"

"Because those delusions ensure they don't really listen to me."

"Why do you care if they listen to you?"

He drew up short at that and simply stared at his grandmother, waiting for her to say something else. When she didn't, he sputtered out the first thing that he thought of.

"I'm not a statue on a pedestal. I don't like the special treatment or the idea that whatever I say is some sort of weird, celebrity gospel."

"But you've chosen not to be a part of the town. What opportunity have they had to know you?"

The words struck him like a swift punch to the jaw and he shook his head to clear the sudden ringing in his ears. While he'd always appreciated the fact that his grandmother didn't pull any punches, it was a bit of a shock to hear her being so honest.

"Does that bother you?" he asked.

"Does it bother you?"

"Look, Gran, enough with the pseudopsychology. My point is valid."

"So's mine, Roman." The cool, even demeanor she'd held all through the dinner flared high with a quick burn of anger. "You don't live here. And you haven't lived here for nearly fourteen years. Most of the time, you use wildly expensive gifts to replace your presence here, which, while lovely, only serves to heighten the untouchability everyone feels about you. So maybe you need to start wondering what you've done to become a figurehead instead of a member of the Indigo community."

"You don't think I should have left."

She threw her napkin on the table at that and stood up. "I have never once thought that, nor will I ever. You have a gift and you were given the gift of opportunity to use it."

"Okay, all right. I'm sorry."

Her features softened, but she didn't sit. Instead, she crossed around the table to sit next to him. "Roman. All I'm saying is that when you left, you left. And you have made deliberate choices about staying away."

He wanted to argue—wanted to rail that he hadn't done that—but he was a shitty liar to begin with, and exceptionally poor at it with his grandmother.

"I couldn't come back. Not with her here."

"I know, darling. I know." She took his hand and held it in both of hers. "A dream is a beautiful thing, but it has a price. Avery was the price."

"I've always believed I made the choice I had to. But now . . ." He stared at the table, barely seeing the dishes covering the top. "Now I don't know. She's here and I'm here and I wonder if I chose wrong."

"If you'd stayed, it would have destroyed both of you."

He laid his free hand over hers and squeezed. "Yeah, but leaving pretty much did the same."

"Oh, sweetie. Who do you think you'd be if you'd never taken the opportunity?"

"Just another hockey fiend who played on the weekends and watched the games with rabid interest."

"No. You have a rare talent and every single minute of your time on the ice would have been spent with resentment. Is that what you would have wanted to bring to your relationship with Avery?"

"No."

"It's easy to look backward and say 'what if,' but when we play that game, we always like to think the 'what if' would be better. What if it was worse?"

He knew she had a point. He'd spent the last half of the season wondering who the hell he was going to be when hockey was over. At least he'd had the opportunity. Had gone for the gold and swung at the fences.

Even if it had come at a terribly steep price.

It was with that knowledge that another thought struck, swift and hard. "She enjoyed Ireland."

"Very much."

"That's her adventure. Her opportunity."

"Yes, it was. Alicia's illness kept her grounded for far too long. Avery's finally been given the gift of wings."

"I'll only hold her back."

"Would you really do that?"

He thought of the choices he'd made so far where

the two of them were concerned and questioned if he would make the right decision when it counted.

"I don't know. I hope not, but I honestly don't know."

Roman walked the quiet streets of Indigo and soaked up the late-night sun as he thought about dinner. While its beginnings had been a bit rough, the second half of the evening with his grandmother had been more of what he looked forward to each time he came home.

She was always honest with him, and even when she struck a nerve, he knew it was something he needed to hear.

Would he hold Avery back?

That simple question turned over and over in his mind.

He wanted to believe he wouldn't stand in Avery's way. Wanted to think enough of himself and his motivations to believe an adult relationship was something mutually fulfilling. Something they could share.

But was that the right thing? The fair thing?

Oh hey, honey. So glad you waited around for me for fourteen years. Ready to pick up where we left off?

Even as he thought it, he knew that wasn't an accurate assessment of how he felt about her or what he wanted. He wanted to share his life with her. Wanted them to share their hopes and dreams for the future, wherever that took them.

So why did he feel like he was trying to have his cake and eat it, too?

On a sigh, he shoved his jumbled thoughts to the back of his mind. After he and his grandmother discussed Avery, the talk had turned to lighter matters. She spoke of all the odds and ends in her life before shifting to recount the excitement in town as Sloan and Walker planned their wedding.

She also told him all the latest town gossip, including the interest in a female pilot Mick and Jack had hired to help them with the increasing workload of their business. Although originally scheduled to join them in the spring, the woman had been forced to delay her arrival for the fall due to some unexpected commitments with her family.

He'd smiled as she told him of Mick's new partner. There was no doubt she was a hot piece of gossip out at the airstrip.

Roman's thoughts were interrupted by a few late-night walkers, and he waved across the town square before heading into the lobby of the hotel.

Straight into a dancing Avery.

"What's up, Donna Summer?"

Her face glowed brightly as she continued to do an odd swoop-n-waltz around the lobby on tiptoes. "Ask me what just happened a few hours ago."

"Can I guess?"

"You'll never guess it."

"Can I try?"

She shrugged but didn't stand still. "Sure."

"You're being profiled in a travel magazine."

The dancing stopped and she whirled on him, her face falling slightly. "How did you get so close?"

"Close to what? You're going to be in a magazine?"

"I was invited to sit on a panel for a tourism conference."

"That's fantastic."

"How'd you guess?"

He shrugged, but a weird tremor hit at the nape of his neck. "I'm not sure. It just seemed like the right answer."

One foot began tapping as Avery looked thoughtful. "That's peculiar. Did your mother tell you?"

"How would my mother have told me? I haven't talked to her. Have you?"

"No."

"So how could she possibly know?"

"She seems to know everything that goes on in this town."

He crossed the lobby to take a chair. "She's not omniscient, despite the fact I spent the majority of my childhood convinced she was."

"You just got the unlucky roll of the dice to get a sister who had a big mouth."

He laughed at that, even as that strange twitch continued just under his hairline. Roman ran a hand over the tight muscles of his neck, willing the tingles to subside. "Tell me more about the conference."

"It's in Anchorage and they had a panelist drop out at the last minute and invited me to sit in."

"That's great. You're going, right?"

"I just need to get the time off."

He eyed her at that. "You're going."

"I don't want to leave Susan in a lurch."

He glanced around the quiet lobby and knew that was the last thing she needed to worry about. "I think she can spare you for a few days. Besides, she's all too happy to leave you here to take care of things. I love my mother, but she's capable of lifting both hands and doing the work, too."

"We share the load."

"I'm not saying you don't, but this is a big opportunity for both you and the hotel. You're representing us. It's important."

"Oh God." She clutched her stomach. "What if I totally screw it up?"

"You won't."

"But what if I do?"

"You're the one who taught me all my public speaking skills and you were sixteen at the time. You've got this one."

The dancing started again as she swirled around the room picking up glasses and waltzing them back to the bar counter. "Damn right."

Roman picked up a few glasses before he stopped and simply watched her, the opportunity too tempting to resist.

He'd memorized the shape of her face in his childhood. Had seen the chubby cheeks grow and morph into the slender face of a teenager. And now, all he saw was the graceful slope of her neck, the curve of her high cheekbones and the shiny wave of her hair tucked behind her ear.

She was beautiful, in an earthy way that made him think of sunshine and picnics, snow and roaring fires.

And the need for her that had never really dimmed came to life, beating furiously through his veins with a desperate craving that knocked his feet out from underneath him. He knew he needed to give her the space she deserved, but try as he might, he couldn't assuage the desire that filled him when he looked at her.

Nor could he quite get rid of the hope that danced at the edge of his thoughts, whispering that things could be different this time. That they could make things work now that they were both free to make their own choices.

Their circumstances were different.

They were different.

But was that enough to make up for fourteen years and the four thousand miles that had stretched between them?

Chapter Fourteen

$\mathcal{A}$very saw the desire on his face. Where both of them usually cloaked their true feelings, his interest was evident in every line of his body, as if he'd been frozen in ice. At the thought, a helpless giggle rose in her throat she couldn't stop.

His dark eyebrows flattened at her laughter. "What is it?"

"All I can think of is Han Solo frozen in the carbonite."

"What?"

"You. That expression on your face. It's so sweet, and all I can think of is how you and Walker and Mick used to go around and freeze in place, pretending to be Han Solo."

"You're hell on a man's ego."

"Sorry. It popped into my head and once it got there I couldn't get rid of it."

The set of his shoulders relaxed a bit as a warm smile spread across his face. Avery was curious to note the desire still hovered in his eyes as he moved closer, but his movements had grown lazy as he crossed the room. "No one ever wanted to be Luke."

"Farm boy or space pirate. It's not a hard choice."

He walked into her personal space, effectively capturing her back against the bar while his large arms closed in around her body. "That was an easy choice. Other choices are harder."

"I know." She nodded, the moment turning serious and—was it possible?—sad.

They'd lost so much time and wasted so many years.

"I've missed you." She whispered the words, as if saying them out loud gave them power.

Maybe it did, her conscience reminded her. Voicing her feelings made them real. Valid.

And now it was something she couldn't try to take back.

"Me, too."

The carefree laughter was gone, vanished as if it had never been. "Please let me say this. I want to get it out."

"Okay." His face softened, the desire banked. In its place, he stared at her in that way he had when she knew he was truly listening to her. His gaze was firm and direct, his attention absolute.

"I loved you. And losing you was hard emotionally. To have a sexual relationship end, especially my first, was hard, but you are more to me than sex. Our relationship, too. It was more to me than just boyfriend and girlfriend."

"I know."

"Do you, Roman?" She whispered the question, the words solemn. "Do you really understand what your leaving meant?"

"I know what it meant to me. I got my dream and

gave up absolutely every single thing of value in my life to have it."

His words struck, swift and true, to the center of her heart. In all these years—all her moments of struggle and pain and sadness—she'd never thought about it from his perspective.

"You've had new things come into your life."

"They were wonderful. But somewhere deep inside, I always knew I couldn't have both."

"You chose not to have both, Roman. There's a difference."

Emotion flashed across the deep green of his irises, a mix of frustration and guilt. "It's not that easy. It never has been."

"Did you try? Did you consider bringing me with you?"

"Where would it have gotten you? Us? Your mother was dying, Avery. Slowly and painfully. Could you really have left her?"

"No."

"So how fair would it have been for me to dangle the opportunity to come with me? It would have killed you."

She recognized the truth of his words—the reality of having to choose would have done just that.

With startling clarity, she understood that if she'd been given the choice—no matter which side she'd chosen—she'd have had resentment.

Resentment toward her mother if she'd chosen to stay. And resentment of Roman if she'd left.

"How did you know?"

"Because I know you. You're sweet and loyal and

you do the things that are hard. Your mom was hard, yet you stood by her. That's who you are."

"I'm not sure I'm sweet."

"I'm sure."

He bent his head, his mouth finding hers. His arms still caged her against the bar and she laid her hands on his biceps, the hard muscle underneath her fingers flexing slightly as he maintained a rigid control.

She wanted him to lose that restraint. To let the fire rage and consume them both.

And she also knew if she allowed it to burn, they might never get it back under control.

Pulling her mouth away, she kept firm pressure on his arms. "I have to get an early start tomorrow."

"Sure." Passion glazed his eyes, and the muscles in his arms flexed again at the frustration that rode him.

"I'll see you in the morning."

He stepped back and dropped his arms at his sides. "Good night, Avery."

"Good night, Roman."

Avery left the glasses on the bar. They could be dealt with in the morning. She knew to her very core that if she stayed one moment longer she wouldn't leave.

At the arch that capped off the hallway to her apartment, she turned to look at him. "Thank you."

"For what?"

"For not asking me to make a choice all those years ago. I never understood before what a gift that was."

Roman stood before the wall of mirrors in the workout room, pushing through his third set of reps. The simple motion of pushing his muscles up and down, his breathing in and out, had gone a long way toward calming his raging body.

It hadn't done a fucking thing for his mind.

Why did they continue to dance around each other like this? The attraction was there, of course, and so was the fear. Avery wasn't a tease—she never had been—but waiting for her had him so twisted up he didn't know if he was coming or going.

Even as he understood why it wasn't so simple as falling into bed with each other.

The face of his cell phone lit up where he'd set it on one of the benches, the loud, insistent ringing pulling him from his thoughts.

"Forsyth."

"Roman? It's Bill Farley. From the network."

Roman grabbed a towel and water bottle and sat down on a weight bench. "Bill. It's good to hear from you."

"Look. I'm going to call your agent but wanted to talk to you first. You're the odds-on favorite here to take the open sportscaster spot."

The news hit him, his competitive nature glorying in the fact that he was the front-runner. "Thanks, Bill."

"You really wowed them a few weeks ago with the interviews and the read-through was spot on. You've got a bright future and we're hoping it's with SNN."

Roman knew the Sports News Network was one of the most respected in all of broadcasting and he knew it was an opportunity most worked a lifetime for.

So why did the knowledge that he might have a future with them feel so empty?

He forced his attention back to the conversation,

well aware what he said in the next few minutes would dictate his future. He also knew the producer had jumped protocol by calling him and not his agent, Ray.

"Look. Why don't you give Ray a call and discuss details. As I told you when we met, I'm evaluating my options right now and appreciate the timeline you've laid out for me to consider things."

"Sure, man. Of course." The jovial tone lowered several notches as the guy realized he wouldn't get any hint of Roman's ultimate plans on the phone. "I'll give Ray a holler in the morning."

"Fantastic."

They exchanged a few more pleasantries and Roman gave his stock answer about how hard everyone worked in the off-season before he hung up.

He stared at the phone as he rested with his elbows on his knees. A professional sports gig would set him up for life. Would ensure he kept active in the sport and could likely even maintain many of his endorsements.

But the harsh reality of never playing hockey again left him with a cold, empty feeling he'd only ever had once before.

The day he walked out of Indigo, leaving Avery behind.

Excitement whispered on the air as the town of Indigo descended on the hockey rink to whip it back into shape bright and early Saturday morning. Roman had sketched out a rough set of instructions and jobs so they could manage as many people who chose to show up. But as he looked up from his list, he could only shake his head.

Who knew it would be every single member of Indigo, minus the three families who were out of town on summer vacation?

He knew he'd have an audience, but hadn't expected a throng like this.

Ignoring his increasing nerves, Roman refocused his attention in the same way he did on big game days. He forced himself to think about something else.

Today, that meant Bear, Indigo's ageless denizen who had a heart as big as his sizable body.

Bear had already been given one of the heavy-lifting jobs, and Roman couldn't hold back a smile as the big man preened around the outdoor boards, pointing out various places that needed work.

"You could have named him mayor of Indigo and he wouldn't be this happy."

Roman glanced down at Avery—dressed in a long-sleeved T-shirt, jeans and work boots—and tugged on the bill of her baseball cap. "I sort of made him mayor for the day."

"I won't tell Sophie."

"Probably a good idea."

"What can I do to help?"

"You want to direct them inside? The boards and bleachers both need a lot of work. You saw what I wasn't happy about the other day."

"Aye, aye." She gave him a jaunty salute and headed for the front doors of the arena. Try as he might to go back to his list, Roman took the few moments for himself to watch her go.

"She's a beautiful woman. Even more so in the midst of sunshine and friends."

Roman felt the heat creep up his neck at being caught by Doc Cloud. The man had approached on his right side and Roman never saw him. "Thanks for coming out today."

"I'm happy to help."

"A common sentiment."

"You're bothered by that?"

"No, of course not." Roman waved a hand and tried to dislodge the boulder on his shoulder.

"But you are bothered by the fact that it should have been done a long time ago."

On a heavy sigh, Roman nodded. "Yeah."

"I agree. And I think everyone appreciates your willingness to take charge and do something about it."

"I just wonder why they didn't take charge themselves."

"Because if they did, symbolically it might mean you wouldn't come back. That rink is a memorial to you."

Roman simply stared at Doc Cloud, unsure of what he could possibly say to that.

"Avery's not the only one who's missed you, Roman. We all have."

"I've been around."

"You've been a visitor. It's not the same thing."

Where it might have been hard to hear from someone else, Doc Cloud's kind eyes and even tone made it plain and clinical somehow. There was no judgment there. No guilt.

Just simple fact.

"Well, I'm here now."

The good doctor nodded and rubbed his hands together. "Then let's get to work."

Julia manned the water station as Mary and Sophie took care of making sandwiches. She couldn't hold back the smile at Mary's disgruntled complaints.

"How could we possibly have gone through all that turkey already?"

"Dot from the diner is slicing more." Sophie grabbed another bag of bread from the now half-full cardboard carton that had been delivered earlier that morning.

"But I had five pounds when I started."

"You've got an entire town of hungry people." Julia eyed her own dwindling ice supply and glanced over toward the rink to see if there were any men she could call away to help get more over at the hotel.

"I saw Roman and Avery talking to each other earlier."

Sophie's voice stiffened her spine and Julia willed herself to relax. "They do know how to be civil to each other."

"And the more time they spend together the more civil they are getting." Mary's giggle floated toward Julia on the light afternoon breeze. "You can't tell us you haven't seen it."

"Of course I've seen it. They care for each other. But I don't think the two of them deserve to be shoved under a microscope."

Sophie let out a snort. "Oh come on, Jules. You can't tell us you're not excited."

Julia whirled, the cup of water she was pouring

spilling from her hands where she squeezed the thin plastic too tight. "What's there to be excited about? That the two of them might make an even bigger mistake than before? That the hurt they've put each other through for almost a decade and a half should be ignored so they can enjoy each other for a few weeks?"

"Oh, honey." Mary's eyes widened and Julia didn't miss the hurt in their blue depths. She rushed over, her hug tight and immediate. "I had no idea you felt this way."

Julia leaned into the hug, grateful for the support, even as she struggled with whether or not her closest friends really understood. "What if they hurt each other even more? Grown-up, adult hurt that can't be taken back?"

"Or what if this is the time they need to understand what they lost?"

"It's not that easy, Mary."

"What if it is?"

Julia held back the sigh and kept any further thoughts to herself.

This was the exact reason she didn't want to discuss Roman and Avery with them. Why couldn't anyone understand what it would do to both of them if they lost each other?

"Grandma!"

Julia pulled out of Mary's arms and turned to find Roman heading toward them.

"Are you okay?"

"Of course." Julia swallowed hard and tried to dislodge the unshed tears in her throat. "What's going on?"

"Would you come with me?"

"Sure."

She glanced back at Mary's and Sophie's sympathetic faces, but followed, curious why Roman would pull her away.

"Are you sure everything is all right?"

"Oh sure, honey. Mary was upset we wouldn't have enough food."

She saw his confusion that a lack of turkey would necessitate a hug but he shrugged it off. "I think we have enough to eat for a week, Grandma."

"Well, people are working hard, we wouldn't want anyone to go hungry."

He wrapped a large arm around her shoulders. "Can't have that."

"Food equals love and hospitality."

"And the overabundance that passes for hospitality in this town could feed several third-world nations."

"Only on special occasions." She patted his stomach. "Now. What do you have up your sleeve? You look excited."

"I have a little surprise."

She felt the excitement in his frame and couldn't hold back the smile. "Does the fact that you pulled me away mean I'm getting a sneak peak?"

"You bet."

"I've hammered over one hundred boards and haven't hit my thumb once." Grier's bright, triumphant smile showed over the top of her sandwich before she took a large bite.

Avery finished adding mayo to her ham and cheese

but couldn't resist giving her friend the eye. "You dropped that hammer on your foot twice."

Grier was prevented from commenting because of the large bite, but Mick took up the slack as he took the seat next to her, dropping a kiss on her head before he sat. "There's a boatload of clumsy in that small, petite frame."

When she could finally speak again, Grier elbowed Mick and shot Avery a dirty look. "Neither was my fault. There are so many of us in here I could barely find a spot against the boards to call my own."

"There *are* a lot of people here." Mick eyed the room. "Wonder if we can find a way to move some of them out of here. I don't think Roman expected quite this big a turnout."

A large shout went up before any of them could agree with him, and Avery turned to look at the far end of the rink. A bright slice of light appeared, first narrow, then wider as the large barnlike doors at the back of the rink opened up. A loud murmuring echoed off the walls as people turned to see what the fuss was about.

"What's going on?" Grier stood to look, her small frame stretching as she tried to get a good glimpse.

"Oh my God." Avery breathed. "It's a brand-new Zamboni."

"No way." Mick scrambled off the bleachers to get a better look. "I'll be damned."

The large, oversized ice-resurfacing machine came rolling through the doors of the rink, and a shout of excitement went up around the arena. Avery couldn't hold back the smile as Julia waved from the driver's seat.

"Would you look at her." Avery marveled at the bright-eyed stare on Julia's face, her arms stiff as she drove the enormous machine.

Avery shifted her gaze and sought out Roman where he stood at the heavy wooden doors that he'd opened to let his grandmother drive through. His eyes met hers and he let up a small shrug. She mimicked the movement before offering him the same salute she'd given earlier.

The heated look he offered in return hit her so hard in the stomach she felt her knees buckle. Desperate to keep her footing, she reached for the row of bleachers behind her with her hand.

How did he keep doing this to her?

And how could she possibly be all worked up over a Zamboni?

But as she watched Julia make a perfect path down the ice, a smooth layer in her wake, Avery felt her heart open, melting along with the surface of old, well-used ice.

She loved him as much as she always had.

And like the old ice that vanished as if it had never been, she couldn't find a reason to keep clutching her old hurts.

Her old pain.

All she wanted to do was open her arms and run toward her future.

Chapter Fifteen

"*A*re we really going to play a game?" Mike's excited voice yammered in his ear as Roman walked the perimeter of the rink one last time.

"Yep. We'll split you up seven and seven. We're playing five on five, two alternates always trading in and out." Roman pointed toward the ice his grandmother had resurfaced like a pro earlier. "We'll only play one period's worth, but I think you all have earned the inaugural skate on the updated rink."

"Holy shit."

Roman grinned at the kid's enthusiasm and knew it was the tip of the iceberg. "Let's go get suited up. Round up your teammates and wait in front of the locker rooms for me."

Mike hollered to the various boys scattered around the rink before bounding outside to call up anyone who was still finishing up there.

"I'm not sure they're going to make it through a minute, let alone twenty." Mick's good-natured tone greeted him as he finished circling the oval.

Avery, Mick and Grier stood waiting for him.

"They'll calm down."

"Around Labor Day." Avery's smile was warm and she pointed toward the smooth ice. "The Zamboni was a nice touch."

"I ordered it after I was home last winter. Someone had mentioned the kids were getting a workout resurfacing the ice the old-fashioned way and I thought it might be appreciated."

"The other one couldn't be fixed?"

Roman thought about the old wreck that was taking up space in the back bay of the building. "Let's just say it's being retired to the Zamboni factory in the sky. The town bought it when my father was a kid."

"It's a very generous gift."

Where he'd once thought Avery was mocking him or angry about that fact, her gentle smile ensured she meant what she said.

"I'm actually excited about a different gift. Come with me."

The three of them followed him down the ice to where the kids huddled at the entrance to the locker rooms.

Roman saw the large boxes where he'd asked Bear to set them earlier. "You want to give me a hand with these?"

"What is it?" Mick asked. "I don't remember seeing any of this in the hangar this week."

"I had the guy who brought in the Zamboni bring it down."

Roman saw where Avery stood by the boxes and he knew, without her saying anything, that she knew what was in them.

"Avery. You do the honors."

She dove into the first box, her hands ripping the heavy packing tape off with expert movements. When she popped the top, he saw her smile falter as she lifted out a new jersey. Just as he'd asked, Stink's shirt was on top.

"Oh, Roman."

"What is it?" Grier moved toward the next box and began the process of unpacking it.

"He got the kids new equipment."

"Oh." Grier pulled the tape off her box and saw the heavy padding layered under the flaps. "Oh wow."

Avery stood straight up, Stink's jersey still tight in her fists, the heavy white letters of his last name stiff under her fingers. "Let's show them."

The wave of emotion threatened to pull her under once more and it took every measure of cool Avery possessed to keep dragging jersey after jersey out of the box.

"Miss Avery! Is that mine?"

She tossed Mike his jersey, then dove back into the box.

After fourteen jerseys, pads and brand-new sticks were produced from the boxes, she couldn't keep a lone tear from falling.

"Hey. There's no crying in hockey." Roman hip-bumped her before picking up one of the empty boxes and turning it over to rip the tape off the bottom.

"There is when you do something like this." She leaned up and pressed her cheek to his ear. "This was for Stink, wasn't it?"

Roman shrugged, but she saw the answer flash in his gaze.

"The kids needed some new stuff and I had the means to do it. And the manufacturer was more than happy to help out when I called."

"You got this for free?"

"I told the owner I'd donate my time to an upcoming ad shoot. My agent worked it out with him and the owner thought it was a more than fair trade."

Way more than fair. While the equipment was expensive, Avery knew an afternoon of his time was worth far more. She was touched he'd think to do it and had to acknowledge she'd been a terribly harsh critic.

He'd given so much of himself to the kids throughout this process.

But it was the look on Stink's face when he walked to the locker room—the new pads clutched tight in his arms—that had her reaching for Roman's hand, linking their fingers. "Thank you."

"You're welcome."

"No, really. Thank you." She reached up and placed a hand on either side of his face, pulling him close for a kiss. "This means so much to them."

Their lips met and he pulled her close, his arms wrapping around her in a crushing hold. Dimly, she heard someone let up a cheer but she ignored it as his mouth plundered hers.

What she'd intended as a quick kiss of thanks turned heated and carnal, flashing over into overwhelming need in mere seconds.

"Wow." She murmured against his mouth, not entirely sure what had just happened.

He grinned at her as he pulled his lips back from

hers, then put a few steps of distance between them. "I'll take that for luck."

"You're coaching both sides."

He gave her one quick smacking kiss on the lips before he headed off toward the locker room. Over his shoulder, he hollered in her direction. "See? Lucky. I'm sure of winning."

Avery watched him go, unable to do anything but admire the firm lines of his butt where it filled out his jeans.

"That is one delightfully awesome specimen of a man." Grier whispered the words as Roman disappeared through the locker room doors.

"He's a professional athlete."

"He's got the body of a Greek god. And this is coming from a woman who likes her man's body way more than just okay." Grier patted her arm. "But you don't really see any of that, do you?"

"Of course I see it. He's gorgeous."

"But it's not what you see first."

Avery turned toward her friend. "He's just Roman."

"Well, let's go grab a seat and watch Just Roman whip those kids into shape."

The game ended up going two periods, but the assembled crowd didn't seem to mind. Everyone cheered on the kids, half of whom were disappointed the coin toss meant they had to wear their old jerseys so they could tell who played for what team.

Avery was secretly glad Stink was able to proudly wear his new jersey.

The teams were evenly matched and it also didn't

escape Avery's notice that a few days with Roman had already improved the kids' technique. She couldn't imagine how unstoppable they'd be with a real coach who knew how to develop players.

"That was quite a game."

"It was." Avery turned to see Stink's mom, Candy, sidle up next to her. The name "Stink" was nearly out of her mouth before she caught herself. "Mark looks like he's died and gone to heaven."

"He has. All he can talk about is Roman this and Roman that. He nearly died when Roman showed up the other night to talk to him."

"Roman did what?"

Candy nodded and she looked momentarily embarrassed before she continued. "Mark came home from practice upset about being told to take a few days off and Roman came over to talk to him about some drills to run on his own."

"I was there. At practice."

"Heard that's where you got that shiner."

Avery touched her fingers to her cheek. "Very few secrets in Indigo."

"And since it happened in front of a group of teenage boys, you'd have better luck hiding it from a reporter."

The two of them laughed at that before Candy pointed toward the ice. "This means a lot to a lot of people."

"It does."

"Look. I hope I'm not overstepping here." Candy worked the strap of her purse where it was slung over her arm. "But that man's crazy about you."

"He and I have a lot of history."

"I know." Candy stared at the frayed purse strap. "I know what it's like to lose someone you love. And it's even harder when they don't come back. But. Well. People can change. I believe that. And maybe he's worth a second look."

Her son came running over, and Candy didn't say anything else as her boy stood, towering over her. "I got the assist on that last goal."

"You were fantastic."

"I knew the good-luck charm would work. Just like Roman said he wears his." The boy proudly dragged out a white pointed tooth from around his neck, hanging on a thin black cord. "Mine's not a horseshoe, but a wolf's tooth means lucky to me."

For the second time that day, Avery felt her knees buckle from underneath her. "Horseshoe?"

"Yep. Roman wears his every time he plays. Says it's the only thing lucky he carries. The rest of the time he just works his ass off."

Candy reached up and swatted the back of her son's head. "Language. Please."

Stink blushed. "Anyway, me and the boys want to go to the diner. You okay with that?"

"Go."

Candy watched her son go, pride filling her face so the lines and stress faded away. "He's going to float through the next week."

"An assist's a big deal." The words came from outside herself and Avery fought the urge to sit down.

"And we will dissect each and every moment of the

play at each and every meal." Candy smiled. "Which means I should go home and enjoy my quiet evening."

Avery felt the gentle pat on her arm before Candy walked away.

And as the loud shouts continued to echo through the cavernous space, Avery couldn't erase the mental image of a small horseshoe charm she'd lovingly wrapped up and given to Roman on his sixteenth birthday.

Roman had agreed to go to the diner for burgers after the game and had assumed Avery would find her way along. He'd been sorely disappointed to sit through a meal alone, especially after the moments they'd shared at the rink.

Fortunately, the boys had been so involved recounting every moment of their game that he was able to sneak out as soon as he'd finished his burger and assured them that they would have at least two more games before he had to leave and go back to New York.

His mother had gone out with friends, and one of the girls who took shifts for Avery was on the desk when he walked back into the hotel so he couldn't even find her there. Where the hell had she gone?

The urge to go to her apartment was strong, but he headed for his own. Clearly she wasn't interested in seeing him this evening, especially with her disappearing act after the game.

He'd be damned if he was going to go chasing her.

A hot shower didn't do much for his mood, but at least he'd washed off the funk of the day. He headed for the fridge and snagged a beer, determined to drown his shitty attitude in a Mariners-Yankees game.

He was screaming at the umpire's crappy-ass call when a knock on his door interrupted him midbellow.

"Yelling at the game?" Avery stood on the other side of the door, clad in a long, flowy dress and bare feet. He ached as he took her in, the long lines and slender strength of her body calling to him with that particular siren's song that was 100 percent Avery.

"Occupational hazard. I hate shitty calls, no matter the sport."

"That umpire can't see to save his life. He's already screwed the Mariners on two plays."

"Come on now. You mean you're not a Yankees fan? Aren't they sort of the America's team of baseball?"

"And root for a team from the same city you live in?" Her smile was full of mischief and a note of something more seductive that reached out for him with sly fingers. "Never."

"Right."

"So?" She peeked past him and into the room. "Are you going to invite me in?"

"Oh. Yeah." He stood back and let her through, closing the door behind her.

She crossed to the couch and picked up the remote. "Are you that involved with the game?"

"No. It passes the time."

"Good."

Roman watched her point the remote at the TV. Heard the sound wink out before the flash of the screen that discolored her skin tone with its neon wash followed.

He still felt like he was missing something.

"How was dinner?"

"Fine."

She lifted her eyebrow in a deliberate gesture. "Just fine?"

"It was burgers, not a gourmet meal. Besides, I thought you were going to join me."

She gently laid the remote on the coffee table. "I had other things I needed to see to."

"Oh. It just seemed funny you didn't say anything."

"I couldn't say anything."

"Why the hell not?"

"Because then I wouldn't have been able to get my nerve up."

The sensation of walking through water surrounded him but underneath the sluggish confusion the heady stamp of arousal began to beat in his veins. With a smile, he took a few steps toward her. "Your nerve?"

"That's right."

"What do you need to get your nerve up for, Avery?"

"For this."

Before he could reach her, she had the material of the dress fisted in her hands and up and over her body. He saw her gorgeous legs first, then nearly lost his breath when he saw the small triangle of hair at the apex of her thighs.

The proof she was naked under the dress broadcast to his cock in a wave of need and longing so intense he would have gladly walked over broken glass to possess her.

Clearly, though, she wasn't done with him.

Her sinuous movements continued as she dragged the silky material over her body until her small breasts filled his gaze. Then the dress was over her head, floating lightly toward the floor.

And then she was there, moving into him, wrapping her hands around his neck as he pulled her into his arms.

The only thing he could see was Avery. The only thing on earth he knew was Avery. The only thing he needed besides the breath that filled his lungs was Avery.

"I needed time to get ready for this, Roman."

"You could have told me."

She pressed closer. "Like you could have told me about the Zamboni?

"Or the hockey equipment?"

And then the last. "Or the charm you still wear around your neck for luck that I gave you when you were sixteen?"

She'd closed the space between them and her hand snaked up and wrapped around his neck, her fingers brushing the cord.

"I didn't do those things for sex."

"I know you didn't. In fact, if I thought that had been the motivation, I wouldn't be here."

"How'd you know about the necklace?"

"Stink has a wolf's tooth he's wearing around his neck for luck. He proudly showed it to me earlier and let me know that a necklace was the only luck you bothered with."

"I didn't tell him you gave it to me."

"But I knew." She moved on her tiptoes and pressed

her lips against his as her thumb came around and fondled the small charm. "I knew."

"Sold out by a fifteen-year-old." He muttered the words against her lips before wrapping his arms around her waist and dragging her to him.

His already-heated body exploded with need, and the pressure of her stomach against his erection had him seeing stars. "Are you really sure?"

Her gaze was honest and true as she lifted her lips to stare at him. "I'm completely sure."

"I want you. There's an aching longing that nothing else can fill." He pressed his cheek against the side of her head and pulled her against him. "Nothing, Avery."

"I know."

Whatever they needed to say didn't matter anymore. Words had been the only thing to exist between them for fourteen years, and now, by unspoken agreement, they allowed other things to fill the space.

Touch.

Taste.

Love.

The reality of being back in his arms kept winging through her mind, and Avery fought to focus on the here and now. There'd be plenty of time to think later.

Time to contemplate and remember and relive every single feeling.

Right now, she wanted to consume. Feed the need that had never gone away and feast on the reality of being back in Roman's arms and of having him back in hers.

She reached for the hem of his T-shirt, the material

soft under her fingers. The heat of his body scalded her as she lifted the shirt up and over his head, and she nearly lost her breath at her first sight of his wide chest.

The body she'd remembered at eighteen had grown and changed. This was a man's body. A man in the absolute prime of his life. Grier's description earlier—Greek god—came back to mind.

With curious fingers, she traced the deeply sculpted muscles that descended into a series of tight, rolled ridges over his stomach before forming hard ropes over each hip. The muscles flexed underneath smooth skin as she traced the lines.

"I don't remember these from before."

A dark laugh huffed from his chest. "It's called lots of gym time and boiled chicken for dinner."

"The process sounds painful but I wholeheartedly approve of the results." Her fingers hit the elastic waistband of his shorts and she tugged on the material, careful to work around the hard length of him.

Free of any clothing between them, Avery took a step back and looked her fill.

"Your body is magnificent."

"Right back at ya, slim."

"Seriously. You're like a statue."

His lips quirked at her assessment. "I'm not so sure about that but I do know something that's harder than a slab of marble."

"So I noticed." She moved back into his arms, her hands tracing an unerring path over the hard musculature until she could grip his erection. "Maybe I can do something about that."

She pressed against him, urging him toward the couch with her body.

"Nope. I'm too tall. I want the bed."

The apartment Roman used when he was home was equipped with the extra-large bed Susan had needed to buy him as a kid. He'd started growing in the eighth grade and she had finally gone out and gotten something custom-made to fit him.

Avery had fantasized about that bed for years, the idea of actually sleeping together on a mattress forbidden to both of them in their youth. In all the time they'd spent together, she could count on one hand how many times they'd actually been able to sneak together into one of their bedrooms.

"What's that look for?"

"I was just thinking about all the places we managed to have sex that weren't a bed."

"God, we were good at finding places."

"Except beds."

"Exactly."

The world tilted suddenly as Roman had her up in his arms. "What are you doing?"

"Let's do this right."

While she thought they'd gotten off to a more than okay start, Avery wasn't about to argue. Either about the bed or the opportunity to feel small and petite as he cradled her in his arms.

It was one of the sensations she'd missed in her attempts to date. She was a tall woman and very few men had Roman's height or solid lines. He wasn't this big when they were younger, but he still had an imposing frame that had always made her feel feminine.

The bed beckoned as Roman walked them into the room and she thought about the moments to come. What a contrast to what they'd known before.

"Is this weird?"

"Weird?" One dark eyebrow shot up as he stared down at her. "Not quite the description I had in mind."

"Not freaky weird. I mean, you and me. Us. Together again."

"I like it. We're different and I want to know you now."

"But we're the same in some ways."

Roman shifted, allowing her feet to touch the floor before he pulled her tightly into his arms. "I like the part of you that doesn't change and I like the parts of you that have changed. You're a grown woman and I like who you've become."

"That's the weird part."

"No. It's the amazing part."

Before she could allow her brain to interfere any further, he took over, pulling them both down on the bed. His hands roamed over her skin, lighting bonfires wherever he touched, and his lips did the same. His large hands cupped her breasts, his thumbs teasing the nipples into hard points. "Amazing."

Before she could even respond, Avery felt her world tilt once more as Roman had her on her back. His mouth replaced his hands and she nearly came off the bed as he painted his tongue over one of her nipples. "Amazing," he whispered against the heavy flesh of her breast before shifting to take the other nipple into his mouth.

Avery rode the wave of sensation, peak to peak, as

he made love to her with his mouth. She'd always appreciated his ability to settle in and spend some time, enjoying the entire experience of being together instead of focusing solely on the main event.

And it was when she felt him shift lower, his hair tickling the sensitive skin of her stomach, that she realized he'd remembered *exactly* what she liked.

"Roman."

He ran a lazy finger along the seam of her body, the pad of his thumb hard against her clitoris, looking up at her with his dark, passion-glazed eyes. She reacted instantly, her thighs falling open to allow him deeper access to her body. But it was only when he whispered "Amazing" once more that she saw stars.

His mouth replaced his fingers and the memories that had fueled her for years became reality once more.

Hot, desperate pulses of need ran through her as he made love to her with his mouth. With unerring precision, he brought her to the edge of madness, then pulled back, changing the tempo so she balanced on that tight edge between pleasure and the anxious need for fulfillment.

Avery gave up everything to the moment. She turned her body over to him and allowed him to drive her to the very height of pleasure. It was only when her orgasm was nearly on her, her body so close to completion she need only whisper the thought to make it happen, that she pulled at him, desperate for him to join her for the fall.

"Now, Roman. Now."

The brief rip of foil interrupted the moment and it

brought a small smile to her lips. Thankfully he'd gotten quicker at that part.

He moved over her and she reached for him, gliding the long, familiar length of him into her body. A desperate sigh rose up in her throat, the familiarity of the moment nearly taking her breath as he supported his heavy weight on his forearms.

God, how she'd missed him.

How she'd missed them together.

The memories faded as the present gripped them both. With a hard moan, Roman buried himself to the hilt and stilled for the briefest of moments before he began to move.

Avery matched his rhythm immediately, the give-and-take driving them both crazy as their sweat-slicked bodies rode the wave together.

She didn't know if it was the years apart or the foreplay they'd engaged in—both verbal and physical—since he'd been home, but the moments raced by, both their bodies desperate for fulfillment.

And when she felt his telltale signs—the tightening of his buttocks and the hard, heavy shout as he pushed into her once more—she let herself fall, secure in the knowledge he'd catch her.

Chapter Sixteen

"*I*'d like to go to Anchorage with you. If you'd want to have me along."

Avery was lying spooned in his arms, her hand tight in his. It was only when she turned to face him that Roman realized he was holding his breath.

"For my conference?"

"Yeah. I know you have to work during the day, but we can go out in the evening. Spend some time together."

"You'd really want to do that?"

Even though he had braced for rejection, her question voiced in a quiet, thoughtful way caught him off guard. "Yeah."

"Even if you won't get a moment alone with people asking for your autograph and stuff?"

"It's not that big a deal."

"Then I'd love to have you join me."

The tire iron that had settled on his chest lifted slightly at her agreement before another concern rose up in his mind. "Does it bother you people know who I am?"

"No. Why?"

"Some people find it annoying."

A small smile hovered at the corners of her mouth. "Some people being ex-girlfriends?"

"No. Oddly enough women seem to find it enjoyable. I meant friends. Hockey players don't get the same attention as football players, but there's usually someone who makes the connection and once one person does, others tend to follow."

"I'm sure you're more than capable of fending them off."

"Most of the time."

"What's it like?"

"The attention?" When she only nodded, he continued. "It's heady at first. Crazy because someone actually recognizes you because of this thing you do and love. But it gets tiring pretty quickly. People in New York are better than other cities."

"Is it strange? That they know all about you and you don't even know their name?"

"Sometimes. But overall people are pretty cool. Every once in a while you get a crier, which is a bit unsettling."

"People have actually cried on you?"

"After winning the Cup it's especially bad. And there's actually another side to it. I was out one night and nearly got decked by a guy who'd lost his mortgage payment betting against us."

"Sucks to be him."

"In more ways than one. Especially when security ensured he'd work off his drunken rant in jail for the night."

She ran a hand down his arm and he enjoyed the feel

of her light touch and the physical awareness that hummed between them. "It must be hard to be responsible for others' dreams. Their happiness and joys. Their sadness and losses."

"I hadn't ever considered that."

"You've always had a lot of that here in Indigo, but I never thought about the fact that you have it from legions of people who follow what you do."

"There are worse problems to have."

"True."

"I mean it, Ave. It's a privilege to do what I do. Sure, there are elements that suck, but for the most part, I'm one of the lucky ones."

"Yet another reason your adoring public loves you."

He couldn't resist poking at her. "I thought it was my sexy assets."

The words had their desired effect when she moved her hand from his arms to swat him on the ass. "And you've been known to flaunt those *ass*-ets a time or two, too."

"It was one lousy calendar. And the towel was strategically placed."

"Myrtle and Chooch bemoan that towel every time they look at it."

An image of the two older women ogling his photo elicited a dull throb at the base of his neck. "Please tell me you didn't just say that."

"Maybe I can take a picture for the women of Indigo and confirm just what they were missing?"

She pressed on his shoulders to force him onto his back as she slid down his body. With quick fingers, she flung the light sheet that covered them both toward the bottom of the bed. "Yep. I'll do my best to make a full inspection."

Roman pillowed his hands behind his head, secure in the knowledge he needed to lie back and take it like a man while she took one for the girls of Indigo.

Julia walked her favorite path along the river, bright morning sunlight accompanying her on the walk. Her thoughts were full of those moments she'd spent with Ken earlier in the week as they'd walked the same route. His quiet advice had been sound, and she'd used much of it in the conversation she'd had with Roman when she had him over to dinner.

In fact, she admitted to herself, it had been nice to share her concerns with a man. Gain his point of view and hear his assessment. It was a different perspective from that of her friends, and she'd appreciated Ken's thoughts.

So why was she thinking about a reason to call him up and ask him to do it again?

She'd nearly invited him to join her, Mary and Sophie for a burger at the diner last night, but had let the opportunity pass at the last minute.

Was she afraid? Embarrassed? Confused?

She dismissed each in kind, knowing it wasn't any of those things.

What she really was, she knew, was out of practice.

She hadn't been with a man in over forty years. There were days that knowledge chafed and then there were other days when she knew she'd made the choices she'd wanted to make. She'd dated on the rare occasion she went out of town or was fixed up, but no one had ever caught her fancy, and after a while she'd stopped worrying about it.

Only now, she was worrying about it. And thinking about it.

Because there finally was a man who *had* caught her fancy.

"Julia!" She turned at the sound of her name and stopped short. There he stood, his solid, fit frame waving at her from about fifty yards closer to town.

With a wave of her own, she turned and walked toward him as he narrowed the gap between them.

"I thought I might find you here." His smile was broad when they were close enough to talk to each other.

"I told you I liked this path."

"Which is why I hoped I'd find you on it."

A wave of butterflies took wing in her stomach, but she kept her smile bright and her tone casual. "Care to walk with me, then?"

"I'd love to."

They walked in companionable silence for a few minutes, and Julia turned over in her mind what she wanted to say to him. "Thank you for your advice about Roman. I'm no closer to knowing if there's anything wrong, but I do feel better after talking to him."

"He'll come around. And I've been gently keeping an eye. I don't sense he has any serious physical issues. The boy is shockingly fit, especially keeping up with those kids on the ice the way he does. He is in prime condition."

"The gals in town certainly think so." She knew it

was unkind of her to say, but she'd lived with the giggles and whispers for the last two decades.

"That bothers you?"

"I just think people could pay a bit of attention to the fact that the boy's my grandson. Dear Lord, the way Myrtle and Chooch passed around those damn calendars." She shuddered. "And I know Mary and Sophie took a peek."

Ken grinned broadly, his dark eyes crinkling at the corners, but his tone was as gentle as always. "There's nothing wrong with a healthy libido, at any age."

Julia found herself chuckling. "I know, but it seems so sordid when it's my grandson in the photo."

"I'll grant you that."

"So what about you? There isn't a Mrs. Cloud. Why is that?" The words were out before she could stop them, and Julia felt her cheeks growing warm.

What had possibly possessed her to ask the question?

"There was a Mrs. Cloud, a very long time ago before I moved to Indigo."

"Oh, I'm sorry. Well, sorry since you're obviously not still together."

"We married young and divorced young."

"No children?"

"Fortunately, no."

"Fortunately?"

"My wife and I didn't have a very good marriage, nor did things end well. I've always been grateful we didn't bring children into the world who would have had to bear the brunt of our mistakes."

She nodded, not sure she understood but respectful

of his feelings. While she'd always believed children were a blessing, she could see where someone's view might differ if they didn't harbor any fondness for the person they'd had children with.

"Do you mind sharing what happened?" Another rush of heat filled her face and she quickly amended her question. "Goodness, but I'm nosy today. I'm sorry for the intrusive questions."

"It's not that big a secret. We married very young, overjoyed with the passions of youth, and had very little idea of the responsibilities that awaited us. Add on two families who didn't care for our spouses and you've got a recipe for disaster."

"What wasn't there to like?"

"Her family resented my Alaskan native heritage. My family wasn't much more understanding in return."

"That seems so sad."

"It was almost fifty years ago. Things were different then." He hesitated for a moment, before adding, "And clearly we weren't willing to try hard enough to get past it, either."

"I suppose. We're so stupid when we're young."

"I'm not sure we're all that much smarter when we get older, either."

Julia stopped, something in his tone pulling her up short. "Oh, I don't know. I think something finally kicks in and we start to figure things out."

"Well then, maybe I can try something stupid because I believe I've finally started to figure out a few things."

With dawning awareness, she watched as Ken

moved closer, pulling her into his arms. "I'd like to kiss you, Julia."

"I'd like that very much."

As the summer sun beat down on them, the lost years of her personal life faded away. And as her arms came up around his neck, pulling him closer against her body, she felt a little bit stupid. A little bit wise.

And a whole lot of happy.

Avery held up an outfit from her closet and faced Grier. "Trying too hard or not hard enough?"

"Depends."

"On what?"

"How much cleavage you're going to show with the shell underneath."

"None. Not like I have any to show off, anyway."

"You've got plenty." Grier waved a hand as she reached for her take-out cup of coffee. "So which is it gonna be?"

"Which is what?"

"The cleavage, Avery. Are you showing any off?"

Avery thought about the pale pink shell she wore with the outfit. "Maybe a modest amount."

"Code for none. Which means you'll look very professional. Personally, I think you might want to spice up your travel conference and give the guys in the front row something to dream about, but that's just me."

"My words will be riveting enough."

"Not nearly as riveting as a hint of lace and an opportunity for a wardrobe malfunction." Grier popped a handful of popcorn in her mouth.

"What good are you? You're supposed to be a so-phisticated New Yorker."

"Fashion was never my strong suit. I just buy stuff that matches, which is about as much as I can handle. Sloan, on the other hand. She's your girl."

"Do you think we can text her pictures in Fiji and get her opinion?"

"She's in the glow of island breezes and honeymoon sex. Do you really think she's even got her phone on?"

"She's just Type A enough to have it in her beach bag."

Grier nodded, convinced. "Give it a try."

Avery had her phone in hand before she shook her head and put it back on her nightstand. "No. It's her honeymoon and I will not bother her with something so stupid and trivial. We're two smart women. We can figure this out."

"Okay. So what else do you have in that closet since the outfits you've pulled out so far have been fashion masterpieces?"

Avery shot her a nasty finger gesture before diving back into her closet. "It's not my fault I live in one of the coldest climates in the entire world, ensuring my wardrobe consists mainly of sweaters. And it's not like Susan requires me to dress up for front-desk duty."

"So what dresses do you have?"

Avery poked her head back out the closet door. "I need to wear a suit."

"Why?"

"Because I'm a professional."

"Dresses are professional."

"But a suit is more professional."

"Those suits look like they belonged to Margaret Thatcher. Show me the dresses."

Avery wanted to scream in frustration, but Grier's point was valid. The suits she'd acquired over the years were serviceable and functional, but they weren't all that enticing, sexy or sophisticated.

"Betsy got a great dress line in last year and I have a few of those."

"Let's see."

Avery spent the next half hour modeling whatever she could find in the closet. She also added a dress she'd remembered in her bottom drawer that had been left behind the previous summer when its owner mysteriously left it by the pool. Since said owner had never been found, Avery had had it laundered and added it to her small stash of clothing.

"In order of preference." Grier held up a hand and ticked off her list. "The red one, the turquoise one and that peach sensation you're wearing that really shows off your legs."

Avery bit her lip, the indecision so foreign she couldn't believe she was staring back at herself in the mirror. "Red? Really?"

"You look gorgeous in the dress. It flatters your figure and screams 'woman!' without screaming 'slut!' at the same time. And"—Grier came over and smoothed the lines of the peach dress Avery still wore—"it will make you stand out on the dais."

"I'm not trying to showcase the fact I'm a woman."

"Why not?"

"Because I want the audience to listen to my words."

"Can't they listen to your words and look at your face?"

Grier's logic pulled her up short and Avery had to admit her friend had a point. "I guess."

"Just because we have breasts doesn't mean we don't have brains. The value of what you're saying will win them over. They'll just get a kick out of how pretty you look when you say it. Besides." Grier stepped back and lifted one of the discarded suits from the bed. "This needs to be burned as soon as humanly possible."

"I think it's polyester. I may pollute the town with the fumes."

"We wouldn't want that. Maybe Tasty can bury it beneath the ice next winter when he goes ice fishing. With any luck it'll get buried at the bottom of the lake."

Grier gathered up other discarded outfits and began hanging them on the various hangers scattered around the room. Her tone was casual when she next spoke. "You and Roman looked like you had a good day yesterday."

Avery stopped folding the turquoise dress she was about to place in her suitcase. With an exaggerated motion, she looked at her watch. "I'm proud of you. You've been here over an hour and it took you that long to ask."

"Avery. Come on, you can't blame me for being curious."

She couldn't. And when Grier and Sloan had started dating Mick and Walker, she'd wanted details.

So why was she so hesitant to share?

"Roman's coming with me to the conference."

"He's what?" Grier raced across the room and Avery felt herself dragged into a tight hug. "That's awesome. What brought this on?"

"He asked me if he could go."

"Just like that?"

"Just like that."

Grier stood back but her hands still had Avery's in a tight grip. "You are holding out on me."

"How can I be holding out on you if I just told you he's going with me?"

"There's something else."

"There is one other small thing." At Grier's impatient stare, Avery let it spill. "We had sex last night."

"Where's that phone? We have to text Sloan now. She'll kill us for not telling her."

"We don't need to bother her."

"All right, tell me then. So how did it happen?"

"The usual way."

Avery knew the pillow was headed for her face and ducked before Grier even got a good heft on it.

"You were at the rink all afternoon. And Roman was at the diner last night with the kids."

"It happened after."

"Yeah, but how? The girlfriend code says you need to share sexy details."

"I went to his room and stripped down. It's a surprisingly effective tactic. Men pretty much stop thinking when a naked woman is standing in front of them."

"And when did you stop thinking?"

"About three minutes after he landed in town."

"I'm serious."

"I'm not sure, Grier. I'm really not sure. But I've

spent the last week telling myself I can't have anything to do with him and then yesterday he was just . . ." She broke off, not sure how to explain it.

She hadn't slept with him because of the Zamboni or the hockey equipment or the necklace, but all had been factors.

"He still wears the good luck charm I gave him in high school."

"Oh. Oh wow." Grier's natural sense of humor and usual broad smile faded as a light sheen of tears filled her eyes. "That is so sweet."

"I thought so. He was amazing yesterday and I just finally stopped thinking about all the reasons I should stay away and looked at all the reasons I wanted to be with him."

"I'm glad."

"I am, too. I'm also scared to death."

"That part never entirely goes away, you know. Fortunately it fades as the comfort and the constancy grow."

"A part of me is afraid it will all go away. And the other part already knows I can survive it if it does."

"Do you think it's going to end?"

"I don't think sex can cure fourteen years of being apart." Avery picked up the slacks she'd laid on the bed and folded them, then placed them in her suitcase. "But I have to tell you, it certainly doesn't hurt, either."

Mick was already at the hangar, his plane fueled and his coffee cup in hand when Roman arrived with a sleepy Avery.

"This is an ungodly hour of the day," Avery muttered as she snagged Mick's coffee cup and took a large swallow.

"Hey, hey. Get your own." Mick swatted at her hand and retrieved his cup before she could take another sip. "I've got a fresh pot in the hangar."

Avery muttered something about sharing before turning on her heel and heading for the small office Mick and Jack kept.

"I thought sex was supposed to make them nicer." Mick gave a wide smile as he took another sip of his coffee.

"You know how she is early in the morning." Roman watched Avery's retreating back and couldn't help but smile at the slight wobble to her still-sleepy walk.

"Which I suspect is the reason your mother gives her nights."

"So how'd you know we had sex?"

"Aside from the way you two keep looking at each other, I've got the group grapevine wrapped around me in my own bed."

"According to Avery, I've been given Grier's full endorsement."

"Assuming you don't fuck it up." Mick's slap on the back was little assurance against the knowledge that Grier still had her doubts.

"I'm not fucking up—"

Mick cut him off before he could say anything further. "Do me a favor and don't say it. Don't tempt fate, the gods or whatever else the world can cook up. Just take it day by day and work really hard to treat her right."

Mick's advice was sound and Roman didn't argue with the pilot's wise counsel.

He *was* holding things back. He still hadn't told Avery about his eye, or the career change he was contemplating in the event he wasn't going to play again.

The words had ridden the tip of his tongue so many times the day before he'd lost count, but in the end, he'd said nothing. When he was with her, the end of his career and the confusion that came with having no clue what he was going to do with his life felt a million miles away. He didn't want to mar their rediscovery of each other with the ugly reality of his future.

He slapped Mick on the shoulder. "Go take care of what you need to. I'll go fetch Sunshine and snag a cup of coffee."

Despite her bearlike morning mood, Avery had two cups already poured when he walked into the hangar and was stirring copious amounts of sugar into both.

"Just the way I like it."

"Sugar with a side of coffee." She finished doctoring her own and lifted the cup. "Sorry I'm so grumpy."

"We're used to it."

"I know. It doesn't make it right."

He dropped a quick kiss on her head. "It doesn't make it wrong, either. And you've got a lot on your mind. It's a big day."

"Part of me is exhilarated and part of me is scared shitless."

"Welcome to my world every time I get on the ice."

She cocked her head over the rim of her cup. "Really?"

"Yep."

"Every time?"

"Every time." He saw the doubt in her eyes. "I'm not just saying this to make you feel better, you know."

"I don't think you're making it up, but it's still hard to believe."

"Why?"

"I don't know. You just seem invincible. In person. On the ice. Even with everyone in town. You're just so . . . with it."

"Avery. You know me."

"I know. And I still think all those things. Knowing you doesn't make that any less true for me."

"I'm a human being. Fallible and flawed and goofy and every human thing everyone else is."

"Don't get upset."

"I'm not." He glanced down at his cup and saw how it bowed under his grip. "Much."

"I'm sorry to egg you on but you don't see yourself from everyone else's perspective."

"What is that?"

"The celebrity thing doesn't help, but it's more than that. You're a large, attractive, fit man. People notice that."

He wasn't sure why he'd picked this moment to have this discussion—smack in the middle of an airplane hangar—but it was suddenly important to him to make her understand how tiring it all was. "They don't see much else."

She took another sip of her coffee, her gaze contemplative. "I don't think that's true. You are also incredibly kind, which people don't expect. It's disarming and only adds to your appeal."

"I can go punch Ronnie out if it'll help."

"I don't think so." The first smile of the morning lit her face. "Face it. You're destined to spend your life as Saint Roman. Just learn to deal with it."

"And if I don't want to be the fucking apostle of Indigo, Alaska?"

She stood on her tiptoes and pressed a kiss to his chin. "Unless you're prepared to start kicking Chooch and Hooch's puppies, I think you're stuck with it, buddy."

Chapter Seventeen

The coffee kicked in midflight to Anchorage, letting her shake off her morning lethargy, but nothing had managed to kick the strange mess of thoughts filling her mind. Avery stood back as Roman flagged down a cab at the airport, content to simply watch him move.

I'm a human being. Fallible and flawed and goofy and every human thing everyone else is.

He was human. She knew that.

And because she knew him, she knew about all those quirks that made him as fallible as everyone else. He was wretched at geometry, he couldn't parallel park to save his life and he couldn't win at Monopoly, even if he owned Boardwalk, Park Place and every railroad.

"You ready?" Roman had the cab door open and gestured her forward.

"Yep."

"You doing all right? You look a million miles away."

She looked up at him from the backseat of the cab before she slid over. "You suck at Monopoly."

Roman slid in next to her. "Run that one by me one more time?"

"That's it. Just that you suck at Monopoly."

"And that's relevant because?"

"This morning. Your comment that you're fallible. Most people can play the game by the time they're eight and I don't think you've ever won one game."

His laughter was low and deep when they were both flung back against their seat as the driver pulled away from the curb. "Thanks. I think."

She patted him on the knee. "I just wanted you to know I know you're not perfect."

"Well, that certainly makes me feel better."

"Your dad sucked at it, too, apparently. Who'd have thought? Bad board-game skills are genetic."

She felt it more than she saw his reaction. His entire frame stiffened next to her and she turned, aware the words might have been unintentionally callous. "I'm sorry."

"It's all right."

"No, really. I'm sorry I said anything."

His voice was quiet when he finally spoke, the husky tones strained with emotion. "It's been a long time."

"Your mom talks about him. That's how I knew about the crappy board-game skills."

"Does she?"

His question came out as stiff as his body, and Avery immediately sensed something deeper in the question. "Doesn't she talk about him to you?"

"No. Never."

Avery wondered at that and thought it was awfully unfair of Susan to deny Roman the memories of his father. Especially since she was more than willing to share them over casual conversation at the hotel.

"Have you asked her? I know he died when you

were young. You can't have all that many memories of him."

"No, I don't, and I have asked from time to time. She usually gives me a terse answer and I end up dropping it, thinking it's too painful."

"Oh."

"I take it that means she's rather verbose with what she says to you?"

"Maybe it's a woman thing."

"Maybe."

Avery hesitated, the desire to say what she thought warring with the respect she felt for his mother. In the end, her respect for him won out.

"I've always thought she's too quick to keep things from you. Like she's afraid she'll ruffle you or make your visit home unpleasant. Not just about your father, but even day-to-day issues at the hotel or things going on with your sister."

"I know. I've always felt it was easier not to ruffle her. To allow her to have her illusions."

"Why do we do that?"

"Do what?"

Avery thought about her own reservations. The things she'd held back from her mother, especially when it came to Roman. Instead of using her mother as a sounding board or a sensitive ear, she'd kept her true feelings hidden, afraid her pain would only make Alicia's worse.

Had it been the right thing to do?

Or had she underestimated her mother and missed out on the chance to have someone she loved help her through her own pain?

"Why do we hide difficult things from the people we love? It's like we're trying to protect them, but maybe we do them a disservice."

"Maybe we do." He looked up, his eyes a fervent shade of green. "I know it might hurt, but I'd like to know about my father."

"Why don't you tell your mom that?"

Roman leaned down and pressed a kiss against her temple. "Maybe I will."

His cab ride with Avery still filled his thoughts hours later as he paced their hotel room. She'd gone down to get set up for her panel and he had a few minutes to kill before heading down to watch.

He'd never thought his father's death was that big a driver in his life, but looking back on it, he knew losing a parent at a young age hadn't been meaningless, either. Both his father and his grandfather's shortened lives had left a sense of urgency within him.

Maybe he'd have had it anyway, Roman mused. No one really knew the path not taken and he was no exception. But that desire to take it all in—to go after his goals with everything he was—beat strong and true inside him. It was why he'd spent so many extra hours a week above and beyond the standard practice times.

Why he still did it, to this day.

He had always pushed himself, striving for more. Striving to be better. Never settling until he *was* better.

Until he was the best.

Proving to himself that he was strong and able-bodied. That he'd done his damnedest to outlive his legacy.

He was thirty-four years old and he'd accomplished every professional goal he'd ever set for himself. Was that his own doing? Or was it a result of the veil of loss that had framed his upbringing?

Maybe it was both.

The ringing of his phone pulled him from his thoughts and he let out a soft sigh. His agent, Ray, had already left several messages to discuss the SNN deal, and he clearly hadn't been put off by the three text messages Roman had sent him over as many days.

The irony didn't escape him that the very same reason he paid Ray a generous salary was the reason he had no desire to talk to the man right now. Dogged pursuit of his future outside the hockey rink wasn't a conversation he looked forward to.

Facing the inevitable, he hit the answer button. After briefly catching up on how he'd been spending his time, Ray launched into the specifics of the offer. "It's better than we anticipated, Roman. They want you."

"They know I'm not ready to make a commitment."

"They're willing to give you some time, but I can't hold them off forever."

"I'm not ready to pull the trigger with the Metros yet."

"Can you give me a ballpark?"

Roman held back the frustrated sigh and kept his tone even. Ray was his business partner, but he didn't know everything. "Give me two weeks."

"I can hold them off until then."

"Good. Thanks."

Roman hung up and continued pacing the room. The conversation had held few surprises—other than just how much money SNN was willing to throw around. While the money wasn't the main factor in his decision, it didn't hurt to know he'd be compensated handsomely for continuing to maintain a travel schedule that would fell more than a few flight attendants.

The small voice that had gotten progressively louder since he arrived back in Indigo screamed at him to come clean with Avery. He knew he should share his medical condition and its impact on his future. Add on the very telling conversation they'd had in the cab about hiding the difficult things and he knew he needed to say something.

And even as he knew he should, he continued to push it off, as if keeping the secret would stave off the inevitable.

Like somehow telling Avery would finally make it all terribly, horribly real.

With his thoughts roiling, Roman paced and stewed on his options until it was time to go down and watch her panel.

The room was packed, with the crowd humming in an upbeat murmur as everyone took their places. He'd snagged a spot in the front corner and passed the last few minutes watching her read and reread her notes in quiet preparation.

It was funny that the look on her face was nearly an identical match for the tight focus she used to get studying for finals. She pushed the hair behind her ear in an unconscious gesture that made him think of study hall and he had to admit just how far gone he was.

Even now, he could conjure up an image of her sitting at her desk, two rows in front of him and three rows over, that was as vivid as if he'd sat in the classroom yesterday.

Was there any moment with her he'd ever forgotten?

He knew her.

And he loved her.

The knowledge rang so true, he also admitted to himself he'd never really stopped loving her. It was the reason he'd stayed away. And it was the reason for the lavish gifts.

He'd desperately wanted to bring her some joy. Give her something that he knew she loved as a way to make her happy.

The fact that those same gifts were looked at as an insult had hurt, but he finally understood why. The loneliness he'd lived with for fourteen years could never have been assuaged by a gift, no matter how well-meaning.

And even the most thoughtful gesture eventually became meaningless.

God, he'd been such an ass. A well-intentioned one, but an ass all the same.

And now that he finally understood that fact, he only had a week left in Indigo.

Of course, he could have had a month and it likely wouldn't have made a difference. His life wasn't in Alaska, no matter what choice he made for his future. He wasn't ready to retire completely at the age of thirty-four. And no matter how sweet the memories, the last few weeks had proven to him that he and Avery weren't the same people after all this time. They'd moved forward as individuals.

Bright, vibrant people who had bright, vibrant futures ahead of them.

Futures that continued to push them in different directions.

Julia quietly closed her bedroom door, but not before she stopped to look her fill of a sleeping Ken, sprawled across her bed. For such a mild-mannered man, he was rather expansive in sleep and she'd enjoyed seeing that side of him.

The day before had been a revelation, the night yet another.

She loved.

It was so simple—so swift and immediate—she wondered how it was possible she could feel this way.

Her kitchen looked the same as it always did when she walked into it a few minutes later, the warm yellow walls greeting her as they did every morning. The summer sun streamed in the windows, the same way it had for the last month. And the summer before. And all the summers that she'd lived in the house.

But everything was different. *She* was different.

A small giggle lodged in her throat. Had she really made love to a man? At her age?

She most certainly had and she was damn glad to know all the equipment still worked, thank you very much.

Wouldn't Mary and Sophie be surprised?

And maybe she'd hold off telling them for a couple of days, as the opportunity to hold the delicious knowledge all to herself felt too lovely to give up quite yet.

Goodness, when had she become so secretive? First her concerns about Roman and now this.

She went to work filling the coffeepot and getting it

on to brew, then turned to the fridge to find the makings of breakfast. She had the sudden desire for pancakes and waffles, bacon, eggs and a side of hash browns.

"Greedy, insatiable woman," she admonished herself with another giggle before she reached for the carton of eggs.

"I'd say so."

She nearly dropped the eggs before turning to see Ken standing in the doorway to the kitchen. "I didn't hear you come down."

"I'm sorry if I startled you." He crossed the room and gave her a light kiss on the cheek before heading to the cabinet to pull down a couple mugs.

She watched him, bemused that he knew where things were. And in that moment, it hit her. "Things between us have been building for a long time."

He turned from the cabinet. "I wanted to think so. To hope so."

"We know each other well."

"We do."

All the years—all this time—Ken had always been there. Watching out for her. Being a part of her social circle.

Being there for *her*.

While she'd depended on him a bit more than usual for her concerns about Roman since her grandson had returned home, he'd always been a confidant. A trusted friend that she shared her life with.

How had it taken her so long to realize it?

"Were there times you wanted to shake me?"

"I didn't want to pressure you. And I never knew if

your feelings were something more, and I didn't want to lose what we had. Have."

He set the mugs next to the gurgling coffeepot and came over to take her hands.

"I care about you and having you in my life. That has always been paramount to me. The rest is—" He broke off, his normally serene face drawn as he searched for words. "The rest is wonderful, but having you in my life has always meant more."

She pressed her hand to his cheek, enjoying the light scratch of beard under her fingertips. "Thank you for giving me space." She moved in closer and pressed a kiss to the other cheek. "But maybe next time you want something as fun and enjoyable as last night, you find a way to tell me? We're not going to live forever, you know."

Their mutual laughter was cut off as he pressed his lips to hers, pulling her close. It was a long while later before either of them thought about their morning cup of coffee.

"In closing, there are many benefits of an exchange program, but the opportunity to both encourage your staff while you allow them to bring valuable learning back to your establishment makes the program a win-win for everyone."

Avery sat back in her chair, relieved the prepared remarks were over and excited at the applause and clear interest from the audience. She'd maintained eye contact with various people during her speech and all had worn that keen look of interest as she spoke.

The moderator moved the panel into the Q and A

session and she relaxed, waiting while the first question was directed at a proprietor from Juneau.

She scanned the room, surprised to realize there were people she knew. She'd attended this conference several years ago and had made many friendships, which she'd nurtured, mostly via e-mail, over the years. She continued her assessment and saw Roman smiling proudly from the front row.

The fact that he was here was heady unto itself. The fact that he saw her at her professional best and encouraged and believed in her was something else entirely.

It was wonderful.

The next question was directed to her and she refocused her attention on the person asking about the logistics of instituting an exchange program. She answered, describing her experience, the company she'd used that matched her and Lena up, and how she'd originally enrolled herself and the Indigo Blue in the program.

As she spoke, her mind whirled with the conversation she and Roman had shared earlier in the week. The choices she'd have been forced to make if he'd asked her to go with him.

She wouldn't have only had to choose about leaving her mother.

She'd have had to choose about her career, too. She wasn't just some girl from Indigo who mopped down the bar and checked people in. She'd become a member of the community. An active hospitality resource in their region, with connections to events and activities, tour groups and travel packages.

She had a career.

And she'd have had none of it if she'd left Indigo to

follow Roman Forsyth around the country as he followed his dream.

For far too long, she'd laid her sadness at the feet of Roman and her mother. And maybe it was time to face the fact that the reality of her life was right where it belonged.

With her.

"Here's to you." Roman lifted his glass of Chianti and waited for Avery to lift hers as well.

"I'll toast to that."

She took a sip of the rich red wine, her expression so light he was surprised she wasn't hovering about three inches off the chair.

The wine was particularly good and he enjoyed the taste of it almost as much as watching her. "It was a good day. Thanks for letting me come along."

She reached across the table and took his hand. "I'm glad you're here. Really glad."

"I am, too."

Their waiter arrived to take their orders and Roman got the chicken Parmesan while Avery ordered her perennial favorite, lasagna.

She watched the departing form of their waiter before she turned back and took Roman's hand once more. "Today it hit me that I have a great career."

He nodded, not sure where she was going. "Of course you do."

"I never realized that before this week. And, well, before Ireland."

"That trip meant a lot to you."

"It did."

Roman knew he wasn't nearly as supportive at first as he should have been. He had been in Indigo the previous winter when she'd gotten the call that she had been accepted, and his inner selfish streak had roared with indignity at the idea of her going that far away.

"I should have been more supportive about that trip. Especially at first."

"It's okay."

He squeezed her fingers. "No, it's really not."

"After Sloan, Grier and I dissected it a million different ways, we kept coming back to the same answer."

"What was that?"

"You were jealous of my adventure and convinced I'd meet someone wonderful, abandon my post under your mother's care and run off to roam the world."

He couldn't hold back the laughter at her words, especially since she wasn't all that far from the truth. "You know me too well."

"While I think women spend far too much time assigning meaning where it's not meant, in this case we figured we sort of had something."

"And you did meet someone wonderful."

"Declan is wonderful." Her warm gaze grew hooded. "But he deserves someone who will love him back. Fully. That person isn't me."

"I've had a few of those myself. It's like no matter how hard you try, no matter how great the other person is, you just can't be what they need."

"The old *it's not you, it's me* situation." Her smile was gentle as she spoke, and he took a deep breath of relief that they could actually discuss this subject.

"Yep."

"I bet you left a path of broken hearts strewn all over Manhattan, Mr. Forsyth."

"Fortunately, relatively few. And from the last I heard, all had been accounted for in new relationships, most of which led to marriage."

"Well, the Internet's quite active with sites devoted to you. Posts go up almost immediately after a game, lovingly detailing your prowess on the ice, your heroic hockey skills, and just how hot you looked when you pulled your helmet off in the penalty box during the second period."

"I haven't seen those."

"It's sweet in a stalkerish, teenage fantasy sort of way."

"Then it's lucky for me sixteen-year-old girls out-grow their celebrity crushes once a real boyfriend arrives to put the stars in their eyes."

The laugher in her eyes faded until all he saw was the past shining back at him. "Most of them, anyway."

Chapter Eighteen

The heavy weight of Roman's arm rested over her shoulders and Avery asked herself when she'd last felt so good. They'd walked to dinner, the restaurant a few short blocks from the hotel, and now they were taking their time to meander back.

Anchorage came alive in the summer, with the long days a natural incentive to get people out and enjoying the city. Add on the numerous visitors who came to the city before or after a cruise and the streets were full of life.

That rush of activity had also ensured they were recognized by more than a few people. The attention had been good-natured, but it had slowed their walk back to the hotel. True to her word, Avery didn't mind the notice paid to Roman, but she did wonder at it. He was so kind and patient, answering the same questions over and over.

How did he deal with it day after day, year after year?

"You weren't kidding about being the belle of the ball." She patted his stomach as they turned up the long, curving driveway to their hotel.

"Did it bother you?"

"What? The people who stopped us? Not at all. I think it's sort of sweet."

"You're a masochist."

"No, it's just neat to see that side of you. I've seen how everyone from Indigo treats you, but they at least know you. Perfect strangers actually light up when they meet you. Your picture will be on Facebook walls and flying through the air in text messages before the hour is out."

"It's nothing to do with me. It's for the idea of me."

Before she could say anything to such a cryptic statement, Roman pointed toward the horizon. "You just don't see a sky like that anywhere else." The late evening light was breathtaking, the colors so bright and golden it drew the eye to its glorious palette.

"Manhattan's a far cry from Anchorage."

"There are some nights, though. The way the sun sets over the Hudson. It reminds me of this a little bit, especially in the fall."

"I bet New York is amazing."

"You've never been?"

She couldn't help but smile at that. "I did a layover at JFK for my flight to Ireland, but that's it. Similar to my disdain for the Yankees, I couldn't come to New York and get that close to you. What's it like there?"

"Everything you've ever heard it is and then more. It also changes how you look at what you need in life."

"How so?"

"A car, for one thing. I didn't have one for the longest time, but I finally had to give in because my professional commitments had me out in Jersey or on Long

Island. Other than that, though, I don't really need one. I take the subway everywhere."

"You don't mind being closed in underground?"

"It's the easiest way to get around. And it's not that hard to get used to."

Avery tried to imagine traveling everywhere in tunnels under the earth and came up short. "I just can't picture what it's like. I also can't imagine that it's comfortable for a man of your size."

"People give you space. And most people are in their own world, headphones on or a book in hand. It's a strange system, but it works."

He extended a hand and gestured her through the front door of the hotel. "You up for a nightcap?"

"Sure."

"I'm sure your adoring public is waiting to greet you."

"I think you're mistaking your life for mine."

He raised his eyebrows and extended his hand toward the crowded bar. "I wouldn't be so sure."

She followed the direction of his finger and saw several people who raised a hand in greeting, large smiles on their faces. Walt Singer was the first to reach her, his arms extended for a hug. "Avery. You were fantastic today."

"Thanks, Walt."

"You did me such a huge favor," he whispered in her ear. "At least let me buy you and your friend a drink."

She eyed Roman and saw him nod with a good-natured smile. "That would be great."

Before she knew it, a glass of wine was thrust in her

hand and a beer in Roman's. And within a few more moments after that, she was dragged halfway across the bar to meet a colleague of one of the panelists.

When she finally looked up a half hour later, it was into the bright, smiling face of Roman as he watched her silently from the bar.

"She's quite a looker."

Roman turned toward the man next to him. "And you caught me staring."

"She's the whole package. Inside and out." The man extended his hand. "Chris Morris. I'm with the Luxotica hotel chain."

Roman introduced himself in return. "They're beautiful properties. I've stayed in several myself."

"You're with the Metros."

"Yep."

"You had an incredible season. I was at that game against the Red Wings last November. That hat trick was particularly impressive. The fact that it was your second that week especially so."

Roman couldn't hold back the smile. "That was a good week."

"As of the end of the season, you're two shy of Gretzky's record of fifty."

"It's the one record I'd most like to beat." Roman's stomach tightened. It had been his highest goal—to beat the Great One on that particular stat and he knew the chances of doing it now with the condition of his right eye were slim to none.

The guy lifted his beer for a toast. "Here's hoping you do it, then."

Roman clinked glasses and tried desperately to ignore the dark, hollow emptiness that settled in his chest and spread through his limbs with cold, creeping fingers. It was killing him to keep the situation with his eye injury to himself. But he knew if he admitted it to Avery, he'd also be forced to acknowledge how real the problem was.

It was a career ender.

He knew that. Had known it the moment he'd come to on the ice after taking the hit. He'd fought around it through the end of the season, depending more heavily on his teammates and passing the puck when he had the chance rather than take a shot on goal himself.

He was just lucky the injury had happened late in the season, allowing him to fake his way through the last few games without too much trouble. The team doctor had checked him out when it first happened and Roman had used his leadership position to bully his way into playing the last few games, claiming he was fine.

He knew damn well he wasn't, especially since the problem wasn't getting any better. Add on the three specialists he'd seen since the off-season began—each with answers he didn't want to hear—and he knew he needed to make a decision.

It wasn't fair to his teammates to play at less than 100 percent.

"How do you know Avery?"

Chris's words pulled Roman from his morose thoughts. "We've known each other since we were kids. You?"

"I've heard her name off and on for several years

now. After seeing her on the panel today, I'd like to talk to her. See what she'd like out of her future."

Roman heard the professional interest in the man's voice and keyed in on it immediately. "You want to hire her?"

"I'm not opposed to it, but I'd take her as a consultant if that's all I can get. She's got a lot of energy and some really innovative ideas."

"Our entire hometown of Indigo loves her. My mother most of all."

"Your mother?" Chris took a swig of his beer, his confusion evident.

"She owns the Indigo Blue."

Chris cracked a broad smile at that. "Then forget I said anything. I'm interested in having her on a consulting basis only."

Roman waved the bartender over and ordered them two more beers. "My mother would be the last one to stand in the way of her advancement. You talk to her if you think that's what you want to do."

Chris accepted the beer with a quick thanks. "I'll plan on it."

Roman glanced back across the bar, where Avery and her red dress stood out in sharp relief to the crowd of men in suits who surrounded her. "She deserves a chance to spread her wings."

Avery stripped out of the dress and tossed it onto the bed. She had to hand it to Grier, the red was an inspired suggestion. She'd spent the evening feeling like she had the room in the palm of her hand and she knew the dress helped.

What she couldn't quite shake was the sense of melancholy coming from Roman.

"You okay?"

"Yep."

"I'm sorry I abandoned you in the bar."

"Don't be. You were working the room just as you needed to be. I told you your adoring public awaited."

She watched his face, waiting for the note of censure or annoyance to appear, but all she saw was the same unwavering support he'd projected all day.

"It still had to have been a bit boring for you."

"I met a nice guy at the bar. He's part of the Luxotica hotel chain. I've stayed in several and they're fantastic hotels."

"Very high-end boutique hotels."

"You do know your stuff."

She grabbed her toiletry kit and headed for the bathroom, still concerned there was something she was missing, yet unable to put her finger on what it was.

Or maybe it's nothing, Marks. Despite the last few days, you don't know each other all that well anymore.

She tried to believe her own pep talk but something held her back.

Coming back into the room, she eyed where he lay on the bed clad only in shorts, a sports magazine in hand. The urge to just stand there and stare at him was strong, but she pushed past it to get to the root of her concerns. "Is everything okay?"

"Yeah. Why?"

"I don't know. You seem sad."

"I'm good."

"All right." She was almost back to the bathroom

when she stopped and turned once more. "Because if this is too much. Us. Here. Together. I get it. I can give you space. It's not like with your mom. I can discuss tough stuff with you."

"I asked you if I could come along."

"Yeah. But. . . ."

"Avery." Roman sat up and tossed the magazine onto the end table. "Come here."

She walked over and stood between his knees. His large hands circled her waist, his thumbs lightly teasing the waistband of her shorts.

"There's nothing wrong. At all. I just have to come to grips with the fact that you're a woman on the rise and I'm an aging athlete whose career has seen better days. I'm not sad about it, but maybe I am a little melancholy."

Of all the things he could have said, this was the last she'd expected. "You're not that old."

"My career's on the downswing."

"You were the MVP last year."

"And this year I was another player in the league. The stakes rise every year and so does my age."

"But—" She broke off, the truth of his words sinking in. No matter how fit he was or how skilled, mother nature and the sheer passage of time conspired against him.

"You, on the other hand, are coming into the prime of your career. You've got the experience to be useful, but you're young enough to have the energy and drive to keep succeeding."

"You make it sound like we're several decades apart."

"Career-wise we are."

His hands shifted to the hem of the tank top she'd put on after changing out of her dress. "Fortunately, we're far more age compatible in other ways."

Pleasure lit up her nerve endings wherever he touched and she allowed him to pull her closer until his hands came around her body, coming to rest on her ass. He pressed his lips against her stomach, in the small space where the tank rode up and her shorts rode down. With his clever tongue, he ran the tip over the sensitive skin exposed there and she saw stars as her legs quivered at the sexy, tantalizing play of his mouth.

How had she never realized the skin around her belly button could be so sensitive?

She rested her forearms on his shoulders and reached her hand out to weave her fingers through his hair. The thick strands were soft to the touch and she enjoyed the way they curled slightly over his neck. Her other hand drifted over the large span of his upper back. Hard muscles flexed and stretched as he moved against her and she marveled at how in tune they were with each other.

At how their bodies fit.

His movements grew more impatient and she felt more than saw him grip the straps of her tank and pull it down to bunch at her waist. He kept a tight grip on the material and dragged it along with the shorts the rest of the way down her body.

"Step out of your shorts." His voice was almost a growl and she did as he asked, lifting first one foot, then the other before kicking the material away. His hands returned to her, pulling her down on top of him on the bed.

"I want you."

Joy unfurled through her, warming every inch of her body like the sun on a summer day. "I certainly hope so. You know, since I'm naked and all."

"You're cheeky."

"I'm happy."

His eyes darkened with something so deep—so honest—she almost couldn't look directly into his gaze for fear she'd get lost there. And then the moment was gone as fast as it had come and his smile matched hers. "Me, too."

Their lips met once more, the always-fevered give-and-take a carnal prelude to what was to come. Avery matched his movements, mimicking the slide of his tongue before sucking his lower lip between hers.

"You don't play fair," he whispered against her mouth when she finally released him.

"I aim to win."

"This is one game we can both win."

"Then by all means. Game on."

Roman heard the promise in her words and recognized the meaning behind her tease. The game *was* on and they were going to drive each other to the very brink of their physical capabilities—and beyond, if he knew Avery.

And he did know her.

He knew the arch of her neck and the fine bones of her face. Knew the soft swell of her breasts and the long lines of her thighs.

He *knew* her.

Every time she was in his arms, it was like they were kids again, falling in love for the first time. And yet, this time he felt even more for her.

His feelings as a young man didn't have much depth or breadth or the understanding of loss. For all the pain it had caused, their time apart had also made the feelings more real, somehow. The need for her more intense. He craved her.

And he needed her so desperately he thought he'd never be sated.

Roman shifted underneath her so her body was fully seated over his hips, then used his hands to trace a path over every inch of her skin. He began with that sensitive area near her belly button, gratified when her eyes lidded to half mast at his touch.

With unerring precision, he then traced his fingers out over her stomach and down the taut muscles of her thighs. He felt them quiver under his touch, especially when he worked his thumbs back up the inside of her thighs, narrowly avoiding her rapidly heating core.

She shifted against him, telegraphing her interest in having his hands back there but he kept up the torment, moving on to her torso. The small, pert breasts he'd fantasized about since he was a horny teenager beckoned him and he captured her nipples between the V of his palm, massaging her flesh while he dragged on the tight points. Her head fell back and the subtle writhing against his hips continued, and he knew to the depths of his soul he'd never seen anything more beautiful.

His woman, taking her pleasure at his hands.

The need and passion he'd managed to keep at bay, content in the joy of simply remembering and memorizing her with his touch, fled as the need to brand her rose up and snapped at him with fierce teeth.

Holding on to her hips, he gently rolled her off so he could stretch out next to her, then went to work. His hands ran that same unerring path down her flesh, but this time he stopped at the apex of her thighs, his fingers sliding into her beckoning heat.

A heavy moan escaped her in a hard exhale and Roman kept up his assault, determined to win this round with her first orgasm. Her body arched and he leaned forward to take one nipple in his mouth, the ripe taste of her flesh on his tongue driving him to an even darker madness as he feasted. And when he knew she was close, he added his thumb to put further pressure on the tight bundle of nerves at her core and trigger her release.

Avery clutched at his arms and he watched, mesmerized as pleasure suffused her face. Like the previous week when he came upon her in the sauna, his gaze was everywhere—on her face, on her body, on the undulation of her waist—taking her in and watching her in this moment of such powerful vulnerability.

He leaned down to press a kiss to her lips, unable to hold back a laugh when she smiled against him. "Round one goes to you."

"Funny," he murmured, "I was thinking the same thing."

She lifted her hands to the back of his neck, bringing him close for another kiss before she shifted to press her lips to his ear. "Don't think you're going to take round two."

"You think you can take me?" He tossed out the challenge and wasn't disappointed with the immediate response.

"The real question is how long you can take it."

With a set of speedy moves a wrestler would admire, she had him on his back, pinned under her hands. Similar to his own explorations, she traced his skin, her hands lingering over his shoulders before moving down to his torso. He felt his stomach muscles quiver as she painted the ridges of muscle there, then felt them contract on a hard pulse of need as she dragged her tongue over one of his nipples.

She'd always known his erogenous zones, her ability to follow the reactions of his body absolute, even when words were unspoken, and this was one of those areas. She lapped at him like a cat after cream before moving down to run her tongue over his stomach muscles, the gentle suction replacing what she'd so recently stroked with her fingers.

Roman knew her destination and braced himself for the onslaught. True to her promise to take round two, she once again moved lower. He wanted to watch—wanted the joy of seeing his woman take him in her mouth—but the needs of his body trumped everything and he nearly arched off the bed as her mouth closed over him. Wet warmth surrounded the most sensitive part of his body and Roman simply gave himself up to it.

Gave her control and settled in to enjoy the ride.

Avery played his body like a goddess, drawing pleasure with her tongue and her hands in a fantasy come to life. Never before, Roman knew, had he enjoyed such an erotic experience. The scent of her—uniquely Avery—wrapped around him and brought with it the loving sense of the familiar and the exciting knowledge of sharing something special with her.

The woman he loved.

The pleasure of the moment rapidly faded under the increasing demands of his body and he reached for her. "Join me."

Her eyes were dark and dilated with passion as he dragged her up until she was seated over him. "I want you, Roman."

"I want you, too."

She fitted her body to his, taking him deeply inside before she began to move. Her long, athletic body rose up and over him and he kept a steady hand on her waist, matching their movements as he lifted to meet the downward thrusts of her hips.

A hard, desperate feeling he couldn't define settled in his chest as they rode the madness together. He ignored it, enjoying their passion as they both drove the other ever closer to fulfillment.

When he heard her breaths shorten—heard the low moan that started in her chest—he pushed them both harder until he felt her quiver around him at the start of her orgasm. Roman thrust once more, riding the demands of her body as she pulled his own response in hard, tight bursts.

Avery fell over his body, looking utterly sated, and he reached up to wrap his arms around her before shifting them to their sides so he could cradle her in his arms.

That strange desperation that had gripped him during their lovemaking rose up once more in his chest as she nestled against him.

He'd spent the last fourteen years missing the girl he knew and remembered. But only now did he understand that his memories were of a younger woman with an innocence about life.

The Avery in his arms was a woman with experience and wisdom, and hopes and dreams for her future.

He couldn't take that away from her.

Couldn't ask her to give those things up as he moved to the next phase of his life. Even if playing hockey wasn't it, coming back to Indigo wasn't part of his life plan, either.

How had he failed to understand this? To see this?

She had a future in front of her—a bright one, golden with opportunity. She didn't need the challenge of juggling something with him, both of them traveling constantly.

Catching time with each other when they could make it work.

It was finally Avery's time to reach for the brass ring.

Chapter Nineteen

$\mathcal{A}$ very sat across from Chris Morris and marveled at how her life had changed in the last week. One of her best friends was now married, Roman was back in town for longer than a weekend and she was about to be offered a new job. Chris was kind and cordial and she'd made the requisite small talk as they got acquainted over lunch, but all the while her mind whirled with the reality of the changes in her life.

And, despite the impending job offer, Roman was foremost in her thoughts.

Where she'd feared intimacy in the past, she now realized it was the one thing—no matter the eventual outcome—they could give each other without reservation. She'd mistakenly thought sex bound them together, but in reality, it was a gift they could share that didn't have the same boundaries that defined the rest of their lives.

But it didn't have to be the only definition of their relationship.

And this time, she was determined she wouldn't lose someone so important to her.

Along with that understanding, she'd grown increasingly concerned. Sex the night before had been amazing but she'd felt something shift. Even as they drew closer to each other, it had felt like somewhere inside he was pulling away.

First was the lingering melancholy that had haunted his eyes when they got back to their room. Then, there had been a strange urgency in his lovemaking that went beyond the physical tease of driving each other to madness.

The nagging sense she'd had all week that something was wrong had only grown more purposeful and more convincing. Roman was dealing with something in his life and she was determined to find out what.

If their renewed time together had taught her anything, it was that she valued Roman's presence in her life. He mattered and she wasn't going to let him go so easily this time. She was a grown woman who understood that the physical needs of her body were only a part of who she was.

The people in her life and the emotional places they filled inside her were as important, if not more so.

"So I'm not sure if Roman mentioned anything to you about our conversation last night."

Avery keyed back in on the conversation and smiled as she buttered her roll. "I saw the two of you talking but he didn't say anything other than the fact that you'd met."

Chris's eyebrows rose but he kept his voice light. "So he didn't mention I'd like to hire you at Luxotica."

"He mentioned some consulting work."

A small, tight ball settled in her stomach and she

wondered at the news. A job offer was a big deal and Roman hadn't said anything about it.

"After he told me his mother is the owner of the Indigo Blue, I amended my interest in hiring you to a consulting gig only. He seemed pretty adamant about not standing in your way, though. Said I should talk to you."

Which only reinforced the point that he was planning on leaving.

The knowledge wasn't a surprise and it made her even happier that she truly had found a sense of distance between the physical and the emotional.

But damn, why couldn't he have said something?

Avery kept her tone light, but she couldn't help question in her mind what it all meant. "He's a good friend and wants what's best for me."

"Which is Luxotica, I know it. Look, Avery. I'd settle for you on my team as a consultant so you could maintain your ties in Indigo, but I think your talent can take you far. Far beyond one of Alaska's remotest areas."

"I like my home."

She kept her tone gentle, but deliberately floated the words to see what sort of reaction she'd get. He wasn't the first to suggest she could get more out of life—could find more *in* life—if she left her home.

"Of course, and what you manage in Indigo is an impressive hotel. You're a favorite of tourism companies throughout the state and you know your business and your area. But imagine putting that to use for a bigger company with bigger resources."

"What role do you see for me?"

"At first? I'd like you in one of our West Coast properties. We still have some service gaps to fill versus
many of our competitor hotels in L.A. and San Fran-
cisco, and I need someone with good ideas who can
find a way past that."

"And after that?"

Chris sat back as the waiter set their salads down.
"The sky's the limit."

Avery wondered at that but kept her thoughts to
herself. Chris wasn't kidding about their West Coast
properties. She'd looked into them this morning and
had put out a few calls before taking the meeting. The
Luxotica line did tremendously well in Europe and
Asia but wasn't hitting the mark in the United States.

Was she up to the challenge of fixing it?

Even as she asked herself the question, she already
felt the excitement rising at how she might come in and
make a difference.

"Why me? To your point, I work in a small town in
Alaska. What do you feel I have to offer in a market as
high-end and expensive as California?"

"You've got a passion and a fire about you. The
packages you started offering at the Indigo Blue—
they're original. And your social media presence is impressive. You've built over ten thousand followers on
your Facebook page for a small hotel in the middle of
Alaska."

"We've gotten some good press. And we've got a
ready-made attraction in town with our bachelor auction. It draws attention."

"It's more than that. You're not afraid to take risks.
Your weekly moose-sighting photos are a favorite, and

one of the videos you put up on YouTube last year went viral."

"Which is why I have to ask what you think I can offer you to fix the California problem. I'm not a native of the area. And I hardly think a high-end establishment like yours wants the California equivalent of moose sightings."

"You'd be surprised."

"Would I? I don't want to dismiss the offer, Chris. In fact, I'm more than a little intrigued. I'm just not sure why you think I'm the right one."

"You're a risk taker. That's what I look for. People can teach you Los Angeles. Hell, I'll get a limo to drive you around for a week if that's the only concern you have. But your ideas. Your ability to work with people. That's what I'm hiring you for."

Avery was still thinking about it a couple of hours later as she walked to her room. She'd made a quick stop into one of the panel discussions after lunch, but rather than try to cram another in, she was ready to relax and think about Chris's offer.

Could she really leave Indigo?

A part of her knew the answer was that she could. She'd spent too many years longing for something different—to get away—and she knew she could handle it. She was also pragmatic enough to know that she could always come home again.

She'd gone to Ireland and had four of the best months of her life and had come home and easily readjusted. Home was where you chose to make it—it was as simple as that.

"Hey." Roman glanced up as she keyed herself into

the room. He was in workout clothes, and from his wet head and the towel in hand she could see he'd just come back.

"Someone got a workout in."

"They've got a nice gym."

She moved in and pressed a quick kiss on his lips. "And no getting flabby in the off-season."

"The horror." He lingered over the kiss before stepping back. "How was your lunch?"

"Chris offered me a job."

"Really?"

She raised one eyebrow as her gaze met his. "Don't act so surprised. I know you know."

"He said he wanted you and wanted to offer you a consulting gig."

"Well, he said he'd settle for that but he really wants me on staff." She tossed the light sweater she'd worn over her dress onto the bed. "He also said you wanted what's best for me and didn't want to stand in my way."

"I don't."

"But what does that mean? Why didn't you say anything to me about talking to him?"

"You've got your whole future ahead of you. It's not my place to hold you back. Honestly, it's not even my place to have an opinion. You're being given your shot at the brass ring and you've worked long and hard to get there. You don't need my thoughts ringing in your ears."

"Would you want to hold me back?"

The question was out before she could censor the words or think of a different way to get at her question.

Did she want him to hold her back?

Or was she looking for something else? Something, maybe, that suggested he'd make a choice and follow her.

"You need to make the choices that are right for you." There was that same look she saw the night before in his eyes. A mixture of sadness and, she thought, a strange inevitability about where things between them would end up.

Roman stared out the window of Mick's plane and took in the sight of Denali where it rose up in glorious splendor. Like pretty much everyone who saw it, he'd always been fascinated by the mountain. The harsh peaks and the sheer awesomeness of nature had always made him feel small.

Helping to put his life in perspective.

So why the hell couldn't he get any of it now?

The time he'd spent with Avery in the last week had been some of the best moments he could remember in a long time. The sex was outrageous, but even that couldn't overshadow the simple joy of being with her.

So why was he acting like such a sullen jerk?

And what would it hurt to try to have both? His career was going to change. Even if he could find a way around the current injury, he didn't have a lot of years left in him. Her mother couldn't stand in the way any longer, either. They could live the life they wanted. Carve out a life that worked for both of them.

But what sort of life would they have? He'd still be married to the game of hockey, just on a different stage.

And if she took Chris's offer, she'd have a new career to focus on.

New demands on her time and an equally grueling schedule, if the job description was any indication.

Excuses, Forsyth. Excuses.

His conscience beat a rapt tattoo behind his eyes, jackhammering a headache along with the harsh assessment.

None of this was about his career or hers. Nor was it about what happened fourteen years ago, and he damn well knew it.

He loved her.

And Roman knew the feeling would live with him for a lifetime.

If given the chance, he'd like to try a relationship with her once more. Their time together since he'd returned to Indigo had proven that there was a reason he'd never found another woman to take Avery's place.

Because there *was* no one who could take her place.

But he wasn't the man she fell in love with all those years ago. And he wasn't the man he thought he was, either. The boy who'd been born on skates had grown into a man who lived on them. And he had no idea who he was without them.

What would happen if they tried to have a real relationship? If he let her in and gave them both hope there could be more?

His career was ending and everything he'd ever known about himself—every achievement, every way he measured himself—was ending with it.

What if *he* couldn't be the man she needed?

If he lost her again, he knew he'd never be whole.

*   *   *

"How was it?"

Avery pushed a bright, sunny attitude into her voice as Grier rolled out pizza dough on the kitchen counter. "Great. It was a fantastic conference."

"How'd your panel go? I'm sure you wowed them."

"I think I did." Avery crossed the living room to the counter that surrounded her kitchen and grabbed the glass of wine she'd poured earlier. "I got a lot of great comments and made some really strong professional contacts."

Grier reached for a large ball of mozzarella on the counter and set it on the bar. "Grate that for me, will you?"

"Sure." Avery was grateful for the small chore and grabbed the ball of cheese like a lifeline. "When do the guys get here?"

"Mick needed some help with a window that cracked in the living room. He figured it would take a few hours to get the new one installed if he had Roman's help."

"So that's why you're making three pizzas."

Grier shot her a grin over her shoulder as she layered sauce on the first pan. "Manual labor makes a man hungry and all that. Besides, this will make a nice batch of leftovers."

"You're so considerate with him."

"What?" Grier looked up from piling sauce on the second pan. "Mick?"

"Yeah. You think about him. And he does the same with you. Like the other day with the pancakes for your wedding hangover."

A light blush suffused Grier's cheeks. "We do nice things for each other that don't involve food, too."

Avery smiled at that. "I'm sure you do, and I'm also sure several of them are things I have no interest in hearing about."

Grier picked up a towel and Avery ducked as the wet cloth whizzed past her head.

"I'm being serious, though." Avery kept her gaze on the smooth slide of cheese as she tried to explain what she meant.

"Well, yeah. Sure. I mean, I love him."

"I think it's more than that."

Grier set down her ladle and turned toward the bar. "Why do I get the feeling this is part of a bigger thought?"

"Because it is."

"And?"

"And I'm confused and happy and sad and feeling sort of scattered, all rolled up into one large ball of crazy."

"What happened down in Anchorage?"

"I slept with Roman the whole time. I got offered a new job. And I figured out he's holding something back."

"That's a lot of stuff to pack into a couple of days."

"Tell me about it."

"Why don't we take it piece by piece." Grier picked up her wineglass. "Tell me about the job first and let's get that part out of the way."

"Luxotica hotels wants me to be instrumental in running their West Coast operations."

"Avery!" Grier circled the bar and pulled her in for a tight hug. "That's awesome news!"

"And just like the Ireland trip, it means not living here." Avery whispered the words as they hugged. "A more permanent version of that."

"Is it something you want?"

"Sort of."

Grier pulled back. "Define 'sort of.'"

Avery blew out a heavy breath. "It is something I want. But I want other things, too."

"Is this where we get to the Roman part?"

"Yes and no. Yes because I can't stop thinking that he's a factor now. And no because the decision to leave my home is bigger than Roman. I live here. And I like it here. I'm not sure I want to go live in L.A."

"It's a hell of a lot warmer."

Avery thought of her closet. "Which is code for I'd need a whole new wardrobe."

"Despite my limited fashion sense, even I know that would be a fun problem to fix."

"And I'd be away from everyone I know and love."

Grier nodded and took another sip of her wine. "There is that."

"And then there's the other part, which is that Roman lives in New York."

"He's not going to play hockey forever. I know he looks invincible, but there's a time limit on his career, Avery. He can't do this forever."

Avery knew that. It was the one small detail that gave her hope they might be able to figure something out, even if they split their time between places for the next few years.

"Have you talked to him about it?"

"I tried earlier but he sidestepped it and went to

shower before we headed for the airport." At the pointed stare, she added, "I will talk to him. I have to talk to him. I owe Luxotica an answer in the next week."

"What if Roman asked you not to take it? What would you do?"

"Truth?"

"Truth."

Avery looked into the deeply concerned gray gaze and voiced what bothered her even more than Roman saying no. "I'm more afraid he's going to tell me to take it."

Chapter Twenty

Roman stood in Mick's living room and hollered out instructions as his friend stood on the other side of the window. "No gaps. You've got it in there tight."

Mick's muted voice echoed through the window they held between them. "Hold it still. I want to grab the level." Roman nodded and braced his feet as he held the glass in place.

He'd been surprised when Mick had asked for the help installing a new window, but the promise of cold beer, manual labor and easy friendship were too good an offer to pass up. His mind had been so full of choices involving Avery for the past week the opportunity to do something physical was a welcome change.

Roman watched as Mick used the level, then switched to his tape measure to confirm the window fit properly before he secured a series of temporary nails. He'd never thought of himself as physically inept, but watching his friend walk through the installation step-by-step forced him to admit how rarefied his life had become over the last decade and a half.

If something broke in his penthouse apartment, he

called someone to fix it. And if he needed something, he ordered it.

He did nothing himself.

And the knowledge chafed a bit.

"You okay, man?" Mick tapped on the glass.

"What? Yeah. Sure."

"It's secure. Come on out here and help me finish up this side."

Roman crossed back through the house, smiling to himself at the small touches that were clearly Grier's doing. A mix of colorful throw pillows dotted the sofa, and several plants were scattered through the room. A pretty rug—in shades that matched the pillows—spread out from the large, oversized fireplace.

Yep. All the signs pointed very clearly in one direction.

Mick had a woman. More than that, Roman knew. Mick almost had a wife.

Another thing Roman had managed to miss out on in his adult life.

Shaking off the maudlin thoughts, Roman continued on outside and met Mick at the window. They worked in companionable silence, adhering the waterproofing that came next.

"That ought to hold her. And if I'm lucky, cut down on the draft we always seem to get in the living room." Mick grinned as he reached for the beer he'd settled against his toolbox. "It's funny. I never cared much about that before. If I got cold, I dragged on another sweatshirt or grabbed a blanket. Now it bothers me."

"Because Grier might get cold?"

"Yep. Man, I am so fucked." Mick rubbed a hand over his jaw as a broad grin split his face. "And I'm loving every single second of it."

"Yeah, well don't forget to nail the rim back on."

"What?" Mick had already dropped his hammer into his toolbox and was kneeling over it, closing it up.

Roman pointed to the piece of wood that rested against the side of the house. "You leaving the window frame exposed?"

"What was that I was saying?"

"Oh, I think your besotted grin and the cupids flying around your head say it all."

"They probably do," Mick said on a sigh as he unlocked the toolbox and pulled the hammer back out. "They probably do."

Avery knew men ate a lot. Heck, she saw it at the hotel all the time. But when Mick and Roman started in on the third pizza, even she would admit to a serious case of surprise. "Hungry much?"

"We did manual labor today," Mick muttered around a mouthful of pizza.

"It was one window, not the entire house."

Roman elbowed Mick as he swallowed his bite. "It was a long, sweaty job. Mick had to open his toolbox more than once."

Avery didn't miss the subtle exchange between the two of them as Mick let out a low guffaw at Roman's comment, but she opted to ignore it. The two of them, along with Walker, had always shared a strange half language she'd never been able to understand.

She certainly wasn't going to try to start now.

"I guess there's no room for my strawberry short-cake, then."

"The one with the pound cake on the bottom?" Mick's mouth dropped.

"The very same."

The man laid down his pizza before turning his apologetic gaze on Grier. "I'm sorry, baby. Your pizza's awesome but Avery's shortcake is so good I may need to propose. To her."

"You do that a lot." Grier's voice was dry.

"Do what?"

"Propose to women because of food." She turned toward Avery and Roman. "He has the hots for a cook up in Fairbanks because of her chicken potpie."

"Her husband's a bruiser."

"Didn't stop your googly eyes."

Mick leaned over and planted a solid kiss on Grier's lips. "The only googles are for you."

"Disgusting," Avery said in an overly loud whisper.

"Whipped," Roman added in an equally loud mono-tone.

"And damn proud of it." Grier and Mick said the words in unison before pulling away.

Avery stood to cross to the kitchen and waved Grier down before she could join her. "I'll get it. Finish your pizza."

Avery pulled the strawberries and the can of whipped cream out of the fridge, then grabbed bowls out of the cabinet before she moved back to the counter. The pound cake had baked up just as she'd hoped, golden yellow in its rectangular pan. She cut slices—

extra large ones for Roman and Mick—and ladled strawberries over each piece.

Without warning, a memory slammed into her so hard she grabbed for the countertop to keep her legs from going out from underneath her.

"Where'd you learn to make this?"

Avery felt Roman's lips on the nape of her neck before a wash of sparks shot down her spine. She'd started wearing her hair up for this very reason. He couldn't seem to resist that spot, and her body never failed to show its appreciation.

"Mrs. Taylor's misguided attempts at home ec during study hall."

"Is this what you and the girls were doing while we got sent down to the gym to learn how to keep our engines from freezing in winter?"

"At least no one can say sexism isn't alive and well at Indigo High School."

Roman shook his head as he leaned forward and dipped his finger into the bowl of whipped cream she'd made from scratch. "Home ec and shop. It's like something out of 1955."

"At least I got something tasty out of it."

"You sure did. And now so did I." Roman smiled before diving in to kiss her. She could taste the subtle cream on his lips and sank into him, the taste of something she'd made on his tongue a surprisingly satisfying sensation.

"What are you two doing in here?" Avery's mother walked into the small kitchen and Avery moved out of Roman's arms, putting some distance between them.

"Nothing, Mom."

"We're kissing, Ms. Marks." Roman grinned broadly. "Your daughter tastes delicious."

"Roman!"

Avery's gaze darted between her mom and Roman. She knew her mother knew they kissed—and likely understood a whole lot more—but he didn't need to go broadcasting it.

"Oh, honey." Her mom waved an arm but Avery didn't miss the sharp look that had come into her mother's eyes. "I was young once, too."

"I know, Mom."

"I know what it's like to have a beau."

"Of course you do."

"I know." Alicia crossed to the cabinet on the far side of the kitchen and snagged a bottle of brandy from the cabinet.

Avery felt Roman's quiet gaze on her but she refused to meet his eyes. She'd had this conversation with her mother before. Alicia's desperate need to emphasize she'd had relationships in the past had only gotten louder and harder-edged as Avery's own relationship with Roman had progressed.

"Anyone want brandy on their strawberries?" Alicia held up the bottle as she approached the counter.

"No, Mom. We're good."

"I know you are, baby." A heavy wash of anger flooded her mother's gaze for the briefest of moments before it was replaced with a sadness so deep it sucked at Avery's soul.

Avery pulled her thoughts from that long-ago day and focused on the four bowls spread out on the counter. That look in her mother's eyes had haunted her more than once—a shockingly clear streak of jealousy at the relationship she shared with Roman.

A sort of love her mother had been denied, yet had wanted with quiet desperation.

"The natives are restless." Grier came up behind her,

and Avery keyed back in to the noise coming from the small dining alcove in Mick's kitchen. "Can I help?"

"No, no, I'm good."

The bright smile on Grier's face fell as confusion narrowed her eyebrows. "Are you sure?"

"Yes." Avery painted on a bright smile, hoping it rivaled the sun. "I'm good."

"You okay?"

Avery looked up from the stack of dishes on the counter she was methodically loading into the dishwasher and smiled at Roman. "Sure. Why?"

"I don't know. You looked about a million miles away during dessert."

He saw it—that immediate urge to downplay something unpleasant—before a resigned look came over her face.

"I had a memory as I was putting dessert together. It just sort of stuck with me and left me a little melancholy."

"Was I there?"

"You were, but you probably don't remember it. There was a day, years ago, when I made strawberry shortcake for dinner when my mom and I had you over."

"I remember it."

Roman did remember that day. Had thought about that sad evening for years, in fact. It was the first time he saw the full extent of Alicia's problem.

And what Avery was living with.

Up until that time, he'd believed Avery when she

told him her mother was an alcoholic, but he hadn't really understood what she lived with. But that day, it was different. He'd seen how insidious Alicia's disease was. How it could ruin a perfectly nice dinner or sully a simple conversation.

"You do?"

"Yeah. You tasted delicious, as I recall." His grin faded as he summoned up the rest of the afternoon in his mind. "But your mom was off that day. Weird."

"She got really weird those last six months before you left." Avery's voice dropped. "After things got more serious between us."

"Do you think she was jealous?"

"I think she was a lot of things. Jealous was likely one of them."

"Did you call her on it?"

"I tried. I don't know. My whole life, I wanted to lash out at her, but the few times I had the chance to do it, I chickened out. She was weak, you know? And not just because of the liquor."

"How so?"

Avery closed the dishwasher and leaned against the counter. "It took me a long time to understand it. Liquor was the outward expression of my mom's weaknesses, but it wasn't the reason she was a weak person."

"Is that why you're not afraid to have a drink?"

"Probably. I like liquor. Have a healthy respect for it, obviously, since I also serve it as part of my job. And I'm also fine to ignore it. Grier and I had a glass of wine earlier, as we made dinner, and then I felt like a Coke with dinner. It's just there, you know. Fun at times, but not *necessary*." She shrugged and a harsh laugh escaped her lips. "My mother couldn't open a bottle of anything without emptying it."

"But you think she had other weaknesses?"

"I know she did. They made themselves known in lots of little ways. When she was still actively holding down a job she traveled on occasion. She came home from Anchorage on one trip, positively glowing about this guy she'd met."

"What happened?"

"He never called and she went into this massive depression. She couldn't get out of bed, Roman."

"She was lonely."

"I know that. And for a long time I accepted that as the reason why. But now I believe it was more. She couldn't process the world around her. Couldn't see it with clear eyes."

"Grief is a horrible thing."

"What grief? The way she mourned my father, you'd have thought they had a relationship for years instead of a few weeks' fling that ended as casually as it had started."

"Do you ever wonder about him?"

"As a kid I did, but not any longer. It's hard to miss something you've never had and he's just never been there. I do have a picture of him and, for me, that's been enough."

"Do you resent her?"

"I did. For a very long time, I resented her. And then I stopped resenting her and started living my life. I got more involved at work. Started doing some of those dopey things I put up on the website and planning travel packages for our guests."

"And going to Ireland."

"Yes."

Roman grabbed the mug of coffee he'd abandoned on the counter and took a sip, trying to gather his thoughts. "I think she'd be proud of you. And I'd like to think whatever jealousy and anger dogged her in her life is long gone, replaced with peace and understanding."

He didn't miss the hopeful flare that rose up in her deep brown eyes like a flame. "Do you really think so?"

"Yes, I do."

Her arms came around his waist and Roman tightened his to pull her close. He bent his head, taking her mouth with his in a gentle act designed to give warmth, understanding and comfort. Her lips opened under his, their tongues sliding together in that familiar mating that was as old as time, yet unique to Avery.

His Avery.

Roman pulled back and laid his forehead against hers, taking and giving support in the quiet moment between them. Unlike his friends, he'd found his match at a very young age.

Maybe he was finally old enough to understand it.

Roman was still thinking about Avery and their future as he borrowed his mother's car the following morning. He'd promised his grandmother he'd pick up some things for her in Anchorage and wanted to get everything delivered.

He pulled out of the Indigo Blue's parking lot and squinted in the bright sunlight coming through the windshield. The sun—and the subtle pain that laced his right eye as he squinted—was a vivid reminder that he needed to make some decisions.

And he *needed* to tell Avery.

Last night would have been the perfect time to tell her. They'd shared that quiet moment about her mother in the kitchen. It would have been the ideal time to tell her what was going on with his life.

So why had he held back?

Because you're not fucking perfect anymore.

The voice that had taunted him for months reared up and gave him a mental kick to the head, adding insult on top of his already irritated injury.

Roman deftly ignored it and tried to focus. He knew full well—when he got past the insecurity of it all—that he was incredibly fortunate. He had options and a future that wouldn't end when his hockey career did.

A lot of people didn't have that and—injury aside—he'd be foolish to think he was immune to the march of time any more than other people.

So why was he holding out on Avery?

The question coursed through his mind, like an errant puck that raced down the ice but stopped short of the goal.

Since he'd arrived at *his* goal—his grandmother's house—he decided he'd worry about it later. He had a practice session with the kids at the rink. He'd tell Avery about it after that. All of it—his future and his options—and discuss it with her.

Roman pulled the large box he'd picked up at the airport from the trunk and headed toward the front door. It was the perfect time, now that he thought about it. The hockey rink was the definition of his past and could possibly be the root of his future, if he took the broadcasting job. He also knew Avery needed to make some decisions on her job offer.

He juggled the heavy box and knocked on the door, his thoughts still playing over his imagined discussion with Avery. They could discuss their futures, there at the newly repaired rink. Could figure out what they both wanted and needed and see what options they had.

They *could* find a way.

He knew it.

With renewed confidence that he wouldn't have to say good-bye to Avery a second time, he knocked on his grandmother's door again, curious that she hadn't answered on his first knock.

When there was still no answer, he dug into his pocket for his mother's keys and unlocked the door.

"Grandma!"

His voice echoed down the long hall that led back to the kitchen and Roman headed that way, his concern increasing with each step.

Where was she?

Bright sunlight colored the back of the house with its morning rays and he again reached up to rub his right eye, the bright light sending a subtle throb into his eye socket.

It was the only reason, he realized moments later.

The only reason he didn't see his grandmother through the back screen door, her lips pressed firmly to Doc Cloud's.

Chapter Twenty-one

*J*ulia heard the loud thud of the screen door and it pulled her attention from Ken and their mind-bending kiss. A subtle irritation at the interruption flooded her veins until she looked up.

Straight into the eyes of her grandson.

"Roman! What a lovely surprise."

"What the hell is going on?"

She kept her smile bright as she stood and crossed the patio toward him, unwilling to admit to even the slightest twinge of embarrassment. She was an adult, for heaven's sake.

And thankfully both she and Ken were fully clothed.

"Would you care to join us for breakfast? I just put coffee on a few minutes ago."

She felt Ken's quiet strength in the steady hand he put at the small of her back and she sensed he wanted to say something, but was holding back. Reaching for him, she gave his hand a quick squeeze.

With brisk efficiency, she headed for the kitchen, all the while ignoring Roman's gaping mouth, and wasn't surprised when her grandson followed her.

"What is going on, Grandma?"

"You've got an imagination. Figure it out."

"That's all I get?"

"What do you want?"

"I want to know what the hell's going on."

"I'm seeing Ken."

Roman sputtered before recovering himself. "Define 'seeing.'"

"I hardly think that's an appropriate question, young man."

"You're my grandmother."

"Yes. And a grown woman. I'm entitled to a life."

"But—" He shook his head before turning to glance toward Ken through the window. "That's Doc Cloud."

"I know."

"And you're having a relationship with him?"

"I most certainly am."

"What do Mary and Sophie think about it?"

The question speared through her and Julia crossed her arms. She knew the pose was a classic defense mechanism, but she didn't care. "They don't know yet."

"Why not?"

"Because I wanted to enjoy it and keep it to myself for a few days."

"It just happened?"

"I think it's been building for years, but yes, we recently took things to the next level."

He winced at that and she almost regretted the words, until he spoke once more. "Well if it just started, you can end it just as easily."

"I'm not ending anything."

"You have to. You're a grown woman, for heaven's sake. What will people think?"

"Hopefully, they'll think how lucky I am to be so happy."

"Grandma. It's not decent. Did he sleep here?"

"It's perfectly decent." Julia felt the anger creeping up on her and realized she had no desire to hold it back. To take the polite route and keep the peace.

"*I'm* perfectly decent. And I'm in love. And I'm going to do whatever I please because that man is the best thing to happen to me in years. I'm just lucky he hasn't given up on me, waiting for me to come around."

Roman's jaw hardened and he glanced once more out the window before turning back to her. "He's been planning this?"

"He's been interested in me but he's been gentlemanly enough to give me space."

"I don't believe this."

"Why?"

"Because you're my grandmother."

"Don't you think I deserve it?"

Whatever anger fueled him faded at her question and, instead, she saw him practically slump before her. The broad shoulders that always looked so strong and solid seemed to shrink. "Of course you do."

"Then what is it? What's the matter?"

"Beyond the shock?"

She let out a hard sniff. "It's not that shocking."

"You're not the one who saw what I was looking at."

She couldn't resist poking at him. "I had the far better seat."

"You're still my grandmother. I don't know what to do with this."

"Don't do anything with it." The words were casual

but she knew it wasn't that simple. Roman's reaction might have been a bit extreme, but she'd give him a bit of leeway due to how he found out about them.

But others?

She knew others would have something to say about her and Ken's relationship. It was why she'd wanted to savor it for a few days before becoming the latest topic of the town grapevine.

"Why haven't you told Mary and Sophie?"

"They don't need to know when I sneeze."

"You're doing more than sneezing."

She couldn't hold back the triumphant smile. "I most certainly am."

"Okay." He held up his hands. "I need to leave."

"You don't want breakfast?"

"No."

She watched Roman walk to the large box he'd obviously dropped at the sight of her and Ken. He retrieved it before crossing back to place it on the counter.

"Thank you for bringing my things."

"You're welcome."

She'd nearly let him leave—was going to—before the urge to say one last thing stopped her. "Roman."

"Yeah?" He turned at the entryway to the kitchen.

"I'm happy."

"I know."

Avery blew hard on her whistle, ending the current ice drill. The clock had run down almost fifteen seconds ago but Roman missed it so she took it on herself to call the halt. Loud, jumbled shouts echoed off the bleachers as the kids yelled good-natured insults at each other.

"Take ten minutes and go get some water!"

After watching the boys race off to the water stations they'd set up at the far end of the rink, she skated over to Roman. "What's up with you today? Do you want to call practice short?"

"No."

She laid a hand on his arm, trying to break through whatever bad mood had taken hold of him. "What's wrong then? You've barely looked at the kids since they started the first drill."

"I walked in on my grandmother this morning."

Several images floated through her mind, but she figured he could only mean the obvious. "Was she naked?"

"Not at that particular moment."

"What did you walk in on then?"

"Her and Doc Cloud kissing on the back porch."

"Oh!" The image she had of Roman accidentally finding his grandmother naked shifted to something more interesting. And all-together wonderful.

"That's fantastic! I've been hoping for them."

"What's so fantastic about it?"

"They like each other."

"They're in their seventies."

The sheer stubbornness that set his face in hard lines had Avery pulling back. "So?"

"So it's weird. And a bad idea."

"There's nothing weird or bad about it."

"Oh don't pull that shit. You can't tell me you wouldn't find it odd to walk in on . . . on that."

"No."

"Liar."

"I mean, it's awkward to walk in on any couple having a private moment. But do I think it's weird that they were kissing? No. Not at all."

"What if he's taking advantage of her?"

"Your grandmother?" The idea of anyone taking advantage of Julia Forsyth was as outrageous as it was laughable. "Yeah. Right. Besides, it's Ken. He's just so awesome. I've really been hoping for them. I can't wait to call her and get all the details."

"You knew about this?"

"No. But I've had an idea he likes her and I kept hoping he'd get his butt in gear and find a way to let her know."

"Why didn't you tell me?"

"Tell you what?"

The long-suffering sigh that greeted her was as melodramatic as the kids' complaints when she'd made them run another drill. "That Ken likes my grandmother. I could have talked to him."

Anger sparked under her skin at the continued evidence of his stubborn, pig-headed reaction. While she'd grant him the surprising nature of how he found them, his blindness to the fact that his grandmother had the normal, healthy, human urge to love a man and be loved by that man in return wasn't negotiable.

"You can stop being an asshole about it anytime."

"I'm not."

"Oh come on, Roman. She's more than able to make her own decisions."

"But—" He broke off and she didn't miss the rising anger that matched hers.

"What's really bothering you?"

"Nothing."

"Then why are you acting like an ass?"

"You don't understand."

"Obviously."

Before she could press him or try to get to the bottom of his snit, he shoved off the boards and skated toward the kids, his whistle blowing in three hard, sharp bursts. The kids scrambled onto the ice at the urgent summons and if it weren't for the fact that they needed a second chaperone to keep watch, she'd have left until Roman calmed down. Instead, she skated toward the water station in an attempt to cool off.

A few moments later, she had a large paper cup of water in hand and enjoyed the cold, smooth slide down her throat.

Julia and Ken?

It was about damn time.

She'd had a sense about the two of them. Had even tried to probe at Julia a time or two about her personal life, always to bump up against a gentle wall, full of No Trespassing signals.

Avery was thrilled to think that Roman's grandmother—a woman so wonderful and so deserving of love and companionship—had finally found someone. And as she thought about it, she realized she felt the same way for Doc Cloud. He was a lovely man—gentle and competent, sweet and dependable.

They made a great match.

Avery risked a glance at Roman again. His bad mood still emanated off him in waves, but he'd started to run a drill with the kids and she could only hope the physical activity would help matters.

Yeah, coming in on his grandmother was a little shocking, but it wasn't like she went on a massacre down Main Street. She was in love with a good man. That was something worth celebrating, not being angry about.

Turning back to the ice, Avery watched Roman play. The same serious expression he'd worn at seventeen still etched across his face as he went in for a tough one-on-one or when he broke out of the pack, driving the puck down the ice.

She didn't miss the expression on the kids' faces, either, as they all parted to the side and watched Mike and Roman skate down the ice. Ronnie's kid brother had an ocean of potential and it was easy to see now that he was matched with someone of Roman's skill and ability.

The two of them raced down the ice, headed straight for the goal in front of where she sat. Electricity and excitement suddenly filled the rink as youth and eagerness met age and experience. Roman had the kid beat, but he was breathing hard as they paced next to each other.

And then a huge shout went up as Mike sneaked in, his stick grabbing hold of the puck and catching a skate in the process. Roman went flying, his body off the ice and in the air for what felt like an hour before he landed flat on his back.

"Roman!"

His large body lay still on the ice as Avery leaped off

the bench and raced toward him. The boys circled around them, and without thinking, she started barking orders.

"Stink. Go get my phone and call Doc Cloud. The number's in there."

The kid nodded and raced off before she turned toward Brock. "Go get the clean towels next to the equipment bag and the first-aid kit."

Roman tried to sit up as she knelt down next to him. "Oh no, hang on there, big man."

"It's fucking cold down here, Avery. I'm fine."

"Hold still." She pressed on his shoulders, surprised to feel him pushing back against her so hard.

"I said I'm fine. Let me up."

She gestured for the kids to move back and give him room. "Fine. Get your stubborn ass up."

The motion had the exact effect she expected. No sooner was he on his feet than he stumbled to a knee. She briefly thought about a concussion but was worried he'd do more damage to himself if he were agitated.

"Let's get him up and over to the benches."

Avery skated slowly behind the boys, who helped Roman to the bleachers, then took the requested towels and first-aid kit from Brock as they got Roman settled.

"I'm so sorry, Mr. Forsyth. Really, I am." Mike's anxious face peered over a few pairs of shoulders, his blue eyes darting back and forth with worry.

"It's fine, Mike. I'm fine." Roman brushed it off, but it did nothing to allay Avery's fears, especially now that the blood ran freely down his cheek from a large gash in his forehead.

Avery gently pressed one of the towels against the

gash, reaching for his hand once she had it firmly in place. "Hold this here for a minute."

Roman nodded and it was enough to have her turning toward the boys. "Why don't you guys move back a bit? Maybe go change out of your gear."

A chorus of agreement met her as the kids moved back onto the ice.

Mike hovered a few extra moments and Avery looked at him with what she hoped was a gentle smile. "His head's harder than you think, sweetie. He's going to be fine."

"I'm really sorry."

"You were playing hard. Nothing to be sorry about." Roman's words were quiet, but firm, as he looked at the kid. "You did nothing wrong."

"Oh . . . okay." Mike nodded. "I'll just go get cleaned up then."

Avery opened the kit as the boys skated away and snagged a packet of gauze and some antiseptic. "I don't know much but I do know you should only be seeing one of me."

"I see one of you."

She held up two fingers. "How many fingers?"

"Jeez, Avery. I'm fine."

"Humor me then, because I'm not."

"Two. You've got two fingers up." He lifted a hand to steady her shaking hand. "I'm fine. Really."

"I realize you've got the four-inch gash, but you weren't the one who watched you go flying several feet off the ice."

His smile was lopsided as he looked up at her. "Not my first rodeo."

She ripped open the packet of gauze. "I think it was Mike's. The kid's shaken up."

"He'll get over it. This happens." That grin spread to a full smile before he winced at the movement. "And when he does, I'm quite sure the story will involve him kicking my ass."

"It's a rite of passage."

"Exactly."

Hands steadier at the evidence he could think into the future, she wadded the gauze over an open bottle of antiseptic, soaking the cloth. "This is going to sting. Close your eyes."

She pressed lightly on the still-bleeding wound, nearly dropping the gauze when his knee knocked into hers as his entire body went still. "Fuck, that hurts."

"Which probably means it's working. Ice is dirty."

"Thanks for the medical wisdom, Florence Nightingale."

She ignored the sarcasm and painted a heavy dose of Neosporin over the wound. Thankfully, he wasn't bleeding as profusely, and she could see the wound didn't look nearly as bad cleaned up.

"Here. Press this new gauze over it and Doc Cloud can fix the rest."

"I'm sure I'm the last person he wants to see."

"Probably so."

Avery pulled some tape from the box and fastened the new gauze over the wound. It was a crude fix, but as she put on the last piece of tape, she was satisfied it would hold.

"That was quite a spill."

"Mike's faster than he looks."

"You're no slouch, Roman, despite having almost twenty years on the kid. What really happened?"

"He got the jump on me. There's a lot of energy in those decades I'm spotting him."

"No, I don't think that's it at all." Avery moved and took the seat next to him. "You can keep downplaying it all you want, but there's something wrong. I was watching you. You never saw the kid."

Avery's words echoed in his ears, and in the ringing void, Roman knew his moment of truth had arrived.

"No, I didn't."

"Even though he was right next to you."

"Even then. I knew he was physically there, but I never saw his stick move."

"Why not?"

Roman took a deep breath as the words lodged in his throat in a heavy lump. "I had a big injury late in the season."

"The one against Buffalo."

"Yep."

"I thought you were fine."

A hard, bitter laugh inched out around the lump. "I've been telling everyone I was fine. My right eye has other ideas."

He stared out over the ice, the familiar look of the rink a taunting reminder of all he'd lost. The scent of ice and sweat surrounded him and for the first time since his injury, he felt close to tears.

"What's wrong?"

"I have no peripheral vision in that eye. And the likelihood of it coming back is slim."

"Oh my God. Roman." Her hand gripped his. "Why

haven't you told me? Us? Does your mom know? Your grandmother?"

"Nope. No one. I wanted to see if it came back and there was no reason to get everyone upset."

"You can't play anymore."

"Thanks for the news flash, Ave."

"I mean it. If you're this at risk in practice, you're going to get killed in a game. You're lucky you haven't already."

He knew there was concern underlying her words—he felt it in the tight grip she had on his hand and the way she rubbed his lower back with her free hand.

But in that moment, he couldn't have cared less.

"Thanks for the fucking pep talk."

"What?"

He stood, the anger growing even hotter as a flash of nausea welled in his stomach at the sudden movement.

"I'm well aware of my options, sweetheart. They're figuratively crystal clear, even if I can't fucking see them."

"Roman. What's wrong with you?" Hurt widened her dark eyes into large saucers but his own hurt and anger and frustration was so huge he couldn't pull himself back.

Or calm down.

"You have no idea. What it's like to lose something like this."

"I don't know about loss?"

"Not loss like this."

The hurt mutated—transformed in an instant—and she was on her feet, her fists clenched at her sides. "Don't tell me I don't know what it's like to lose something. I'm sorry you're going through this and I'm sorry this is how you're going to end your career, but whatever you do, don't stand there and tell me I don't know about loss."

"It's not the same."

"Not the same?" Her voice edged up a few octaves as it echoed off the metal bleachers. "The day you left here I might as well have lost a body part it hurt so bad. Whether physical or emotional, loss is loss."

"I have no future."

"If you truly believe that you're a bigger ass than I've ever given you credit for."

"You don't understand."

"No, Roman. *You* don't understand."

Avery felt the anger recede from her body, like water down a drain, as it was replaced with something empty and cold.

Indifference.

She'd spent years upset over losing Roman— wondering if she could have made different choices. Done something different.

No more.

"The human experience includes loss, Roman. It also includes heartbreak, death and sadness. You've tried to ignore that for fourteen years."

"I haven't ignored anything."

"Oh no? Expensive gifts? Rare visits? How would you define your behavior?"

"I've had a life."

"An empty one, if all you've said in the last week is any indication."

"It's my life. My choices."

She nodded, the underlying truth of his words harsh. "Yes."

"You don't understand. You didn't grow up with a ticking clock."

"Life has a clock."

"Not like mine." He shook his head and she saw him search for the words, his face a hard mask.

"No one tells you what professional athletics are like. They're the holy grail. The brass ring. They're also terrifying."

"That's true of any profession. You think I wasn't nervous at the conference?"

"But in your case, each year brings more experience. More wisdom. Makes you better."

"You're better now than you were in your twenties."

"And I'm also worse."

Avery sensed that understanding whatever he was trying to say was important, so she left off with the questions.

"Do you know I peaked professionally at twenty-eight?" His hands clenched on his knees and his eyes misted as bitter memories rose up in his gaze. "That was the year I skated the fastest. Had the lowest body fat. Had the quickest reaction time. Every year after that has been a decline."

"You're still considered at the top of your game."

"I know myself and I know I'm not. So I work harder, run harder, play harder, all in hopes of outrunning the inevitable."

"Growing up is hard, Roman. And it's not like people tell you it will be."

He turned to look at her. "What do they tell you?"

"That it's a fairy tale. That there's some magic happy-ever-after and we'll only find it if we find the right job or find the right person or find the right place to live. But there isn't. There's just life, day by day. And we have to make the most of those days."

Avery took a deep breath and realized that was the real lesson her mother had taught her. No matter what pain and suffering Alicia had lived with, she'd never allowed herself to come out the other side.

Had never counted her blessings or enjoyed the good things in her life.

She'd only focused on the pain.

Roman stared at his skates before looking back up to meet her gaze. "I don't know who I am if I'm not a hockey player."

Avery thought she'd erected a wall around her heart, saving her from the fear of losing him again.

But in his words, she heard the truth.

"I know who you are. I've always known who you are. But if you don't know I can't fix that for you."

She stood up and turned to look at him. Her heart broke in half, so like that day so many years ago when she watched his plane lift off at the airstrip.

Yet, the pain was sharper. Deeper.

And full of the knowledge that they were beyond fixing anything.

"You're Roman Forsyth. You're a son and grandson. You're bright and funny and you see the world with a kindness that is rare in many people. You have a physical gift to play a game, but it's really a small part of you. You're good with kids. In fact, you're good with people. And you're loved, Roman. By all those people

I just named." She bent down and pressed a kiss on his lips. "And by me."

"Ave."

She stood to her full height and looked down at him. "I've loved you always. Before I even understood what it was, I loved you. But I love me, too. And I won't spend my life worrying if I'm enough to make you happy."

Chapter Twenty-two

*R*oman winced at the pull of the thread as Doc Cloud stitched up his forehead. "You okay?"

Physically, he knew he'd live. *Emotionally?* Roman thought. That was an entirely different matter.

"I'm numb. I can still feel the tugging, though."

"I'm nearly done."

Ken's normally easy manner was nowhere in evidence as he moved around his office with a cold, clinical efficiency.

"I'm sorry about this morning."

Ken didn't say anything as he reached for a small pair of scissors and snipped off the edge of the stitches. Nor did he say anything as he reached for a fresh bandage and took the time to cover up the wound.

The silence was unnerving but Roman refused to say anything else. It seemed nothing that came out of his mouth was acceptable any longer and the apology was all he had left in him today.

"I want to check your vision."

"All right."

Ken moved back to a long metal counter and grabbed a small light as he turned off the overheads.

Roman submitted to the test, following the small point of light, following Ken's index finger and finally reading a series of letters, decreasing in size, off the eye chart.

"This is the secret you've been hiding?"

"Yep."

"How long?"

Roman shrugged. "A few months. It was the Buffalo game late in the season."

Ken nodded, his expression sober. "Has any of your peripheral come back?"

"Not really."

"What does your doctor at home say?"

"He doubts it will."

"And they keep clearing you to play?"

Roman swallowed hard. "I've downplayed the problem. And my doctor's been understanding enough to cut me a bit of slack."

"That's unacceptable."

"It's professional sports. He wasn't clearing me for this coming year, but he gave me a bit of a pass for the play-offs. Told me a few ways to overcompensate if I needed it."

"You could have gotten hurt. Your head's hard, but the ice is harder."

It was clear nothing would erase Ken's professional ire, so once again, Roman shut his mouth.

Ken crossed the room and flipped the switch. The bright wash of light had Roman wincing and the move was enough to have the slash of the good doctor's mouth turning down once more. "Light sensitivity, too?"

"Only when it's that big a contrast."

"Roman. You can't play any longer. You know that, don't you?"

As Roman stared into the kind brown eyes he'd known for a lifetime, the truth of his fucked-up life came crashing down around his head.

"Yeah. I do know."

"So why are you fighting it?"

"Because I don't know how to be anything else."

Ken shot up out of his rolling stool and paced the room. "That's bullshit and you know it."

The sudden outburst—so unlike the man—had more impact than a swift punch. "Avery's opinion is similar."

"Your profession doesn't define you. I know you're smarter than to think otherwise."

"Hockey gave my life a purpose."

"If you believe that, then you've let the game define you." Ken reached for a folder on the desk, ripping a sheet off the top that was secured by a paper clip. "Here're your papers to check out. Melissa will take care of you at the front."

At the door to the exam room, Ken turned around. "I do have a prescription for you."

Roman glanced up at that. "For what?"

"It's a single dose, from one old fool to a young one. I love Julia. Have for damn near half my life. And I've been a raging moron to wait so long to tell her. I'd hate to see you make the same mistake. You might not be so lucky to find a woman as understanding or patient as your grandmother."

*   *   *

Avery walked through the empty halls of the Indigo Blue, taking stock of each room as she walked past. The large conference room stood empty, the chairs all placed neatly around the long oval table. The lights were off and she smiled to herself at the image of how messy the room had been the previous tax season as Grier set up shop with Chooch and Hooch.

She moved on, passing the dining room they used for meals. The light scent of bacon and French toast wafted toward her as she took in the gleaming silver chafing dishes that stood in a row along the back serving station, clean and waiting for the next morning's breakfast. Each chair was pushed in around the room's tables and a fresh placemat and set of wrapped silverware waited for the next guest to sit down.

She'd chosen those placemats and the silver napkins that went with them. Had selected the framed pictures on the far wall and had encouraged Susan to invest in the coffee machine at the back so guests could get themselves a late-night cappuccino or espresso.

The hallway to the gym and sauna beckoned to her right but she kept on walking, the thought of going back to where things had begun once again with Roman too hard to bear at the moment.

Even now, days later, she could feel the touch of his fingers on her body. Could imagine herself in his arms, the lost years between them fading into nothingness.

She unlocked the door to her apartment, her thoughts still firmly in the hallway. Everything was here, at the Indigo Blue. All her memories, both good and bad.

Her life, in a series of images that flashed through her head on a photo reel.

Could she give it all up and move to L.A.?

Could she afford not to?

Roman nursed his beer at the bar. Where he'd enjoyed a series of good-natured hellos everywhere he'd gone in the past week, the patrons at Maguire's were giving him a large berth.

Good.

He wanted company about as much as he wanted a root canal, and the thought of casual conversation ranked even lower.

"You want another?" Ronnie stood on the other side of the bar, his austere expression making it more than clear that small talk was equally untenable to him.

"Yep."

A fresh beer appeared a few moments later and Roman reached for it, mindless to the light noise and lingering joviality around him.

He had fucked up.

Avery deserved better. His grandmother deserved better. Hell, *he* deserved better, and he knew it.

So why couldn't he get his head out of his ass for more than two minutes and make the decisions that needed to be made?

A few women came up to him a short while later and asked for an autograph. He couldn't place them, as he'd been gone when they grew up, but he could have sworn Avery babysat one of them. He scribbled out a few autographs on napkins, gave them both a quick smile and turned back to the bar.

Roman knew the gesture was rude, but in addition to avoiding small talk, he had no interest in flirting with women half his age.

He never had.

"Heard my brother kicked your ass today." Ronnie laid another fresh beer on the bar, whisking away the second empty.

"He's good."

"I know he is. I think he can get a scholarship."

Roman nodded. This was something he knew. Something he could talk about without second-guessing himself. "Where's he looking?"

"He hasn't made up his mind so I keep telling him to see what the scouts say and make his decision then."

"I can talk to a few people. Let them know a trip up here is more than worth their time."

The hard glint in Ronnie's eye softened. "Thanks."

A shouted order pulled Ronnie away and he walked down the bar toward a couple of guys who came in. A few minutes later they took the seats next to Roman. "You're Roman Forsyth."

"Yeah."

"You had a great season."

"Thanks." Roman smiled. It wasn't his Hollywood special, but it was far more gracious and kind than he felt.

"What happened to you?"

He'd blessedly forgotten his bandaged head wound and the whole thing came barreling back. "Accident at the rink."

"Heard you've been playing with the kids."

"Yep."

"Some of 'em are pretty good."

Roman nodded. "Some of them are."

"Glad you got the rink back in shape."

The ire he hadn't quite gotten rid of exploded like a hot pan that you fling away when you finally feel the burn. "Not sure why you all needed me to come home to fix such a fucking disgrace."

The guy nearest him put his beer down as his eyes widened. "You got a problem?"

"Yeah, I do. That rink was a mess yet this entire town let the kids play on it for years and years. What if someone had gotten hurt? What if a visiting team had gotten hurt?"

"It's fine now, buddy."

"No, that's the problem, *buddy*." Roman emphasized the words. "It's not fine. Not to me."

Ronnie must have noticed the fight brewing because he was around the bar and Roman felt his hands on his arm. "Why don't you get out of here, Roman? I know Doc Cloud gave you a pretty heavy dose of sedatives for that head."

He'd taken none of them but Ronnie's words had their desired effect. Whatever irritation rode the bar patrons' features faded at the news their town legend might not be feeling quite himself.

"I'm fine."

"Still. Why don't you let me get you out of here for a few minutes. You can go get some coffee at the diner or something."

Although he had about four inches on Ronnie, the kid was solid. Roman also knew you didn't tend bar and not learn how to take care of yourself.

"Come on. This round's on me."

"Fine." Roman shook off his hands but walked out of the bar through the back entrance a few feet away. He'd nearly walked away—knew he needed to walk away—when he turned on Ronnie in the back parking lot.

"You like her. Why the fuck won't you ask her out?"

Before Ronnie could even answer—his slack jaw and widened eyes evidence he knew exactly who the "she" was—Roman had his fist headed for the guy's face.

A combination of the beer and the still-fuzzy eyesight on his right side had him grazing the punch and Ronnie came back swinging. Roman felt the hit to his jaw before he stumbled backward and landed against the wall.

"Fuck, that felt good." Ronnie stood across from him, his arm still up.

"Good?" Whatever fight was in him faded at the broad grin that split Ronnie's face. "And what the fuck are you smiling about?"

"First my brother gets the jump on you and now me. I'd call this a pretty good day."

"Asshole." Roman spit out a small mouthful of blood. The hit was more irritating than painful, especially compared to the hits he took in a game. "What'd you do that for?"

"You really need to ask?"

"I punched first, I know."

"Oh hell, that's not why. You have the best thing walking completely in love with you and you're pissing it away."

"She deserves better than me."

"She probably does."

Roman winced at that, the words more painful than the hit to his jaw.

"And for the record, I did ask her out. The other day at the picnic."

"Oh." Memories of that day and how upset she was when she left flashed in Roman's mind. "I take it she said no."

"Yep. Flat out, but she was nice about it."

"That has to hurt."

"It does, but it's what I needed to hear."

"There seems to be a lot of that going around."

Roman didn't miss Ronnie's puzzled gaze before he pushed himself off the wall and extended his hand. "Thanks for the beer. And the ass kicking."

"I didn't kick your ass."

Roman smiled—his first easy one of the day as he gripped Ronnie's hand. "No, but by the time you're done telling the story, you will have."

Ronnie's gaze softened and a wicked grin played the corners of his mouth. "So my brother didn't really get the jump on you?"

"If that's the story the kid wants to tell, who am I to ruin a dream?"

Roman walked off, satisfied he'd slightly redeemed himself.

Avery opened the door, only half surprised to see Roman. A part of her had expected he'd come. And the other half had wondered if he'd simply avoid saying anything.

"What happened to you?"

"I fell on the ice."

"I mean the fresh bruise on your face. That wasn't from earlier." She gestured him into her apartment before she turned and headed for the kitchen and an ice pack.

"Ronnie."

She turned halfway to the kitchen. "You fought with Ronnie?"

"*Fought* isn't quite the right word."

On a shake of her head, Avery continued on for the freezer. When she came back with the ice pack, wrapped in a towel, she slapped it into Roman's outstretched hand. "Define it for me, then."

"He was attempting to save me from myself."

"Too late." Avery heard her voice—dry as day-old toast—and realized she didn't care how she sounded. She was still pissed.

And hurt.

About the secret of his injury. And even more hurt by the wall that had suddenly sprung up between them when they'd made so much progress toward tearing it down ever since he'd come home.

"When did this get so hard, Avery?"

"When you made it hard."

He turned to look at her, his eyes going wide. "Me?"

"Yeah. You. This isn't rocket science, Roman. It's life, and while it's got its challenges, it's not always as hard as we make it."

"I love you. I've always loved you. You have to know that."

"I do. And I love you, too. I just wonder if it's enough."

"It has to be."

His mouth came down over hers as he flung the ice pack onto the floor. His hand and cheek were cold where both pressed against her face but she ignored it as the familiar heat and passion flared up between them.

She opened her mouth to kiss him, the quick slide of his tongue sending an immediate shot of lust spiraling toward her core.

This worked.

The physical they'd figured out long ago and it was a familiar pattern to fall back into.

Why was the rest so damn hard?

As she wrapped her arms around his neck, Avery promised herself she'd deal with it later. After.

For now, she wanted to give and receive in the only way they seemed to make any sense.

Roman wrapped his arms around her waist and pulled them both backward toward her bedroom. The need to sink into her and forget all the bullshit that clouded his mind rode him as he whipped off the shirt and shorts she wore.

They moved into the bedroom and Roman felt the bed brush the backs of his legs. Avery's hands had already fisted the material of his T-shirt and he felt her draw it up his body and over his head.

"Your pants. And hurry."

"Bossy." He nipped a quick kiss on her lips before complying, toeing off his sneakers before the jeans.

"Absolutely."

Her hands dove for the waistband of his briefs, and a hard moan rose up in his throat as her hand wrapped around his cock.

"Avery."

"Mmmmm." She kissed him again, her open mouth hot and wicked as she pleasured him with her hands.

With a firm hold on her shoulders, he pulled her toward the bed. "We're taking this trip together."

"It's not like I'm across the room."

He smiled at her as they lay face-to-face on the bed. "That's not what I meant."

Her dark, laughing eyes turned serious. "So what did you mean?"

"I'll show you."

Rolling forward, he pressed a soft kiss to her lips as his hand drifted down her cheek, over the arch of her neck until his fingers ran along the ridge of her collarbone. "So soft."

He continued his gentle exploration of her skin, the light play of their lips, teeth and tongue an increasingly hot counterpoint to the gentle caresses.

The urge to make love to her was strong, but the urge to savor her was equally powerful.

And no matter how many times he touched her, Roman couldn't banish the thought that this might be the last opportunity he ever received to do so.

The sensual moments spun out, one after the other, as the late-night sun streamed through the windows. Roman saw the various colors—deep reds and golds that bathed Avery's skin in a warm glow—and for the first time in a long time, he had clarity.

She was the only woman he would ever love. And

he loved her with a madness that haunted the very deepest parts of him.

And it was because of that love that he had to let her go. Had to give her the chance to see the world and live her life freely and not be tethered to him and his choices.

Even if he took the broadcasting job, he'd miss out on hundreds of days a year, spending so much time on the road. And his evenings would be filled with commitments. That was no life for her.

And it was no way for two people who'd spent their adult lives apart to get reacquainted.

"Roman?"

Her voice was a quiet whisper as she moved on top of him and straddled his hips. With easy movements, she lowered herself onto him, her body sheathing his with tight warmth.

"Are you ready?"

He nodded, the demands of his body quickly overtaking the questions that wrapped his mind in knots.

"Yes."

The long, lithe lines of her body called to him and he ran his hands over her, eager to touch her as they both pushed onward toward their pleasure. Her fingers clutched at his shoulders and he felt the imprint of her touch like a brand.

He lifted his hips harder—more urgently—desperate to make the moment last.

Frantic that they both find fulfillment.

He felt her response first and nearly came as her body clenched around him, but he held on. Willed himself to make it last for her, as if each moment could bind them more tightly to the memory.

More tightly to each other.

Something that would last, even after they were both gone from each other's lives.

Chapter Twenty-three

*R*oman left Avery sleeping several hours later. After slipping back into his clothes, he slipped out of her apartment, restless and looking to clear his head.

He'd never done bittersweet well and he knew it.

The thought of going to his own room was even less enticing, so he headed for the front office and a stack of books he'd seen on a shelf there. If nothing else, a thriller might keep him mindlessly entertained.

The light to the office was on, as it usually was, but he was surprised to see his mother sitting at her desk, fingers tapping away on the keyboard to her computer.

"Mom."

"Hi, sweetie." She looked up and smiled before she pushed the keyboard away and came around the desk. "What happened to you?"

He realized he'd not seen her since the accident earlier. "A little mishap at the rink. Doc Cloud sewed me up."

Her fingers were on his chin as she turned his face right and left. "You've got a cut and a bruise on the opposite side of your face."

"The eye happened at the rink. The jaw at Maguire's. In a fight."

"Roman Andrew Forsyth. What's wrong with you?"

"A freaking boatload, Mom. But that's probably not what you were asking." At her not so subtle grimace he nodded toward the door. "Can we go sit out there in the chairs? They're more comfortable. I need to talk to you."

He followed her to the lobby bar and one of the large, cushioned chairs that served as a conversation area.

"I'll make some coffee and will be right over."

It was a while later—their coffee mugs long empty—that Susan finally nodded at him and spoke up. "Why didn't you tell me about your sight?"

"I kept hoping it would come back. And if it came back, then it never was a problem to begin with."

"You knew it wasn't coming back." The words had a hard, clipped edge to them.

"I hoped."

"No, Roman. I think you knew all along."

"So what if I did. It's the first real threat to my playing."

"I think you're forgetting age." Her harsh tone gentled and she added a small smile, he thought, to remove the sting.

"Yeah, but that's always been in the distant future. My eye is an immediate problem. One day I was fine and the next I lost twenty percent functionality on one side of my body."

"So what are you going to do about it?"

"There's a broadcasting job I've been offered. It's

based in L.A. but they're happy to let me keep living in New York if I want to."

"You and Avery can still be together if you take it and choose to live in L.A."

"Mom. That's not going to happen."

"Sure it is. Especially if you're in the same city."

Roman stared into his empty mug, wondering how to make his mother understand. "That's the problem. We won't be in the same city. The job involves nearly as many days on the road as I am now. More, even, because at least now I have home games. I'll be out on the road, covering games, most of the year."

"But when you're home, you'll both be home in the same place. I have to tell you, it makes it a lot easier for me to give her up knowing you'll be there with her."

His mother's bright smile and oddly serene look struck a nerve and, just like the rink discussion earlier in the bar, he had no ability to dam up the emotions that came next. Why did she see everything between him and Avery as some sort of fairy tale? "Why won't you listen to me about this?"

"About what?"

"Avery and me. It's not happening. We can't make it work."

"Why not?"

"We've been apart too long and we can't put us back together."

"You've been doing just fine the last week."

"Sex isn't fine, Mom. It's just sex."

Her eyes widened at his terse response and the apology sprang quickly to his lips. "I'm sorry. That was crude. You know she's more than that to me. But it's not something I should be discussing with my mother and I'm sorry."

Roman looked at his mother—really looked—as she nodded, accepting his apology. While still attractive and relatively young to have children in their midthirties, she was beginning to look her age. The lines around her eyes were more pronounced and there was a hesitation to her movements that hadn't been there in the past.

It saddened him. Not because he thought she was old, but because the lines were a visible reminder of all he'd missed.

And what he was still going to miss.

"I'm not staying, Mom." When she only stared at him, he kept on. "Here. In Indigo. It's not my home and it hasn't been for a long time."

"You think I don't know that?"

The ethereal hopefulness that had possessed her like some demented fairy morphed into a very real anger as tears welled in her eyes. "I've supported you all your life, Roman. Believed in you and understood that your dream wasn't here, in Indigo. I've done the same for your sister. But I won't sit here and act like I'm happy while watching you throw away something good and worthy."

"It's not your decision to make."

"I'm not suggesting it is. But I'm also not going to sit idly by and keep my mouth shut. I've suffered loss, Roman. I know what it is to lose someone you love more than your own life. And now I'm sitting here, watching you voluntarily give up that same love. Why won't you fight for it?"

"It's not the same."

"It's exactly the same. Only in the case of your father, I lost him to something out of my control. You have a choice."

Avery was up when he got back to her apartment. The conversation with his mother, while strained, was productive and Roman was pleased to feel the heavy burden of keeping his injury a secret lifting from his shoulders.

It didn't change the decisions he needed to make, but sharing the burden did make it easier to think clearly.

Avery looked up from where she read a book on the couch, her legs tucked up under her. "I thought you went to your room."

"I was headed that way. I guess we're on the same wavelength. Thought I'd get a book from the lobby and I found my mom instead."

"And?" Avery set the book aside and he winced inwardly as she cracked the spine.

"And she knows about my eye. The end of my season. All of it."

"What'd she say?"

"After she drubbed me for not telling her?"

"That's a given."

"She's convinced you and I are going to live happily every after."

Her eyebrows shot up at that. "She said that?"

"Not in so many words, but it's my takeaway." He crossed the room and took a seat next to her on the couch. His pulse began a heavy throb as everything he wanted to say—everything he needed to share with her—welled up inside him. "She said if we both take jobs in L.A. we'll be near each other. We can be together."

"We can."

"And then we can pick up where we left off."

"Like we have been?"

The words were deceptively innocent, but Roman heard warning bells loud and clear hidden in their meaning. "That's what she seems to think."

"What about what you think?"

All the fear and anxiety he felt for his future poured out. "I think we're fooling ourselves if we think our little Alaskan oasis of travel and sex and living ripe on the town grapevine is going to be anything like starting two brand-new careers in a strange city. That is, of course, if either of us even wants the jobs that have been offered to us."

"What if we both want the jobs that have been offered to us?"

He turned to stare at her, the probing words pressing into him like a battering ram. "You want the job?"

"You didn't answer my question."

"What? You don't have some thoughts on the matter? Why's it all what I think?"

"Because I think you've already made up your mind and I haven't. Because I think you're hoping I'll let you off the hook by being the one to make the choice."

"What hook?"

"The one that says you have to step up and take responsibility for what you want, Roman. And accept that what you want—while very valid and very important—has an impact on others. You need to talk about it with me. That's part of a healthy adult relationship and not travel and sex and grapevines."

He cringed as his own words were flung back at him.

And then he did the dumbest thing he'd ever done in his entire life.

For the man who lived calculating angles and odds that came down to the briefest of moments—most often with great success—he took a shot he knew he had no hope of making.

"That's handy. Now I'm the bad guy."

"That's not what I said."

"It's implied. I was the shit all those years ago and now it's up to me to do it again."

The almost serene façade cracked as she leapt from the couch. "That's fucking bullshit and you know it! What have you missed about the last two weeks? The fact that I not only forgive you, but I've also come to understand you made the only choice that was right for both of us?"

"That was fourteen years ago."

"I get that. So why are you so damned interested in repeating history? We've got a chance to start fresh. To begin anew. Don't you want that?"

"I already got what I wanted. I got a career that was all about me, four thousand miles away from home. I don't have a right to make the choices anymore."

"Why can't you accept the forgiveness that's been given to you? What happened in the past doesn't change your right to an opinion now. What. Do. You. Want?"

"Hockey's all I've ever known. The job is tailor-made for me."

He saw her gaze shoot toward the ceiling as if asking for divine relief before it settled back on him with a feverish intensity. "So you want L.A."

"Yes." The agreement popped out and he didn't even choke on it, even as the simple acquiescence burned on his tongue.

"Then you need to accept the job."

"What are you going to do?"

"Accept the job."

"So we're agreed."

"On what?"

Cold seeped into his body, as if he lay flat on his back on the ice, as he fought the panic that rose up at her words. "On moving to California."

"You mean together? Like two people who want to share their life with each other."

"Isn't that what you want?"

"I did until we started this asinine discussion."

"What changed your mind?"

Avery crossed the room toward him and he watched as the light framed her face, before she leaned over and pressed her lips to his before standing back up. "You, Roman. You changed my mind. You're talking about your future. And deep down inside, I don't think you're ready to have me in it."

He reached for her hands but she pulled away.

"I think you should leave."

That seeping cold began to blow through his body on a harsh, driving winter wind. "Avery. Come on. We can figure this out."

"We already did." She walked to her bedroom and stood inside the doorframe. "You need to go now."

"You're really leaving? Even before Sloan and Walker get back?"

Avery glanced up from where she folded a dress into her suitcase. Grier sat on the edge of her bed, folding and unfolding a pair of slacks. "I'll be back in a few weeks. I just need to get to L.A. for a week of meetings. I'll come back after and wrap some things up here."

"I can't believe you really took the job."

"Yep."

"So why don't you seem happier about it?"

"Of course I'm happy about it."

"What did Susan say?"

"She's excited for me. Says she wants what's best. We haven't said much else."

"Maybe because you've been hiding in your room for two days."

"I'm not hiding."

Liar, liar, pants on fire, her conscience taunted her. Loudly.

"Or not much. I have a lot of preparation to do. I've been going through things and thinking about what I want to take and what I want to leave behind. And these were my days off anyway, so it's not like I'm shirking my hotel responsibilities."

"Aren't you upset about Roman?"

The busywork she'd used to avoid facing Grier faded as she stilled and looked into her friend's concerned gaze. "I'm very upset. But I'm not crying about it anymore. I've already grieved once. It's not necessary the second time around."

"Mick said Roman went to L.A. the other day."

"Yep. He's got a job offer. My guess is he's there to formally accept it."

"He's switching teams?"

"Not exactly."

On a sigh, Avery patted the bed and took a seat. "A lot's happened in the last few days. Let me catch you up."

Roman shook hands over the table as he and Ray, his agent, stood up from lunch. "You're making the right choice, Roman. It's a good choice. Although I wish you'd have told me about the eye."

"I keep getting a lot of that."

"Rightfully so. You could have gotten hurt a lot worse or you could have tanked a big play-off play."

Wouldn't want that, now would we?

He knew Ray saw his career in strictly professional terms—and knew that's why they worked together—so Roman held back the barb, instead focusing in the present. "Bill at SNN seems like a straight shooter."

"And he's got a career plan for you. That matters and they don't do offers like this unless they're serious."

At Ray's hopeful gaze, Roman nodded. "Have the paperwork drawn up. I'll be in Alaska through the end of next week and then headed back to New York."

"Which brings us to our next big hurdle. You need to make the announcement to the Metros."

"I know." At the thought, the cobb salad he'd had for lunch curdled in his stomach. Tamping down on the discomfort, Roman gave the answer he knew was expected of him. "Get it set up."

"Will do. Need a lift to the airport?"

"I've got a car. I'm going to get out of here."

A few minutes later Roman had retrieved his overnight bag from the coat check and was in the town car on his way back to LAX. The last two days had been a blur, but at least he had direction once more.

Purpose.

He glanced at his phone and saw messages, so he made quick work of them to pass the time.

And was pleased to hear one from Tucker Jordan.

He pressed the call-back button and in moments heard an all too familiar, smart-ass voice. After some ribbing and the expected sports insults, Roman dug into the heart of the matter.

"I've been up at home in Alaska and working with the kids in town. They need a full-time coach and I thought of you for the job."

"You know I don't coach kids."

"Don't bullshit me. You know as well as I do the minors are a bunch of barely grown kids."

"With the ability to buy beer."

"Exactly."

"Fine. Tell me more."

As he got out of the car at LAX twenty minutes later—an agreement in hand from Tucker to come visit and check out the team—Roman couldn't hold back the smile.

His life might not be where he wanted it, but maybe

he'd just done something to help a heck of a lot of kids in Indigo.

Avery sat in Julia's sunny kitchen, the familiar colors a soothing welcome amid the constant thoughts of change that whirled through her mind.

"I want to hear all about Doc Cloud."

"After you tell me about L.A."

"Julia. Come on. You've got juicy details and I want to hear them."

"You sound like Mary and Sophie," Julia said on a huff.

"Good. I don't blame them for wanting details, too. It's the girlfriend code."

Julia smiled as she poured two cups of tea. "I've not had a lot to share under the code in a long time. I'm out of practice."

"Not for long." Avery couldn't resist teasing Julia and received a satisfied smile for her efforts.

"He's wonderful."

"I know that! How'd it happen?"

"I'm not sure, really. I needed someone to talk to about Roman. Someone other than Mary and Sophie. And he was there. And he understood what I was feeling."

"About what an ass Roman can be?"

Julia's hand gripped hers and Avery took comfort in the small gesture. "Yes, that. But also my concerns about him. About whatever he was hiding, which, for the record, still pisses me off."

"Me, too."

"Yes, well. Anyway, Ken. He listened without making judgments." Julia giggled, the sound light and happy. It tugged at Avery's heart and brought a smile to her lips. "And then he finally made a move and kissed me."

"All I can say is it's about damn time."

"I couldn't agree more."

"Do you think women make judgments? Is that why you couldn't talk to Mary and Sophie?"

Julia's smile fell. "I think we all, men and women both, make judgments. I just think women are sometimes too stubborn to realize when it's not theirs to make."

"Like everyone wanting Roman and me to get together?"

"That. Other things as well. I think we often mistake the physical power men have and assume that translates immediately to their thought processes. I've begun to accept that's not always the case."

"Or ever the case."

"Why don't we settle on rarely?"

"Deal." Avery thought through the last few weeks. "Roman pulled away a while ago. When we left Anchorage, as soon as he knew they wanted me for the job."

"He doesn't want to hold you back from achieving your dreams."

"Why can't he see that it's not holding me back if we figure it out together?"

"It's taken me a long time to understand this, but for all the successes my grandson has received in his life, they've been shockingly empty."

"He said the town doesn't know who he really is."

"I'm not surprised."

For all the things her future might bring her, Avery realized, one of the gifts that would never be replaced in her life was her friendship with Julia.

The woman who had started out as an authority figure who inspired anxiety and a subtle dose of fear—her boyfriend's grandmother—had become one of her closest friends.

"I'm not sure what I'd do without you."

Julia leaned over and Avery reveled in the tight embrace. "Me, too."

Avery dashed at the tears that had dripped down her cheeks. "I haven't written him off, you know. But I'm not willing to sit in limbo, either. I needed to make a decision and I made one."

"I haven't written him off, either. But I do hope he gets his head on straight soon."

Since Roman's head was still firmly planted in his ass a day later—after he'd been home a full day and still hadn't found a way to talk to her beyond polite platitudes in the Indigo lobby as she worked the bar—Avery continued with her plans.

The Luxotica team had already e-mailed her a bunch of documents and she was devouring them with equal parts interest and sheer panic that she was expected to fix things.

And then she'd find herself thinking of ideas in odd moments and realized the fear was well and truly outweighed by the excitement of the challenge.

"Hey."

Avery turned from where she was stacking bottles of

their latest wine shipment on the marked shelves in the stockroom, checking off her inventory as she went.

"Hey."

Roman stood with his hands in his pockets, his shoulders painfully stiff. The bandage over his eye had changed to a simple Band-Aid and the bruise on his jaw had faded to a greenish yellow.

"You've been a ghost around here."

"I've been hanging with the kids for practice. And I was out of town for a few days."

"In L.A. I know. Your mother swore me to secrecy since things haven't been announced with the Metros yet."

"It's strange to think that's coming."

"You ready for the press onslaught?"

"That's part of what I've been prepping for the last few days."

"It's time for the next chapter. And soon you'll be the press, hounding someone new."

His eyes widened, evidence he hadn't thought that far forward. "I guess so."

The quiet returned and the need to fill it up with all the things still unsaid between them pushed her on.

"I'm happy for you, you know. Really happy. You're going to keep doing something you love, even if it's in a different form than you're used to."

"I hope so."

"With those Hollywood looks and cultured arguments honed in debate class." She winked. "I know so."

"Look. Avery."

She waited, curious to see if he could find a way out

of it. A way to pull himself back from the idiotic path he'd opted to walk for both of them.

"I didn't mean to start something and then get us here again."

"Here where?"

"Where we act like two strangers to each other, offering up polite chitchat because we don't know how to act."

"I know how to act."

She moved closer to him and laid her hands on his chest. "I know exactly how to act."

She stood on her tiptoes and pressed her lips to his. The immediate reaction—the same one that had pushed them both since they were kids—had him opening his mouth as his arms came around her. She kissed him once more before she stepped back from the circle of his arms.

"I love you. I've always loved you and, like one of those saps in weepy movies, I always will. The difference is, I'm not going to sit around and wait for you to figure it out. Not anymore."

"You deserve a life."

"We all do. With the people we care about most."

She pointed toward the shelf. "There's still a few bottles of Petrus there. On the bottom shelf, hidden at the back. You should take them. Celebrate your new job."

Roman stared at the bottle of wine, where it sat on his dresser. He'd not taken all of the remaining bottles she'd offered, but he had taken one, intending to get drunk on it back in his room.

It was the morning after and not only had he not gotten drunk on the wine, he'd never even opened it.

His phone buzzed with a text message and he looked down to see one from Mick.

YOU SURE YOU AREN'T COMING TO THE AIRSTRIP?

Roman ignored it. Ignored the fact that in mere moments, Mick would be lifting off the ground and flying Avery to Anchorage, where she'd get her connection to L.A.

He could fix this. Could still make the changes he needed to make. He knew it, even as the fear of holding her back lingered like lead casings around his ankles.

The knock on the door wasn't unexpected—he'd been waiting all morning for his mother or grandmother or even Grier—to show up and tell him what a moron he was being.

Which was why he was surprised to see Mike on the other side of the door.

"Hey, Mike, what's up?"

"Miss Avery's left town."

"Yeah, I know."

"So why are you still here?"

Roman looked into the kid's face—they were almost eye level, Mike was so tall—and wondered at the mix of anger and resentment he saw there.

"I let her go."

"Why?"

"Because she got a new job. It's complicated, kid."

"Actually, it's not." Mike moved into the room. "I've idolized you. Absolutely idolized you. And it's really embarrassing to find out you're a big pussy."

The anger rose up swift and strong. "Excuse me?"

"She's awesome."

"I know she is. That's why she deserves a chance at happiness."

"She wants it with you."

Roman shook his head. "I'm not the answer."

"Look, Mr. Forsyth. I know you think I don't know anything, but I do. I know how much I love hockey. And how much I love my family, who pushes me to play and practice hard because I love it and I'm good at it. And I love my girl, Vicky. She's the best thing that ever happened to me. And I sure as hell wouldn't let her go because of hockey."

"I let Avery go a long time ago because of hockey. And now I'm letting her go so she can have her dream." *And I'm letting her go because I was the last in a long line of people who'd failed her and I can't do that again.*

"I thought you let her go because she had to take care of her mom."

Roman stopped, caught at the kid's logic. "There was that, too."

"My brother told me you used to send her mom money."

Roman closed his eyes, the evidence of the town grapevine—and the absolute lack of secrets—shocking. "And just how would he know that?"

"Drunk people talk and Ms. Marks used to talk to him at the bar."

"Oh."

"You took care of Avery and helped her out the best you could. Now you can do better."

The incredible clarity Mike seemed to have at seventeen suddenly started to remove the fog that had clouded his own eyes, shocking Roman to his core.

Was it really that simple?

A glance at the kid's eager—and wise—face suggested it *was* that simple.

And he'd be a monumental fool to continue listening to the irrational fears that had driven him up to now.

"You'll go far, Mike."

"I hope so. But remember how I said playing in the play-offs must be like ice cream and Christmas and sex all rolled into one?"

"How could I forget? It was quite poetic."

"I was wrong."

"How so?"

"Being with the right person trumps it all."

Mike's words were still ringing in his ears ten minutes later as Roman raced over to the airstrip. He'd already caught Jack, pleased he'd gotten to him before the man had started his runs.

Roman put his mother's truck in park and cut the engine, then raced across the tarmac.

"I'm not leaving without you." Jack grinned, his hand held to his forehead to ward off the bright morning sun.

"I'm not worried about you. I'm worried about Avery."

Jack shrugged. "So you follow her to Los Angeles."

There was an odd sort of logic to it, but Roman waved toward the plane. "I need a grand gesture. You can help me figure out one on the way."

Five minutes later they were taxiing down the runway, and Roman turned toward Jack, excitement winging its way down his spine. "I've got an idea."

Avery heard Mick's chatter and tried to summon up something in return, but all she'd managed since take-off had been one-word answers and half laughs to his attempted jokes.

She knew he was trying to make her feel better, but after his third moose story, she decided she'd had enough.

"Mick, I love you like a brother. Honest, I do. But if you don't shut the fuck up, I may have to strangle you with the cords to your headset."

"Sorry."

"So am I. But I still mean it."

"Okay." His grin was gentle as he maneuvered them through the air and she settled back in her seat, trying to focus on the promise at the end of the destination and not what she was leaving behind.

Mick's voice rose up and she turned toward him, prepared to say something else unkind and bitchy when she realized he was talking to the tower. It was only when he caught her eye that she realized he was really talking to her.

"Take the headphones." He pointed toward the pair at her knee. "Put those on."

With a resigned sigh, she picked up the headphones. What could he possibly want to talk about now? "Can you hear me?"

"That's my line."

The husky voice floated through her headset and Avery felt her pulse bump up a few notches.

"Is this the town ass of Indigo, Alaska?"

"You bet it is, coming to you live over Air Indigo."

"Perhaps you've mistaken me for someone who gives a shit. And"—she risked a glance at Mick— "who is not in a good place to have a private conversation."

"I'm not looking for private." She heard a serious edge to his voice. "And for the record, I know damn well Mick and Jack can hear me. So can everyone back at the airstrip."

A loud cheer went up as the women at the airstrip let out a hearty squeal and Avery risked a glance at Mick, who just rolled his eyes and shrugged his shoulders.

"So we have an audience."

"You bet your sweet ass, you do!" hollered back through the headset.

Avery let out a deep sigh. She'd lived her life in the small spotlight of Indigo. Her fellow townsfolk knew her happiest and her saddest moments and had shared many of them with her, even if it was merely through observation.

"All right then, Sexy Voice. What do you have to say?"

"Three things and I need complete silence until I get them out."

When the open line stayed dead, Avery whispered, "Go on."

"I love you. I've always loved you, and I always will."

"That's your three?"

"In the end, is there really anything else?"

"No."

"But now that those things are out of the way, there is something else I need to say."

She couldn't resist the tease. "I thought that was all that ever needed to be said."

"Yeah, well, indulge me."

"Anytime, baby."

A light giggle floated through the headphones, and Avery heard the distinct sound of someone being shushed.

And then Roman's voice came through the headphones again, and Avery was caught. Completely trapped in his words. "I will follow you anywhere. I want you to have a life and a career and I want you to fulfill all your dreams. I'm happy to follow you and if we have kids I'll run them in the carpool when you have to meet a foreign diplomat and his staff."

"And if you have a game?"

"There are no more games. I'm done with all of them. I'm a grown man and my life and the people in it are more important to me than any game. You most of all."

"Thank you, Roman. That was sweet of you. I'm going to sign off now."

Mick eyed her sideways and she covered the speaker. "Turn it off."

"You okay?"

"Absolutely."

"Then why did you turn off the headphones? I've got so much squawking in my ear you have no idea."

She reached over and grabbed his hand. "Because some things should be private."

Avery felt the plane descend through the sky and knew she had a decision to make about her career. She might stick to the L.A. plans or she might change her mind, but whatever she decided, she was going to do it with Roman and not apart from him.

"You're still here." Roman's blood pumped double time as he saw Avery standing at the gate.

"Where'd you think I was going?"

"To L.A. You turned off the headset."

"What I had to say didn't need an audience. And no, I'm not going to L.A. Not today, at least."

He nodded and simply stood there and took her in. The beautiful girl next door he'd spent a lifetime in love with. No matter how many times he'd told himself otherwise, she'd always had his heart.

And he knew with absolute certainty he never wanted to be free of her.

"I love you, Avery. I've always loved you. A part of you lives inside of me, and you're so deeply embedded there, I know nothing can change that. Different cities. The passage of years. Creaky knees and a bum eye." He saw the first hint of a smile in her face. "None of it changes how I feel for you. You've always been the one for me."

"I love you, Roman. And I want to make a life with you. A life that we make *together*. Built on the foundation of both our dreams."

"Even though I got my turn?"

She moved closer and he felt her hand close over his. "And I had my turn doing what I needed, too. I know now I wouldn't give up that time with my mother. With your mother and grandmother. It all made me who I am today and I like that girl."

"I do, too."

"So can you promise me we'll make decisions about our future together from now on?"

"I promise."

"And you won't go thinking there's some enormous score, keeping tabs on our life?"

"No scoreboard. I'm done with them."

"There's just us."

"Just us."

She wrapped her free hand around his neck and pulled him down for a kiss. Unlike the innumerable kisses they'd shared before, Roman knew this one was different.

Monumental somehow.

This was a kiss to seal their future.

He could only thank the heavens he'd gotten to her just in time.

Epilogue

Crisp air surrounded them as the annual Labor Day festival on the town square wound down to a close. Roman delighted in the feel of Avery's shoulders under his arm and the slight buzz from an afternoon spent drinking beer, eating hamburgers and watching the town of Indigo wrap up summer. Already, the hints of winter were making themselves known, with shorter nights and the cold snap of air that had people burrowing under their blankets.

"I'm glad we were able to be here for Labor Day." Avery smiled broadly as she looked up at him.

"Me, too. Aside from battling jet lag, it hasn't been so bad."

She stepped up on her tiptoes to press a quick kiss to his lips. "Not bad at all."

And it wasn't, Roman knew. They'd been able to modify their new jobs in a way that had given them both more flexibility. Avery consulted on a project-by-project basis for Luxotica and he was reporting for SNN on a time-specific basis, most especially around the open of the NHL season and then later for the play-offs. He'd been told his draft analysis was the most spot-on they'd had in years, so he figured he'd started off on the right foot.

His agent, Ray, hadn't been crazy about the change, but SNN was more than willing to accept the new terms in exchange for locking him into a contract after his retirement.

He and Avery had even figured out living arrangements that made sense, splitting their time between L.A. and Indigo. A situation, Avery had warned him more than once, that was going to favor L.A. in the winter and Indigo in the summer.

"Let me see it one more time." Grier came to a hard stop in front of them, her eyes bright with excitement. "I've been telling anyone who will listen how gorgeous it is and Sloan has already suggested a piece on it for the fashion editor at her magazine. 'The latest trends in wedding jewelry.'"

Avery smiled and reached for the neck of her sweat-shirt and Roman couldn't hide the swell of pride as she pulled a diamond-crusted horseshoe charm from beneath the heavy cotton fabric.

"It's awesome, Avery. Really." Grier leaned forward, gently taking the horseshoe between her fingers. "It's the most original engagement jewelry I've ever seen." Her eyes flashed with the slightest hint of tears as Roman felt her gaze on his. "Just gorgeous. Trendy yet wildly sentimental."

Avery reached for his hand, linking their fingers. "And it's us."

"Exactly." Grier smiled.

The moment was interrupted by a tapping sound from the small stage that had been erected at the front of the square. Walker's grandmother stood on the dais, asking for a moment. When everyone had quieted, she began to speak.

"As we bring another summer to a close, I think it's important to reflect once again on the many blessings that have been bestowed upon our town and the amazing people who choose to call Indigo home." Roman listened as Sophie outlined several achievements of various townsfolk, their upcoming plans to expand the town hall meeting center, and a new addition to the high school that was planned for the coming summer.

As he listened, his thoughts drifted over all that was still to come this year. Mick and Grier's upcoming wedding and the plans he and Avery were making for their own wedding. A trip he and Avery would take to Australia in another month for a conference she was attending. And the annual charity banquet the Metros put on at the holidays that he was emceeing.

Good, happy things to look forward to and memories they'd make as they built their life together.

"So it's with great pride and pleasure that I wrap up this year's Labor Day festival with a thank-you to one of our town's favorite sons, Roman Forsyth."

Sophie's words pulled him from his musings as Avery put gentle pressure on his back. "She's calling you to the stage."

"Me?" He saw the hint of a smile in Avery's eyes. "You know something."

"Maybe. Just get on up there."

Roman walked toward the dais, happy shouts echoing around him even as he continued his confused walk up the small set of stairs. "This is a surprise, Mayor Montgomery."

"As well it should be." She pulled him down for a quick hug.

Turning back toward the crowd with an expression of mischief painted on her face, she continued. "As I said, we here in Indigo count ourselves the recipients of many blessings. And a big point of pride for all of us has been Roman's accomplishments in the NHL."

Another cheer went up and he could still only puzzle at whatever Sophie had planned.

"But I'm afraid there may be times we've given the impression that the only thing we care about is Roman's ability on skates."

The cheers quieted as the town focused on Sophie's words. "And I'm of the opinion we've shortchanged some of his other fine qualities. The ones that are most often displayed off a hockey rink."

Roman's gaze sought Avery's in the crowd. She stood next to his grandmother, and at the expression on both their faces, he knew they had a hand in whatever it was Sophie was about to announce.

"I had the great privilege of knowing Andrew Forsyth for many years and I grieved when we lost him at far too young an age. He was a man of strength. A man of quiet integrity. And a man who gave back to his community." Sophie turned toward him, and Roman felt a strange heaviness lodge in his throat. "In his grandson, I see those very same qualities. So it is with great pride that I announce that an annual Forsyth Family Scholarship has been established by the mayor's office. The scholarship is designated in honor of Roman Forsyth and in memory of his grandfather Andrew. Each recipient will receive fully paid college tuition at the university of their choice."

"Sophie," he whispered.

She only smiled in return before adding, "The first recipient is Mark Unger."

His throat grew even tighter as Roman watched Stink's mouth drop before he hugged his mother and headed for the stage. Cheers and wolf whistles echoed off the square while Sophie made a few additional remarks, but Roman heard none of it.

All he could hear was his own heart beating in his chest.

All he could do was mouth "I love you."

All he could see was Avery.

She stood in the midst of the smiling faces of Indigo, her eyes shining with love and understanding.

And Roman knew he'd found his forever.

Now that you've enjoyed a
visit to Indigo, Alaska,
see what happened when Grier
and Sloan first arrived!

Baby It's Cold Outside

Available from Signet Eclipse wherever
books and e-books are sold.

*I*t was surprisingly easy to book a trip to the middle
of nowhere, Sloan thought with no small measure of
amusement as she stepped up into the cold vestibule
between train cars.

Grier had peppered her with a nonstop barrage of
information and instructions for the past two days as
she'd booked her flight and made her travel arrangements. Apparently, a train from Anchorage to Indigo
was the recommended mode of travel by the local tourist board.

Sloan couldn't say she was all that upset to miss
out on flying in a puddle jumper–sized plane to the
town her best friend was presently calling home, but
she was admittedly tickled at the idea of a local tourist
board.

She knew from her editorial work that Alaska had a

booming tourism industry, but a tourist board for a small outpost virtually in the middle of nowhere? It was serious overkill.

The train let out a loud, piercing whistle as they pulled away from the station, and Sloan huddled down in her coat. It was surprisingly cozy in the train car, but she couldn't quite shake the chill that had permeated her after a few moments on the station platform.

She shot a quick text to Grier, letting her know she was on the train and headed her way, then pulled out a book to sink into for the ride. She'd barely gotten through a page when her gaze caught a reflection out the window.

Endless plains of white, snow-covered ground, framed by impossibly tall mountain peaks, were set off by the dusky haze of sunset. Grier had given her a heads-up on the weird daylight she'd find at this time of year—a sort of perpetual twilight that hung around for about five to six hours in the middle of the day before darkness descended for another eighteen.

Her eyes roamed over the landscape again and a small thrill shot through her as she noticed a herd of moose in the distance, their large antlers a distinct identifying marker, as if their long, knobby legs and oversized bodies weren't a dead giveaway. And behind them, growing closer with each passing mile, was the mountain referred to as Denali by the locals.

A small curl of anticipation unfurled low in her belly as Sloan stared at the mountain that dominated the entire landscape. It hadn't escaped her notice they shared a name, and she'd come to think of it as *her* mountain as she'd read up on Alaska over the past few days.

Mount McKinley.

Of course, her mother was anxious for her to get rid of the name and Alaska natives preferred the mountain's given name—Denali—to the politically charged Mount McKinley, so maybe it was apropos she felt this odd kinship.

Or maybe it was just a funny coincidence, she berated herself for her fanciful notions.

A sharp spike of nerves ran the length of her spine as Sloan burrowed down in her oversized sweater—one of five she'd purchased specifically for this trip. The land and the enormous mountain behind it were impossibly beautiful.

And impossibly hard.

How does anyone live here?

She knew that's what people thought about living in a city like Manhattan, but easy transportation, food on every corner and ready access to any type of entertainment imaginable didn't seem nearly as challenging as miles and miles of barren land.

Pulling her gaze from the impressive sight, she turned back to her book. A sense of anticipation filled her in a sudden, steady throb she couldn't ignore and the words lay unread on the page.

Purpose.

It was something that had been missing from her life lately.

This trip had it in spades.

She'd help Grier. She'd pitch a few stories. She'd relax and get out of New York for a few weeks.

The twilight sky spread out on the horizon before her as Sloan turned back to her book.

It was perfect.

And don't miss Kate and Jason's story in

From This Moment On

Available from Signet Eclipse
wherever e-books are sold.

K ate Winston had always thought herself an intrepid soul. Between growing up in the wilds of Alaska and teaching hormonal eighth graders, she could stare down a moose with an attitude or handle a pimple-ridden fourteen-year-old with an eraser stuffed up his nose and still maintain her equanimity.

But nothing in her life could have prepared her for the sight of the three town grandmothers modeling lingerie at Sloan McKinley's prewedding bacchanalia. A strange event that was part bachelorette party, part bridal shower and an all-around peculiar Indigo, Alaska, ritual.

"Sophie! I told you to keep your bra on." Mary, grandmother to Kate's sister's fiancé, Mick, admonished across the room as she played with the fur boa draped around her neck. "The bust isn't supposed to droop that much. Are you trying to scare Sloan off so she runs screaming out of Indigo?"

Sophie—Indigo's mayor and grandmother to the intended groom—waved a hand. "It's fine. Besides, Sloan's sweet on my Walker. She's not going anywhere."

"She will if you flash her one more time," Julia Forsyth—the third matriarch in their triumvirate—chimed in.

"Is this really happening?" Grier Thompson, Kate's recently discovered half sister, leaned over and whispered. "Because it's quite possible I've been scarred for life."

"We hear you," Julia hollered from across the room.

"I meant you to," Grier hollered back as she lifted her wineglass in a toast.

Kate lifted her glass to clink with Grier before downing a liberal sip of her Cabernet. She'd heard rumors of the prewedding ritual, but had never been privy to an actual viewing of one. Bridal showers were a strange tradition in Indigo, dating all the way back to the town settlers.

The older women modeled various nightgowns for the bride and her friends. The idea was to send the bride off with a lot of laughter and a reminder that getting old was well worth it with the right person.

It was also a reminder, Kate thought, that Alaska attracted a certain type of individual. One who could live in the rugged climate and small-town atmosphere and still enjoy themselves and appreciate where they'd put down roots.

It was where she'd grown up—the local environment had molded and shaped who she was—and until recently she had never really appreciated what that meant. Or how she saw the world because of it. Especially now that she lived over four thousand miles away in New York City, a city that had more people in one square block than she'd see all year long in Alaska.

Manhattan was a far cry from Indigo, but it was the home of the man she loved. And the previous winter she'd realized that her life was far better with Jason Shriver in it than staying safe and warm, cocooned up in Indigo with a life that didn't make her happy any longer.

If it ever had.

Even now, she marveled at how much things had changed in the last six months, starting with Grier's arrival in their small town and later Jason's.

"I want to hear all about New York."

Sophie's voice interrupted her thoughts, and Kate dragged herself back into the moment, abandoning her quiet reflections. "It's good. Really good."

Avery, part-time bartender and good friend of the bride and groom, lifted one of the wine bottles scattered around the room and refilled Kate's glass with a generous pour. "You mean Jason's really good."

A smile Kate couldn't hold back even if she'd wanted to—and she didn't want to—broke over her face. "He's very good. And I mean that in a non-dirty way." At Avery's raised eyebrows, she continued on quickly. "And so is the city. I'm adjusting quickly, and that was one of my biggest worries. Sort of Grier's experience in reverse."

"Well, we all know Grier's experience has turned out quite well." Mary extended her glass toward Avery for a refill as she leaned over and wrapped Grier in a tight one-armed hug. "Plus, as a bonus I'm about to get a new granddaughter."

Kate wasn't sure if it was the wine or being home for a visit for the first time since the move or the realization that she and Grier had come out the other side of an unpleasant battle over their late father's will, but tears pooled in her eyes as she took in the women around her.

Women who'd embraced her when she finally stopped fighting and looked up to realize she needed their love and affection as much as they wanted to give it.

Although she would have liked to discover herself without losing her father to cancer in the process, Kate had also come to accept that through horrible loss she had been given new gifts. Good, strong relationships she liked to think would make her father very proud. A sister she loved and a man she could see herself making a life with.

As if she sensed Kate's slight melancholy, Grier pulled her aside a few minutes later with the excuse of needing help opening a few more bottles of wine in Mary's kitchen.

Grier sifted through the detritus on the counter—napkins, discarded corks, various bags of chips and pretzels and, oddly enough, an unopened pair of panty hose—until she came up with a corkscrew. "You doing all right?"

"I am."

"It's hard sometimes. Like no matter how happy you are, you can't help feeling just the slightest bit guilty. Or a little sad that he's not here."

"Actually, I was thinking something else."

Grier looked up from tugging the cork from the bottle. "What's that?"

"I think Dad would be thrilled to see us spend time together. To know that we've become friends. And real, true sisters."

Grier set the bottle down with a heavy clunk and Kate went into her arms as they pulled each other into a tight embrace. "God, I've become such a sap." Grier pulled back.

"It's all those love hormones and wedding planning."

Grier wiped at her eyes. "I've got hormones aplenty, but I prefer to put them to use elsewhere. I will cop to feeling so full of emotions sometimes they get the better of me."

"I know." She did know, Kate thought. Her feelings for Jason were so overwhelming, she had days she could barely sit still for the excitement that coursed through her veins.

And other days she wasn't sure how it was all going to end up.

"Like when we talk. I love our conversations and selfishly I wish you lived closer, but I'm so happy for you."

Grier's voice pulled Kate from her thoughts along with the warm hand that wrapped around hers. "Sometimes I can't believe it's all happened. That I found Jason. That I left Indigo and live in New York City, of all places. My mother is probably turning in her grave."

The image of her mother's perpetually sour disposition—and the realization that she'd never have gone to New York had Laurie Winston still been alive—stretched another thin layer of melancholy over the evening.

"I'd like to think maybe she's now able to appreciate the things that make you happy."

"That's lovely."

"Or hard-won wisdom." Grier winked. "Because we all know my mother has quite a few moments of her own. How is Pattycakes?"

Grier had a strained maternal relationship with Patrice Thompson, which made Kate's own relationship with her mother look like something out of a Hallmark commercial. The two women had mended a lot of old wounds the previous winter when Patrice finally had to come to terms with her affair with Grier's father. Patty had lived with decades of grief that she had been unable to give herself over fully to that love. Despite their progress, the relationship had over thirty years of strain that wouldn't simply vanish overnight.

"I haven't seen her yet."

"Have you and Jason been out for any society events yet? You're sure to see her there."

"We have something next week. An opera function." Kate waved it off like it was no big deal, but the acid churning in her stomach told a different story. She harbored the very real fear that she'd make an ass out of herself with Jason's elite social circle—one she'd only read about in magazines and imagined from books.

Grier took a sip of her wine. "They're not so bad. I wouldn't go so far as to call them fun, but there are worse ways to spend an evening."

Kate had hesitated to ask Grier too much about her old life. While the two of them had moved past the initial harsh circumstances that brought them together—no knowledge of each other while their father was living and a contested will for Jonas Winston's belongings after he passed—Kate hadn't quite worked herself up to talk about Jason with any degree of frequency.

The fact that he was Grier's ex-fiancé was the subject of much speculation in Indigo and she hadn't figured out how to casually ask all the questions and concerns that perpetually hovered in her mind.

Was she going to be able to fit into Jason's rarefied life for the long haul?

Did she have what it took to be a partner's wife?

And did she even desire his lifestyle?

The questions churned over and over, assaulting her at quiet moments, forcing her to examine what it really meant to fall in love with someone who came from a completely different life.

Also available from

Addison Fox

Baby It's Cold Outside
An Alaskan Nights Novel

After a frantic call, Sloan McKinley travels to the heart of the Alaskan wilderness to be there for her best friend, who's just inherited property in the small town of Indigo. Soon Sloan finds herself falling in love with the wild outdoors...and with one of Indigo's most beloved residents. There's just one question that remains: is the town's most confirmed bachelor ready to get caught?

"I cannot wait to return to the wonderful town of Indigo, Alaska."
—Romance Junkies

Available wherever books are sold or at
penguin.com

facebook.com/LoveAlwaysBooks

S0404

Also available from
Addison Fox

Come Fly With Me
An Alaskan Nights Novel

A story of risking it all for love—and the sky's the limit.

When Grier Thompson is called to Indigo, Alaska, to deal
with the estate of her late, estranged father, she meets
pilot Mick O'Shaughnessy, a rugged dream guy. But then
an unexpected visitor from Grier's past unsettles the entire
town. By the time Mick comes out of the clouds to realize
he's fallen head over heels in love, it might be just too late
to win Grier's heart.

"A sexy, emotional journey of the best kind."
—*New York Times* bestselling author Carly Phillips

Available wherever books are sold or at
penguin.com

facebook.com/LoveAlwaysBooks

S0431